Steve Jackson and Ian Livingstone present:

DUNGEONEER:
ADVANCED FIGHTING FANTASY

by Marc Gascoigne
and Pete Tamlyn

Illustrated by John Sibbick

PUFFIN BOOKS

**For MT at the start of his great adventure,
and Joy for asking nicely**

PUFFIN BOOKS

Published by the Penguin Group
27 Wrights Lane, London w8 5TZ, England
Viking Penguin Inc., 40 West 23rd Street, New York, New York 10010, USA
Penguin Books Australia Ltd, Ringwood, Victoria, Australia
Penguin Books Canada Ltd, 2801 John Street, Markham, Ontario, Canada L3R 1B4
Penguin Books (NZ) Ltd, 182–190 Wairau Road, Auckland 10, New Zealand

Penguin Books Ltd, Registered Offices: Harmondsworth, Middlesex, England

First published 1989
10 9 8 7 6 5 4 3 2

Concept copyright © Steve Jackson and Ian Livingstone, 1989
Text copyright © Marc Gascoigne and Pete Tamlyn, 1989
Illustrations copyright © John Sibbick, 1989
Maps copyright © Leo Hartas and Steve Luxton, 1989
All rights reserved

Filmset in 11 on 13 point Palatino by
Rowlands Phototypesetting Ltd
Bury St Edmunds, Suffolk
Printed in Great Britain by
Cox and Wyman Ltd, Reading, Berks.

PUFFIN BOOKS

DUNGEONEER:
ADVANCED FIGHTING FANTASY

You and your friends can create your own fantasy films! No expensive equipment is needed – you will be imagining the scenarios in your sitting-room, and you and your trusty band of heroes will be playing all the roles yourselves! Nor are there complicated rules to learn before you start: *Dungeoneer* explains how you can begin straight away and introduces the rules in easy stages as the shooting of your film progresses. So, are you ready? Then let the cameras roll . . .

Dungeoneer is a companion volume to Steve Jackson's popular role-playing game, *Fighting Fantasy*, but develops the Fighting Fantasy role-playing rules so that you can achieve even more reality in your games.

Steve Jackson and Ian Livingstone are the co-founders of the hugely successful Games Workshop chain and are the creators of the Fighting Fantasy series. Marc Gascoigne is a freelance writer specializing in fantasy gaming and is the author of *Out of the Pit*, *Titan* and *Battleblade Warrior*. Pete Tamlyn works in the computer industry; *Dungeoneer* is his first book.

Fighting Fantasy Gamebooks

Steve Jackson's SORCERY!

FIGHTING FANTASY – The Introductory Role-Playing Game
THE RIDDLING REAVER – Four Thrilling Adventures
THE TROLLTOOTH WARS – A Fighting Fantasy Novel

The Advanced Fighting Fantasy System
OUT OF THE PIT – Fighting Fantasy Monsters
TITAN – The Fighting Fantasy World
DUNGEONEER – An Introduction to the World of Role-Playing Games

CONTENTS

STEP INSIDE!

Gritting his teeth in order to steady his hand, Ulrik Wolfsbane silently unsheathes his mighty longsword. The rune-carved blade glows with an eerie light, as if shimmering with some inner magic. The barbarian creeps forward, every instinct straining to alert him to any hidden danger. Nerves jangling with concentration, he reaches the lip of the parapet and, with a final muttered prayer to his unearthly guardians, peers over to gaze down at the arcane ring of stones.

His green eyes widen as they alight upon the object in the very centre of the circle. The flickering torchlight distorts his vision, filling the scene beneath him with dancing illusions; but there

1

can be no doubt that he has at last found the object of his quest over many long years. The idol, carved from purest Khulian jade, looks so very small and insignificant upon its mammoth granite plinth; but Wolfsbane knows too well its awesome evil power, the power which has cursed his beloved land of Allansia with a foul plague of famine and decay.

Clamping his sword between his teeth, Ulrik Wolfsbane swings his body over the edge and begins to climb down into the pit . . .
AND CUT!

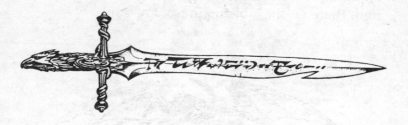

Have you ever wanted to star in your own fantasy movie, or become the hero of an epic swords-and-sorcery novel? The very best fantasy movies and books are wonderful excuses for letting the imagination run riot on an awesome scale, freeing it from the trappings of everyday life and letting it stalk through worlds full of excitement and danger. But think how much more fun it would be actually to *be there*, to be doing all the things your heroes do, to *become* your heroes!

Well, now's your chance. You need look no further than the pages of this very volume to discover everything you could ever wish to know in order to create the fantasy world of your favourite books and movies – and, most importantly, the wildest flights of your imagination – right there on the tabletop in front of you!

Simply turn the page, and let the action commence!

New Adventurers Start Here

You may think that what you have in your hands at this moment is just a book. Well, it is that, certainly, but that's not all it is; it's much more than that. *Dungeoneer* is a complete introduction to a whole new experience, a key to the wonderful world of fantasy role-playing games and the Fighting Fantasy game specifically.

But just what does that mean, you ask. Well, when we say 'fantasy', we are referring to the books of a whole range of writers, including J. R. R. Tolkien, Robert E. Howard and Fritz Leiber, and a whole range of films, from *Conan* to *Willow*; to a dark, medieval world where magic really works – a world of knights and brigands, Dragons and Orcs, thieves and sorcerers, samurai and ninja, proud heroes and crazed monsters. A world where adventure and excitement lurk round every corner. And what we are going to do is to re-create these fantasy worlds via the medium of 'role-playing'.

At its simplest, this usually means that a group of friends sit round a table and act out a story together, solving problems and winning through to the conclusion. It's as if you and your friends are going to create a fantasy film right there in front of you on the tabletop, with everyone playing the part of one of the heroic stars! Unlike a film, however, everyone who plays has a voice in deciding on the script; *everyone* will have to choose what his or her respective character says and does – and do it with sufficient skill, they hope, to slay the dragon, rescue the princess or bring home the treasure.

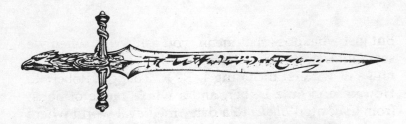

And, finally, it is a *game* for two reasons. First, because we use a few simple rules to decide on the outcome of chancy events: if your hero is having a showdown with the evil wizard, you'll need to know whether you can slash out at him with your sword before he zaps you with a bolt of magical energy. To decide this sort of thing, you roll dice according to the easy rules which we will go into in detail later on. And second, we call it a game because the main intention is for everyone to enjoy themselves and have endless amounts of fun!

So let's go! Skip the next couple of pages, which are for those lucky people who've played games like this before, and let's get cracking on our fantasy masterpiece!

Veterans Start Here

If you have already played the *Fighting Fantasy* multi-player role-playing game or any of the marvellous range of Fighting Fantasy gamebooks (such as *The Warlock of Firetop Mountain* or *Deathtrap Dungeon*), you may well be familiar with some of the concepts and rules we are going to present here. That's quite all right, because there's still plenty of fun and excitement to be had here, even by the most experienced of adventurers!

You'll find that this book updates many of the basic rules found in the *Fighting Fantasy* game and gamebooks. As its title indicates, this is simply *Advanced Fighting Fantasy*. We have taken nothing away from the original rules; we have simply added more details. For example, there is a new individual skill system which allows every hero to specialize and become even more skilful in certain areas, be it swordplay, sneaking or sorcery. There are copious new notes on designing and running your own fantasy adventures too, along with every tip and hint we could cram in for making your games more enjoyable than ever. Finally, we shall be describing the way you play the games using a novel procedure, to ensure that everyone can understand all the unfamiliar concepts we shall be presenting.

Depending upon your experience of the Fighting Fantasy game, you may wish to skip the first few sections of this book – in which we introduce the Fighting Fantasy experience to those people who are about to play the game for the very first time – and head straight for the nitty-gritty, the new rules and adventures. This is quite acceptable. Like any set of role-playing game rules, you need take from this book only as much or as little as you wish in order to have fun playing your own fantasy adventures. If you don't like one particular new rule we've presented, don't use it. The whole point of everything in this book is to have fun creating the most exciting scenes from a range of fantasy books and movies, whether they are familiar ones or new stories you have thought up for yourself! Happy adventuring!

1. Getting Started

If you have ever glanced through the rules of other role-playing games, you may have noticed that there seemed to be hundreds of pages of charts and tables, rules and regulations, which all had to be read and learnt before you and your friends could sit down and get started. In this game, however, we are going to tell you the rules as you go along, revealing them only when they are needed. This way you can get started straight away – at this very minute, in fact, if you so choose!

Just before you start to create your fantasy adventure, though, you will need to gather together a few things. We'll explain each of them in more detail in a moment but here's a checklist to be going on with.

- Some Heroes
- A Director
- Somewhere to play
- Some dice
- Pencils and paper
- A watch or clock
- Props (optional)
- Miniatures and scenery (optional)
- Other items (optional)

The Heroes

Your wonderful fantasy adventure will need a group of actors to play the roles of the Heroes, that brave but foolhardy band of characters who are going to solve all

the puzzles, defeat all the monsters and generally vanquish evil and win through to fight another day. Have you got anyone in mind for these parts? Well, your budget probably couldn't run to Arnold Schwarzenegger or Sigourney Weaver, so you'll have to make do with your own friends. Gather together a motley group of between two and six of them (any more than six and the action will get very confusing; they probably wouldn't all be able to squeeze in round your table anyway).

Dungeoneer players can be male or female, as can the Director: you don't need to be big and beefy to wield an imaginary sword in *Dungeoneer*, and brains can always be as important as brute strength. To avoid getting long-winded, though, in these rules we'll refer to everyone as 'he'.

The Director

Since what you are going to be doing is very like making a fantasy movie, you will need a Director. As this is your book, we think you are the ideal person for the job; congratulations! From now on, we are going to assume that you are the Director.

Just as in a real film, the Director instructs the actors (our Heroes) in their roles, sets the scene by describing what is going on around them, and then lets them get on with their heroic acting. In *Dungeoneer*, the Director is also the person who interprets all the rules of the game whenever anything important happens. (That is why the Director is sometimes referred to in other games as the Referee, GamesMaster (or GM), or Dungeon Master.)

We know what you're thinking: 'This doesn't sound like much fun to me so far! Can't I be a Hero too?' Well, the

11

fact of the matter is, the Director also has to play every character that the Heroes meet. Depending on the plot of your adventure, this could include evil wizards – 'Heh-heh-heh, you meddling fools!' – doomed knights – 'We must duel . . . to the death!' – brutish Orc guards – 'Yoomans! Kill 'em all!' – and any number of other types. All these parts (which some games call Non-Player Characters, or NPCs) will be referred to here as Bad Guys, Extras or the Cast, and you get to play all of them! This aspect of the game is one that you will enjoy, we promise!

As Director, it's your job to read out to the Heroes and interpret to them all the necessary material from the script of the fantasy adventures (which we will get to in a minute). Unless we say otherwise, *only you* should read from this book. Secrecy isn't too important at the moment, but you should discourage anyone who is going to be playing a Hero from reading the script of any particular adventure; it will spoil the surprise and excitement for them, and they won't have so much fun. As we said earlier, so far as the first adventure in this book is concerned, you can sit down and play it through simply by reading it out as you go along; it is *not* essential to have memorized rules and tables or anything like that. If you *do* have some time to spare before your first game, though, it would make things even easier if you read the adventure through beforehand.

Somewhere to Play

Role-playing game sessions can last from as little as half an hour to all night, depending on the complexity of the situations the Heroes find themselves in. The first adventure in this book should last around two hours or so. The second will last slightly longer and will probably need to be played over two or more sessions, depending on how much time you have to play, and how regularly your little band of Heroes can all get together.

We think that the most comfortable and friendly way to play *Dungeoneer* is with everyone grouped round a table, with the Director at one end and at a slight distance away from everyone else; that way, everyone can see what's happening, no one has any excuse for falling asleep, and you're not constantly hunting for runaway dice under the sofa. If you want to create a suitable atmosphere, turn down some of the lights (but not so much that you can't read the adventure!) and put on some appropriately mysterious music in the background. If the session is going to drag on for a long time, some snacks and drinks will be appreciated by everyone, too. Remember, you're all getting together to have fun and be sociable, so enjoy yourselves!

Dice

The rules of this game come into operation whenever something that a Hero or an Extra does will either fail or succeed. For example, if Ulrik Wolfsbane is swinging his trusty longsword at a Goblin brigand, we need to know whether the blade connects or goes flying past its target. To adjudicate at these moments you will need some dice. Ordinary six-sided dice will do; these can be borrowed from a boardgame or bought from most toy and game shops. You don't need to buy the multi-sided dice that some shops sell; these are used in some role-playing games, but not in this one.

You will find it handy to have at least four dice, if you can acquire that many, so that everyone playing can lay their hands on some when they need them. At various stages in the adventure, both the Heroes and the Director will need to throw dice.

Pencils and Paper

Everyone who is playing a Hero will have to write down who their character is, what he or she can do, what weapons they are carrying, and so on. You, the Director, may also need to make notes concerning certain secret matters relevant to the adventure. Therefore, make sure everyone has a pencil and a few sheets of paper – and perhaps an eraser for the inevitable mistakes that occur.

A Watch or Clock

Some things in the game will last for a certain length of time, such as a spell or the effects of a sleeping gas. Have a watch ready for such occasions.

Props

By Props, we mean those few little items which can be given to the Heroes as if they had really acquired them. For example, if your Heroes go into a tavern and decide to indulge in a little gambling with some of the ruffians there, wouldn't it be great if they all had some plastic coins to wager with? Props are of course optional. You never *need* to have them, but they can add extra fun to a game and we'll be offering suggestions for them as we go along. Remember, though, if you don't want to use Props, or if you can't find anything to use, then you don't have to have them.

Miniatures and Scenery

These too are optional; it is not essential for you to use them. When role-playing games first became popular, people started using inch-high model soldiers to represent their Heroes, arranging them on the tabletop so they could see, for example, just who was clobbering whom in a punch-up. These days, whole ranges of knights, wizards, Orcs, Goblins, Dragons -- and just about any other creature you could dream up – are available; many toy and game shops stock them. They are not essential, but they do come in useful sometimes, and they can help players visualize what is going on.

If you are going to use metal miniatures for your Heroes and their grisly adversaries, you might care to think about using scenery too, thus turning your tabletop into a proper set for the adventure you are about to act out. Nor do you need to pay out huge sums for your scenery: books under a tablecloth can become hills; a blue ribbon can represent a stream; walls made of children's building bricks can become the dungeon walls. More expensively, you could buy specially manufactured scenery from your local hobby shop; a wide range of trees, buildings, doors, dungeon decor and more is available, though, again, most of it is quite expensive. Scenery is not at all essential, but, like Props and Miniatures, it can look very nice.

Other Items

Although this book (and the few easily available items we've just mentioned) are all you need to play the adventures contained within it, there are several other books in the Fighting Fantasy series (all published by

Puffin) which you may find will come in handy later on, especially if you go on to designing and writing your very own adventures for your friends and yourself to play. You won't need these books right now; but they do contain information and adventures which you will be able to use in the future.

Titan is a complete adventurer's guide to the Fighting Fantasy world where these adventures are set. It isn't a gamebook; it's an encyclopedia of the world of Titan, with maps and descriptions of places, people, transport, money, the gods and demons, history and legends, and a lot more besides. It will provide you with many ideas for adventures and the background to your characters, as well as information on every aspect of life in Allansia and the rest of the Fighting Fantasy world.

Its companion volume, *Out of the Pit*, describes over 250 different monsters ready for use in your Fighting Fantasy adventures. They range from tiny Sprites and Elementals to enormous Giants, Dragons and Demons. Each creature and being is described in minute detail, together with game information for use with the rules laid out in this book.

The Riddling Reaver was the first book of ready-to-run multi-player adventures written for use with the Fighting Fantasy rules system. Its four linked episodes take players flying round the southern jungles of Allansia in search of that most elusive of villains, the Riddling Reaver. The adventures can be easily adapted for use with these advanced rules, and they really are great fun!

Finally, many books from the Fighting Fantasy range of solo gamebooks can also be adapted for use by groups of more than one Hero, using the *Dungeoneer* rules. Of course, some won't work because the plots require the Hero to be on his own; but so long as the Heroes stick together, most of them will prove fun to play. Anyway, some of the puzzles or situations found within them may lead you, as the Director, to dreaming up similar tight spots for your Heroes.

We shall be giving you more copious notes on creating and playing your own fantasy adventures later on in this book, once we have taught you and the players you recruit how the game actually works.

A Quick Recap

So, now you've got this book, you want to start playing. To sum up, this is what you should do next:

1. Enrol some friends who are interested in playing Heroes in your adventure.
2. If you have time, read the rest of this book; otherwise, read at least the first adventure which follows on page 34.
3. Sit your friends down round the table and give each of them the following: paper and pencil, possibly an eraser and two six-sided dice. If you're feeling really flush, you can also hand out a metal miniature to each player, plus food and drink. If you have time, and if you feel it will help the atmosphere, you can assemble some handy props for use in the adventure.
4. Read on: everyone is now going to be given their own individual Hero to play, and then the adventure can start!

2. THE HEROES

Your first tabletop fantasy movie is about to start – but you still need one more element: the Heroes, stars of the show. In later adventures, your players will be able to create their own Heroes, using the rules we provide; but for this first game we have provided a selection of six ready-made Heroes for them to choose from. You will find these Heroes and their *Adventure Sheets* at the very back of this book. You should either pull out the pages, or photocopy them, or copy the details on to separate sheets of paper.

You should then have one Hero for each player (up to a maximum of six players). Let the players pick which Hero they want to be, rolling one die to determine who chooses first. You don't have the chance of picking a Hero, of course, because you're the Director; you'll be playing all the other characters. Once everyone has chosen a character with whom they are at least vaguely happy, put any remaining *Adventure Sheets* to one side; they won't be needed. Don't fret if you have only been able to drum up enough players for two or three Heroes, as quite a small band of sufficiently valiant Heroes can succeed in this quest. In fact, if your party contains five or six Heroes, on several occasions you will find notes telling you to add more enemies in some of the scenes. However, don't worry about that for now.

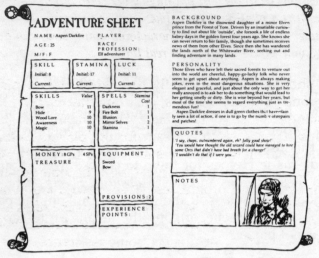

Sample Adventure Sheet

Hero Characters

After you've given everyone enough time to read through their particular Hero's *Adventure Sheet*, you may read out the following to your players:

On each character sheet, a Hero is described in two ways. First, he or she is described in numerical terms, with scores given for SKILL, STAMINA *and* LUCK. *Each character has also been assigned some appropriate Special Skills or magic Spells. These are simply what the Hero is especially good at.*

Secondly, there is a brief outline of the sort of person the Hero is. Remember: you will be playing the role of the Hero, just as you would in a movie. You should therefore try to behave as your Hero would, according to these suggestions, at all times. There is no script for you to learn – you make that up as you go along, acting out the adventure – but we have given you some suggestions as to the sort of things your Hero might say. A lot of the fun in playing a game like this lies in trying to stay in character and acting out the character of your Hero, and doing things you would never do in real life!

You should now run briefly through all the items on everyone's character sheets, ensuring that everyone understands the gist of their Hero's personality and skills. At this stage it isn't necessary for the players to know *exactly* what all the numbers mean and how they affect the Hero's capabilities; that will rapidly become apparent as the adventure progresses. (Players who are familiar with Fighting Fantasy solo gamebooks or the rules as set out in *Fighting Fantasy* will need no explanation anyway.) For those players who do need some assistance, read out the following to them.

Skill

The number given here is a measure of the Hero's expertise, both at fighting in combat, and in a wide range of other activities. The latter could include, say, sneaking about without being heard, climbing up a steep wall, dodging an enemy's arrow, or many other actions. Heroes usually have a SKILL in the range from 7 to 12; their enemies may have less than this – or, occasionally, more!

Stamina

This score shows just how fit and healthy a Hero is, and also how determined he is to survive. It may be helpful to think of STAMINA in terms of 'lives', because every time a Hero sustains a wound, his STAMINA score is reduced by one or more points. If a Hero's STAMINA reaches zero, most probably he is dead! STAMINA points can however be recovered by a prolonged period of rest after an adventure, or by the application of healing magic. STAMINA for a Hero usually lies in the range between 14 and 24.

Luck

Everyone has a certain amount of LUCK, and this can sometimes be called upon when all else has failed. The score given on the *Adventure Sheet* is a measure of the particular Hero's good fortune and success so far, and it usually lies in the range of 7 to 12. Calling on one's LUCK drains it, and it is recommended that Heroes do not resort to trying their LUCK too often; if it runs out, their adventure will end in death.

Special Skills

These are dependent on the Hero's *Initial* SKILL score, and show how expert he or she is in certain specialized areas. (The number given on the *Adventure Sheet* for each Special Skill is worked out according to the Hero's SKILL score. Exactly how these points are arrived at is explained fully later.) Note that a Special Skill in using a *Sword*, for example, can be applied only if the Hero in question is actually fighting with a sword. In a situation in which he has broken or lost his sword and is using an axe instead, his basic SKILL score would apply instead. In certain situations, the Director may temporarily add or subtract 1 or 2 points from a Special Skill score, depending on the ease or difficulty of the task being attempted. If a Hero's SKILL is reduced, through magic or injury, his Special Skills are reduced by the same amount.

Most of the Special Skills given for the Heroes are self-explanatory. A few, though, may need a little more explanation:

Awareness – The chance of sensing something out of the ordinary: this could include hearing someone sneaking up, smelling faint traces of poison, spotting a hidden trap, etc.

Con – The chance of duping someone, for example into believing what the Hero is saying or buying what the Hero is selling.

Dark Seeing – The ability to see in near darkness, especially underground. This Special Skill does not work in total darkness.

Dodge – The chance of getting out of the way of something or someone coming towards you at speed.

Magic – The lore of spells and sorcery; without this Skill, a spell cannot be cast at all; what's more, the Skill also determines the likelihood of its being cast correctly! Incidentally, the choice of this Special Skill requires so much concentration that the Hero will have his SKILL (and hence his other Special Skills) reduced to compensate.

Underground Lore – The ability to survive in a dungeon or cavern complex: not getting lost, noticing rock falls before they happen, etc.

Wood Lore – The ability to survive in woodland, this Skill includes the chance of finding food, staying on a path, tracking someone, finding shelter, and more.

World Lore – The chance of knowing a particular fact about an area's geography or history, or about the weather, local personalities, the right roads to take, and so on.

A comprehensive list of Special Skills and more detailed explanations are to be found later in this book, starting on page 114.

Spells

Magical spells are stored in the mind of the Hero, ready
to be invoked at an appropriate moment. Spells can be
quite powerful if used in the right situations – but they
can be risky, too. Casting a spell first requires a successful check against the Hero's *Magic* Special Skill. Activat-
ing a spell, whether it works or not, costs the Hero a
number of STAMINA points (the number for each spell is
listed after the spell's name). A Hero can continue casting spells until his STAMINA runs out (at which point he
dies – so be careful!). Spells which last for a certain length
of time may be automatically stopped before that time by
the spell-caster. The spells possessed by the characters in
our first adventure have the following effects:

Darkness (1) – Puts out all artificial light (and negates the
Dark Seeing Skill) in a circular area up to five metres round
the caster, for three minutes.

ESP (2) – Allows the spell-caster to read the general
feelings and emotions of any one nominated person or
being (not plants or rocks, unless they are intelligent!). It
can't read actual thoughts or words, and the longest time
it can last is one minute.

Fear (1) – Terrifies one nominated person, sending them cowering as far away from the spell-caster as possible. The effects last for two minutes.

Fire Bolt (1) – Hurls a blast of fire at one target, causing one die of damage to the victim's STAMINA.

Illusion (1) – Creates an illusion that will convince one person of its validity for up to three minutes. If anything happens to reveal that the illusory object doesn't exist or is not the thing that it appears to be, it reverts to its normal form immediately. A wound from, for example, an imaginary sword, will be revealed as having not really hurt only after the illusion has run out.

Levitate (2) – The object upon which this spell is cast is freed from the effects of gravity, causing it to move up or down in the air, under the caster's control. The caster may also levitate himself with this spell, which lasts for a maximum of five minutes.

Luck (1) – This spell restores up to 4 points to one character's LUCK score. A character's LUCK can never be raised higher than its *Initial* score.

Mirror Selves (2) – This illusion, which lasts for three minutes, convinces one person that there are now three of the spell-caster! If fighting, the victim has only one chance in three of choosing the right enemy. However, all three images of the caster may fight back and wound the victim!

Sleep (2) – This sends one person or creature to sleep for five minutes.

Stamina (1) – Similar to the *Luck* spell, this restores up to 6 points of one Hero's STAMINA, up to their *Initial* STAMINA score.

Weakness (1) – This spell temporarily reduces its victim's SKILL score by between 1 and 6 points (roll one die) for five minutes.

Director's Note
Spells which go wrong (that is, when the caster fails to make his *Magic* Skill roll) usually have the reverse effect, attacking the caster instead of the spell's intended victim. It is up to you to decide on the precise results; but our advice is to make it funny, but not unfair or lethal!

Many more spells will be available to Heroes after this first adventure. The full list of spells is given later, on page 125.

Equipment

This is simply what each Hero is currently carrying to help him on his quest. For this first adventure we have allotted every item already, and nothing more can be bought. For future adventures, the Heroes will be given the opportunity to purchase extra items.

Gold – This details what little money our Heroes are carrying. The standard coinage is the Gold Piece (often shortened to GP). The other common coins are Silver Pieces (SP); ten SPs equal one GP.

Background

Just who is the Hero, and where has he come from? This section adds a few relevant facts for the players' information.

Personality

This section summarizes our Hero's attitudes to life, the other Heroes, special enemies, and so on. This section should be used by each Hero's player as a basis for acting out the Hero's character as the adventure unfolds.

Quotes – The suggestions given here are just a few typical phrases that each Hero is fond of saying. Players are encouraged to invent more for their characters; others will surely become popular as the character progresses through his adventuring life!

Once all the players are at least vaguely aware of who they are playing, and are happy that they understand roughly what their SKILL and STAMINA scores mean, we can proceed straight away with the adventure. Are you ready to start shooting the fantasy adventure to top all fantasy adventures? Then let those titles roll!

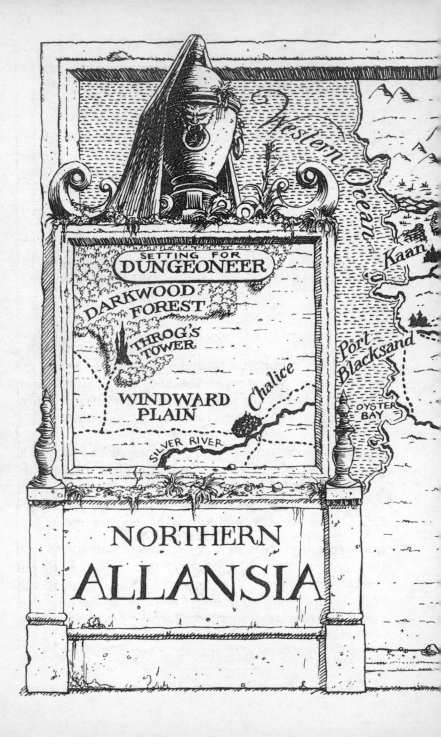

SETTING FOR
DUNGEONEER

DARKWOOD
FOREST

THROG'S
TOWER

WINDWARD
PLAIN

Chalice

SILVER RIVER

Western Ocean

Kaan

Port
Blacksand

OYSTER
BAY

NORTHERN
ALLANSIA

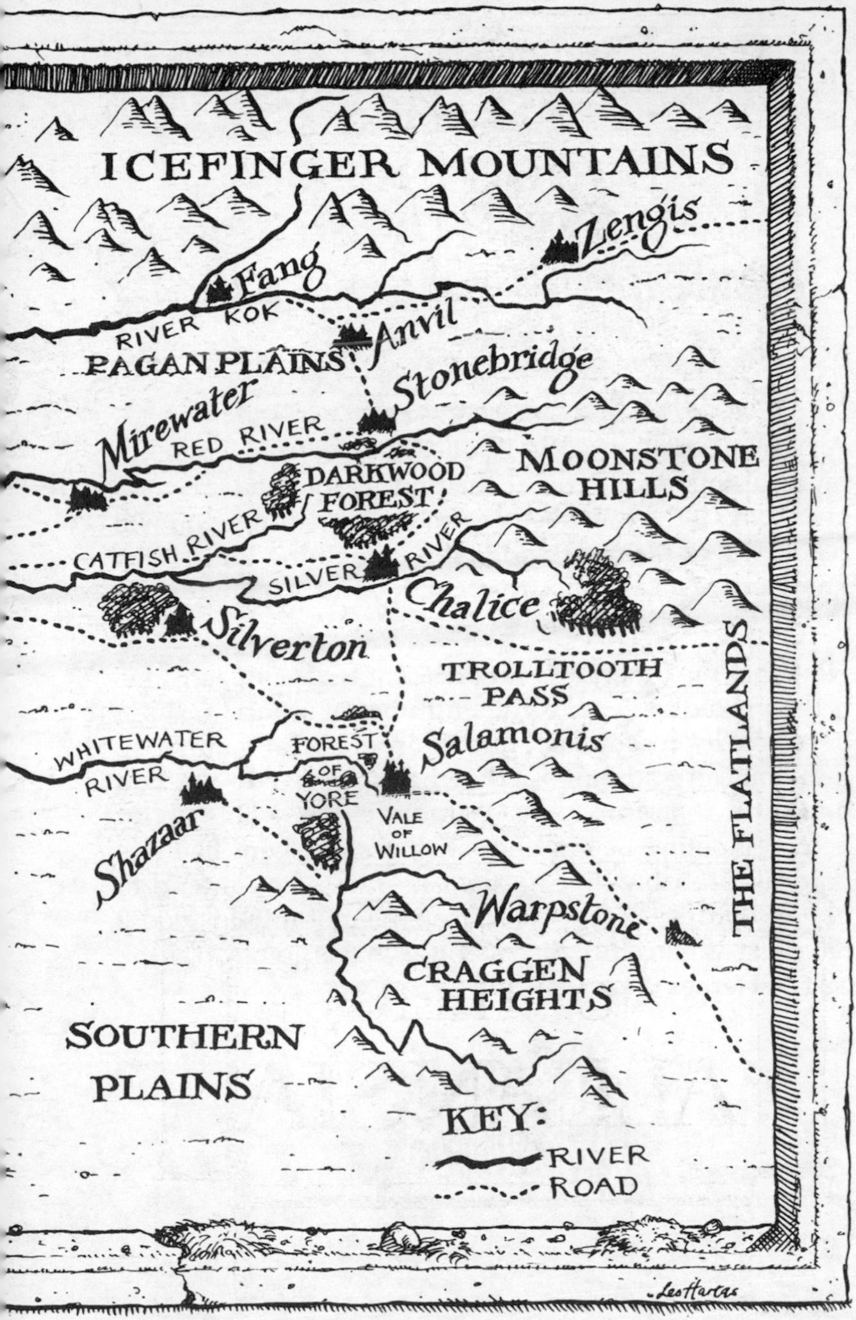
ICEFINGER MOUNTAINS
Zengis
Fang
RIVER KOK
Anvil
PAGAN PLAINS
Stonebridge
Mirewater
RED RIVER
MOONSTONE HILLS
DARKWOOD FOREST
CATFISH RIVER
SILVER RIVER
Chalice
Silverton
TROLLTOOTH PASS
WHITEWATER RIVER
FOREST OF YORE
Salamonis
Shazaar
VALE OF WILLOW
Warpstone
THE FLATLANDS
CRAGGEN HEIGHTS
SOUTHERN PLAINS
KEY:
RIVER
ROAD
Leo Hartas

DUNGEONEER ADVENTURE I: 'TOWER OF THE SORCERER'

Director's Introduction

All the information about this adventure, from this point on until the credits roll at the end, is for the Director's eyes only. If the cast needs to know something, you will read it out to them, provided it is something they *should* know or are able to discover. So, if you are a member of the cast, stop reading now. That's NOW.

Now that the others are out of earshot, Mr Director, this is the procedure: we've got a number of scenes to shoot here. We'll present each one in an identical manner so that you can find out exactly what you have to do. You may find it useful to read through the whole script before shooting begins, but with a short item like this you can probably dive straight in unless you intend to use any props. That way, too, as the plot unfolds you'll have just as much fun discovering what is going on as the cast of Heroes does.

As we come to each new scene, we'll describe the *Location* first. Generally we do this from the point of view of our imaginary camera as the scene opens. You can read this description out to the Heroes to help them visualize what they can see. The parts for you to read out directly will be in *italic text like this*. Sometimes a map will be included for the benefit of those of you who like to use miniatures. On other occasions there will be a picture which you can show the heroes.

Next comes the *Plot Summary*: a few quick lines solely for your benefit so you will know straight away what is about to happen.

This is followed by the *Cast List*. No, not the Heroes; this time we mean all the bit parts, the Extras and, most importantly, the Bad Guys. Most of them appear in only one or two scenes, which is why we haven't allocated players for them. So who plays all these characters? You do – remember? And your friends playing the Heroes thought they were having all the fun, eh? Well, since you are working harder than they are, we've saved the best roles for you. The Bad Guys may just get killed in the end, but all the same they are great fun to play.

Next come the *Props*, those little bits and pieces which are not at all essential to the plot but help liven things up a bit and create a good atmosphere. These things may need a bit of preparation, so, if you do want to use them, make sure you've got everything ready before shooting begins.

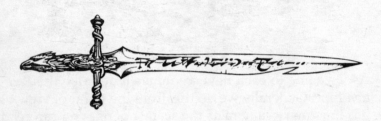

And so to the call for *Action!* In some scenes there will be more than one Action! segment, but some of them happen only if the cast do certain things. For each one we will tell you what is supposed to happen, how to make sure it does (we can't have the cast running away with the plot, can we?) and when to cut that part of the scene and move on to something else. We'll also provide some suggestions for the script, especially when one of the Bad Guys has a big dramatic speech to make!

Of course sometimes a member of the cast will do something so dumb (or even so wonderful) that the whole plot seems to be in danger of being overturned. Because of this, we've included a *Problems?* section for each scene, and this will help you get the show back on the road.

Finally, there are the *Turn To* . . . instructions. In movies, you never have to spend ages watching the Heroes travelling from place to place or sitting around waiting for wounds to heal; but occasionally you need to explain how they got from where they were in the last scene to where they will be in the next. We have the additional complication that the cast have a certain amount of freedom in what they can do. Because of this, they won't necessarily use every scene. So this section tells you which scene to shoot next, and how the Heroes manage to get there.

Are you all set? Have you got your dice ready? Are all the players sitting comfortably and attentively? Here we go then, Scene One . . . Roll cameras!

Scene 1 – Into The Forest

Location

You should read out the following to your players, to set the scene for the action to come:

The adventure opens on a lonely forest road. As the imaginary camera tracks forward, we see a line of mounted soldiers. Their uniforms are splendid; but as we move around to see their faces, it is obvious that they are none too happy with their surroundings. Although picked veterans, they all have a nervous, worried expression. Many of them ride with their hands resting upon the pommel of their sword.

Our camera now pans along the line of troops towards the head of the column, observing the faces as it goes. At the front we see several unusual individuals. Obviously they are not soldiers, yet some of them look as if they could take on the entire column by themselves. These are our Heroes, and as they ride along they are deep in conversation with a richly dressed young man and the commander of the soldiers.

Finally the camera moves forward to view the overgrown path ahead of the company; then it rises into the branches of the forest and beyond. We see a lone, rocky crag towering above the trees. At the top of it is a grim, evil-looking castle. Cue dramatic sound-effects and swirling, epic music on the imaginary soundtrack!

The camera now swings back down to watch the Heroes and soldiers ride past. As they do so, decorative text scrolls up the screen to explain to the viewer (and, in our case, the cast) what is going on, while a deep voice (yours) reads out for the benefit, presumably, of those viewers who can't read:

In the year 285 After Chaos, King Pindar of Chalice, knowing that his aged body would not see many more summers and fearful of the advance of Evil, sought to provide for the safety of his people after his demise. Mindful that a small city-state like Chalice could not stand alone for long, he sought an alliance with mighty Salamonis. It so happened that King Salamon had a daughter of similar age to Pindar's son, and so a marriage was arranged. But before Prince Barinjhar and the lovely Sarissa could be wed, the Princess was kidnapped, even as she rode to meet her intended husband, by Xortan Throg, an evil-hearted sorcerer who dwelt deep in the forests, north of the Catfish River.

King Pindar hastily summoned his counsellors. Chalice was in dire danger, for surely Salamonis would be angry at the poor care taken of its princess, and how could such a small city hope to provide enough warriors to overcome a mighty wizard? Why, his rocky castle looked as if it could withstand the onslaught of every army in Allansia. In desperation, it was suggested that the king hire a small, select band of expert adventurers, the sort of people to whom no odds are too high and wizard killing is all in a day's work . . .

Plot Summary

The Heroes (and their players) learn of their quest and arrive at the wizard's castle.

Cast List

Prince Barinjhar
The prince is the richly dressed young man we saw at the head of the column. His father has trained him carefully and he is as polite and courteous as you would expect an Allansian prince and heir to the throne of a city-state to be. Yet he is no idle, foppish nobleman. He rides as expertly as his bodyguard and is keen to get to grips with the wizard who has stolen his fiancée.

Morval
The captain of the guard is a veteran of many years spent guarding Chalice against the forces of incessant Evil and infernal Chaos. He has never been to war, for Chalice has not fought one in Pindar's lifetime; but he is an able soldier and would doubtless serve well if ever called upon to do so. He has considerable admiration for the Heroes and, were he ten years younger, might well have asked to go with them into the tower.

The Royal Bodyguard
These motley troops are Extras who serve no dramatic function other than to ride along behind the Prince looking worried.

Props

None are needed for this first section, which is all talking and explanation.

Action!

1. The Conversation

As the Heroes ride along, they have the opportunity to question Barinjhar and Morval about the wizard. They should also be taking the opportunity to establish their personalities and reveal some detail of their past background. All the Heroes have been hired from various parts of Allansia, so they will need to introduce themselves to one another too. Let the players ease into their roles gently, but ensure that everyone says something in character before the conversation comes to an end. Hopefully they will ask lots of questions themselves. If not, or if you prefer to take full control to begin with (usually a good idea if everyone is a novice player), here are some speeches for Barinjhar and Morval which will reveal to the Heroes all the information that is available.

BARINJHAR: *'To some extent, my friends, I blame myself. Had I come to meet her as I had wished, I might have been able to do something to save her, but Father persuaded me that the proper thing to do was for us to meet at the city gates. Due pomp and ceremony and all that, a nice spectacle for the people, gives them an excuse to stop work for a bit of a celebration. Still, if these brave men could not save her, what could I have done?'*

MORVAL (bowing his head as he starts to speak to his liege): *'Very little, I suspect, sire. I stayed as close to the Princess as possible. We were on the main forest road, of course, the one that runs east of here, as it's much wider and easier to spot an ambush. We saw the Goblins coming a mile off and I had my men in position in good time. It's almost a routine man-oeuvre; they rush out, we ride them down; it beats me why they keep trying!*

'Anyway, all was going well, when suddenly there was a great scream above me. I looked up and saw a huge Griffin diving straight for the Princess. Fortunately I still had my spear to hand, but not having time to charge I had no speed behind it and my thrust was deflected by the thick feathers on the belly of the monster. The beast took the Princess's horse in the neck, killing it instantly, and as it did so the sorcerer – for he was riding upon its back – reached down and pulled the girl away. I thrust again and took a fair bunch of feathers from its tail, yelling all the

while to my men to get bows, but the wizard had planned his attack well. By the time we had disengaged from the Goblins and readied our bows, the Griffin was away over the trees and out of sight. He's a cunning opponent all right; we'll have our work cut out to get her back.'

BARINJHAR: 'Cunning he may be, Morval, but we have the gods on our side. I wouldn't fancy the chances of anyone assaulting that castle, even if he had a legion of Dragons at his back. But our priests tell us there is a secret entrance to the castle, hidden in the trees at the base of the crag. If this divination proves correct – and who am I to doubt the word of the gods? – then while I distract the wizard with talk of ransom our friends here can sneak in and catch him unawares.'

MORVAL: ''Tis a good enough plan, sire, and, as you say, one with divine blessing. One thing still puzzles me, though, and that is why he did it. Now, granted that most wizards are a pretty bad lot – comes from all that cavorting with Demons and the like, I shouldn't wonder – though this fellow has some pretty disreputable servants, he's never given us any trouble before. Twenty years he's lived there in that keep and the worst complaint we've heard of him is that his Goblins steal the odd sheep from the villages on the edge of the forest. Why, some folk even said the king should make him an adviser. What can we have done to offend him?'

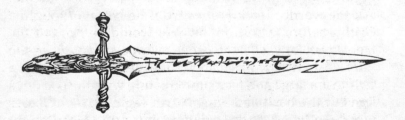

BARINJHAR: *'Naught that I know of, faithful Morval, but men's minds are sometimes turned by other things than offence. After all, if what you tell me of this young princess is true, then any man might take risks for her, especially if he were a lonely old man with none but Goblins and Trolls for company!'*

If you are having difficulty getting your players to speak, try having Prince Barinjhar ask them questions. Have they fought wizards before? Do they know much magic? Ask them individually, perhaps giving a question that will help them display their personalities and back-grounds. If they are included in the party, for example, ask the warrior Jerek Stormgard if he has ever fought a Griffin before (a truthful answer would be no, but the Hero could always lie in order to appear braver), or the Elf if she is at all worried about the quest? (Incidentally, a Griffin is a large and fearsome creature with the body of a lion but the head and wings of an eagle. All the Heroes will have heard of the creature, but none have fought with one.)

Once most of the information has been revealed and the conversation is starting to drag (maybe sooner, maybe later, depending on your players), move to the next part of the scene by having Barinjhar say:

'Hush! This must be the gnarled oak of which our priests spoke. Aye, there appears to be a path through the trees here. Morval, you accompany our friends into the forest. When you report back that they have found the entrance, I will make myself known to the wizard and ask to speak with him.'

2. Finding the Entrance

The Heroes must now dismount and move through the trees on foot, accompanied by Morval. There is a clearly marked path. If present, Aspen Darkfire and Axel Wolfric could look around and use their *Wood Lore* Special Skill here. If either asks to use it, get them to roll two dice. If the total is equal to or less than their *Wood Lore* score (10 or less in this instance), they will realize that the path is used regularly by Goblins. If the total rolled is 11 or 12, they don't notice any clues as to who or what made or uses the path.

After a short while the Heroes arrive at a cave entrance. Here Morval wishes them the best of luck and returns to the prince. They can ask him for any information they might have missed on the way, if they have any further questions – but, once he has gone, they are on their own.

Problems?

Let us hope that the Heroes will not be so cowardly as to try to get out of their quest, but they may ask for some assistance, perhaps a few soldiers to accompany them. Barinjhar says he would love to go but his father has forbidden it, and in any case he has to distract the wizard. As for the troops, they are needed to protect him. Anyway, they are far too nervous of the sorcerer's reputed power to go anywhere where they might meet him face to face again!

Something else the Heroes may do, especially if one of them is the Dwarf (Grimbold Tornhelm), is to ask about payment. Naturally King Pindar intends to reward them as richly as his small kingdom can afford, but the terms are strictly payment by results. After all, if the Heroes fail, Pindar must have the means left to hire others. If this topic comes up, Barinjhar will remind the Heroes that the agreement was that they would be 'handsomely rewarded' by his father once the job was done.

Turn To . . .

Once Morval has left the Heroes, the action moves immediately to *Scene 2 – Into the Crag!*.

Scene 2 – Into The Crag!

Location

This scene begins with the Heroes entering a half-hidden cave at the foot of the crag. They light torches – at least, we hope they do! – and move slowly forward. The cave soon narrows to an uneven passage which climbs slowly up through the rock. The Heroes must struggle forward, heads bent because of the low ceiling, in single file. A small stream trickles down through the tunnel, making the rock underfoot wet and treacherous.

That will do for telling the Heroes what they can see. Read out to them what they encounter, using the above as a guide, as they tell you what they are doing moving forward up the tunnel, we hope! They've got a few decisions to make before you reveal any more, but while we're describing locations we'll let you know what they are going to find further up the tunnel when they get there. Don't reveal the following information to them until they push on up the tunnel.

After a fairly long and clumsy climb, the tunnel ends in a huge natural cave. The weak light from the Heroes' torches will not be sufficient to see right across it. *Dark Seeing* is no use when a torch is lit, and without a torch the Dwarf cannot see any further than the others could with the torch. At the far side is an artificially widened tunnel with stairs which presumably lead up to the castle. On either side of the cave are many small tunnels leading off to the caverns in which Xortan Throg's Goblin hordes live. Unknown to the Heroes (for the moment), the shadowy recesses of the cave are packed with armed Goblin warriors.

49

Plot Summary

The Heroes carefully make their way up the tunnel. In the great cave they are ambushed by an army of Goblins. Many of the Goblins are slaughtered and the rest flee in terror!

Cast List

Large numbers of Goblins who will get carved to pieces (poor Goblins!). The Goblins are armed with long daggers and each has SKILL 5 and STAMINA 5. Yes, we realize that may not mean much to you just yet, but it will in a moment; just bear with us for now.

Props

If you are running this game during the evening or night, you may like to turn the lights down for the first part of this scene and then switch them up again suddenly when the Goblins attack. Don't do this if you can't see to read out what comes next, of course.

Action!

1. Up the Tunnel

You will need to check what the Heroes are doing as they make their way up the rocky passage. *You* know that they are going to be ambushed; they don't, but hopefully they will want to take precautions against the chance of it happening. Do they use torches, or do they try to find their way blind, led by the *Dark Seeing* Dwarf? Torches will be noticed by the Goblins, of course, but in the dark the Heroes will miss their footing and fall, making quite a lot of noise.

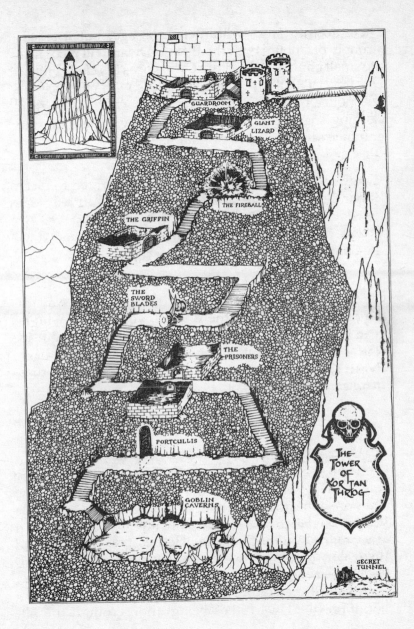

GUARDROOM

GIANT
LIZARD

THE FIREBALL

THE GRIFFIN

THE
SWORD
BLADES

THE
PRISONERS

PORTCULLIS

THE
TOWER
OF
XOR·TAN
THROG

GOBLIN
CAVERNS

SECRET
TUNNEL

51

There are no tracks within the passage, but it smells strongly of Goblin; both the Elf and Dwarf will recognize the smell immediately. If the Dwarf uses his *Underground Lore* Special Skill (by rolling 10 or less with two dice) he will notice other tell-tale signs, such as bits of ragged clothing snagged on rocks. Although well hidden, the entrance seems to be in regular use.

Check the order in which the Heroes make their way up the passage, by asking them to tell you exactly who is where in the line. This isn't actually important, but in other circumstances it might well be, so you should ask about it here as well, so as not to make the Heroes suspicious.

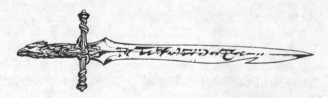

Once you have established the order of march and answered any questions the Heroes may have about their surroundings using the *Location* section, you should be able to move straight on to *Action!* segment 2. However, if the Heroes are engaged in interesting conversation (the Dwarf likes being underground, the Elf hates it, the thief is suspicious, everyone else can invent their own opinions), let them get on with it for a while before moving on.

2. At the End of the Tunnel
When the Heroes get to the end of the tunnel they will probably want to check out the cave before actually setting foot in it. This is a difficult moment for you, as you have to choose exactly the right time to spring the ambush.

Goblin Caverns

The Heroes will not be able to see or hear the Goblins from where they are. If one of them is sent forward as a scout, spring the trap fairly quickly. You will need to leave the scout time to run back to his friends, otherwise he will stand no chance – and you don't want to kill anyone off this early. If the entire group marches into the cavern, then the Goblins can make a better job of it by waiting until they are sure they can surround the Heroes easily.

54

The Goblins don't have anything to say as they leap out from their hiding places, but they can utter all sorts of horrid, inhuman war-cries as they charge forward. (Yell any old gibberish at your players, but make it sound horrid!) Goblins are nasty, green-skinned, humanoid creatures, smaller and skinnier than a man (see the illustration). They are also brutish and ugly but with a self-serving intelligence. They are dressed in scraps of cloth and tattered fragments of armour, and they carry long, jagged daggers. Some of those at the back light big torches, illuminating the whole of the cavern. The purpose of this is to show how many Goblins there are ('lots and lots' – the Heroes don't have time to count the exact numbers!); it also gives you an opportunity to describe the cavern to the Heroes. To inexpert eyes the situation should look quite hopeless.

3. The Fight
The Heroes should have time to move back to back as the Goblins circle them, or, if the Goblins have to attack early, side by side in the tunnel mouth. This means that they need fight only one Goblin at any one time. As the Goblins are pretty feeble fighters, they should die quite quickly. Once each Hero has killed two or three Goblins, the rest of the Goblins flee back into their tunnels. An especially good time to have them retreat is just after one of the Heroes has cast a spectacular spell, if they can (and do!). The Heroes should then be able to make their way across the cave to the staircase. This ends the scene.

Here's how to fight. Each Goblin has similar characteristics to those possessed by all the Heroes, possessing SKILL 5 and STAMINA 5. You will need to keep track of these figures on some rough paper. Each hero should decide which weapon he is using (normally the one in which he has a Special Skill, as he is better at fighting with that one). Only close-up weapons can be used; bows cannot be used. Sort out each battle between one specific Hero and a Goblin before moving on to the next.

The sequence of combat is as follows:

(1) You roll two dice and add the result to the Goblin's SKILL (5).

(2) The Hero rolls two dice and adds the result to the Special Skill score for the weapon he is using (or to the *Initial* SKILL if he hasn't a Special Skill in any weapon).

(3) Compare scores. If the Goblin's score is higher, it has wounded the Hero: turn to (5). If the Hero's score is higher, he has wounded the Goblin: turn to (4). If both scores are equal, the blows have been blocked or avoided. Return to (1) and begin another round of fighting.

(4) Ask the player to roll one die and cross-reference the result with the weapon being used, on this chart:

	DIE-ROLL					
	1	2	3	4	5	6
SWORD	1	2	2	2	2	3
AXE	2	2	2	2	2	3
DAGGER	1	1	2	2	2	2
STAFF	1	2	2	2	2	2

The number given is the number of points deducted from the Goblin's STAMINA because of the injury. If a Goblin's STAMINA score drops to zero, it is dead. Otherwise, turn to (6).

(5) Roll one die on the 'Dagger' row of the above table. The Hero loses the number indicated from his STAMINA score. If any Hero's STAMINA score drops to 1 or 2, the Goblins will run away; no Hero should die here – the adventure must continue! (This last point applies to this fight only. Other creatures will fight to the death!)

(6) Begin the next round by returning to (1), and carry on fighting.

Magic: Any Hero who is able to use magic has the option of *either* casting a spell at a Goblin *or* fighting him. The Hero should choose which he wants to do; if he chooses to fight, use the method we've just detailed. If he chooses magic, let him state which spell he is going to use (we recommend *Fire Bolt*, *Fear* or *Sleep*, if available).

Don't forget that casting a spell requires a successful roll against the Hero's *Magic* Skill using two dice. If the roll is equal to or less than the Hero's *Magic* Special Skill score, the spell works properly (you should check the time on your watch if the spell is one which lasts for a specific duration – and don't forget that, once the time's up, the Goblin may well pop straight back up into the fight!). Any Goblin struck by a *Fire Bolt* will lose between 1 and 6 STAMINA points (roll one die) in a tremendous flash of light which may well scare off several other Goblins. If the *Magic* roll fails, the spell goes terribly wrong – think up something funny that is appropriate to the spell and inflict it! For example, a messed-up *Sleep* could send the spell-caster into a deep slumber!

Problems?

The route into the Wizard's castle should be quite obvious to the Heroes, but there are a few stupid or cowardly things they could do. If they try to flee back into the tunnel they came from, point out that it is low and cramped and that they could not fight, or even flee, effectively in there. The Goblins will catch up with them and fight, though the narrowness of the tunnel means that not everyone will be involved.

It is possible that one of the Heroes has really rotten luck with the dice; they are not supposed to die here, and there are ways of preventing this. For instance, you can make the Goblins even more cowardly and have them flee sooner. This may seem a little like cheating, but this is your film; what's going to become of your fabulous closing battle if all your stars get rubbed out in the second scene?

After the fight, the Heroes may decide to hunt down the Goblins rather than get on with the rescue. This is not very heroic – and it is also very difficult. The Goblins will have retreated into side-tunnels which are only just big enough for them (and therefore much too small for every Hero except the Dwarf, who should be restrained by the other characters if necessary).

Possibly one of the Heroes will be smart enough to capture a Goblin alive and interrogate it (you should dissuade them from torturing the poor thing; these *are* the Good Guys, remember). The Goblin can confirm that the stairs lead up to the castle. It adds that the wizard's hirelings include a few Orcs, an Ogre and the much-feared Griffin. More than this the Goblins do not know – they are not allowed into the castle; furthermore, the wizard has set many magical traps to prevent them getting in. Don't worry if the Heroes decide to take the captive with them – he won't last long.

Turn To . . .

As soon as the Heroes regroup and start to ascend the staircase, move immediately to *Scene 3 – The Wizard's Tower*.

Scene 3 – The Wizard's Tower

Location

The Heroes make their way up through the main tower of the wizard's castle. It is well built and obviously very sturdy. If the Dwarf is present he may well admire the fine workmanship (if he doesn't, you can always point it out to the Heroes). At several points, they will encounter traps designed to keep the Goblins out of the castle; these will be described in the appropriate *Action!* segments. The Heroes will also pass several stout wooden doors which they may check in the hope of finding Princess Sarissa. Again the rooms behind the doors will be described in the appropriate places.

Plot Summary

The Heroes ascend the central tower of the castle, avoiding various traps and encountering prisoners and monsters as they go.

Cast List

This scene features two human prisoners, plus the Griffin and a Giant Lizard. The Griffin, as we have already said, is a very large creature, part eagle and part lion. The Giant Lizard is slightly larger than a carthorse, green and scaly.

GRIFFIN   SKILL 12   STAMINA 15

2 Attacks, Large claws (as Sword)

GIANT LIZARD   SKILL 8   STAMINA 9

Large bite (as Sword)

Props

None for this section. Miniatures, while letting you see where everyone is in the fight scenes, are not essential to play.

Action!

There is a separate *Action!* segment for each trap or room that the Heroes come across. None of these is designed to pose any great danger unless the Heroes do something stupid. Certainly they need not fight either of the monsters. You should try to keep things moving along, especially if the Heroes are having difficulty working out how to get past a particular trap. This scene is an interlude between fights, designed to introduce some of the other skills that the Heroes possess. It should not be allowed to drag on and become boring. Finally, please remember that you are here to present the adventure to the Heroes; it is not sporting to try to kill them off at every opportunity (it's also no fun for the players if you do). In other words, give them a fair chance at solving the puzzles.

1. The Portcullis

At the top of the stairs is a passageway. A loose flagstone in the passage floor triggers a portcullis which thunders down from an unseen groove in the ceiling, hopefully (from the sorcerer's point of view) impaling anyone who is passing beneath. If the Heroes have a Goblin prisoner leading the way, this is an excellent – if messy – way to get rid of him.

However, they will probably be taking more care. If the Dwarf is present, he might suggest using his *Trap Sensing* Skill. He should roll two dice and try to roll a number equal to or less than his Special Skill score (10). If he is successful, he will notice the slit in the ceiling. You need to put at least the weight of a Goblin on the flagstone to activate the trap, so a gentle prod would not activate it.

Should they trigger the trap, they still have an opportunity to roll out of the way. This can be done in one of two ways. If any of the Heroes has *Dodge* Special Skill, he can try to dodge the portcullis as it falls. He should roll two dice. If the result is less than or equal to his Special Skill score, he dodges successfully; if he rolls higher, he gets caught under the portcullis. Alternatively, any Hero can try *Testing his Luck*. He should try to roll his LUCK score or less using two dice. If he does this, he is Lucky and has managed to avoid the portcullis. Whether the roll is successful or not, the Hero must reduce his LUCK score by 1 point (every Hero has only so much good fortune). If a Hero gets hit by the portcullis, it will cause 5 points of damage; subtract this from his STAMINA.

The trap can be avoided by jumping over the loose flagstone or edging round it – it doesn't quite fill the width of the passageway. If some Heroes are trapped on the wrong (cavern) side, the portcullis can be lifted far enough for someone to crawl through (a combined SKILL of 20 is required to do this; add together the SKILL scores of everyone lifting until they total 20 or more). If Axel Wolfric is present, he can attempt to lift it by himself by making a successful roll against his *Strength* Skill. Really smart Heroes may think to fetch a boulder from the cavern below to wedge underneath the dropped portcullis so that everyone can wriggle under in safety.

2. The Prisoners

After the passageway with the portcullis in it, some more stairs lead up and round a corner, to reveal another passage. The Heroes should get the impression that they are ascending a tower. There are two wooden doors here on opposite sides of the passage. No sound can be heard at either (but don't tell the Heroes unless they ask to listen). Both doors are locked.

Someone with a lock-picking skill could probably open them. Since none of the Heroes has this, though, a *Fire Bolt* spell or a hefty kick from a strong character like Stormgard or Wolfric will break the lock, though you should comment on the amount of noise they make. The noise doesn't mean much: the intention here is simply to make the players increasingly nervous as their characters creep through the sorcerer's tower.

Prisoners' Cells

Behind the doors are two cells, but neither contains the princess. Instead the Heroes find two wretched, misshapen peasants whom Xortan Throg has been using for his experiments. They are suitably grateful at being rescued, profusely thanking the Heroes with much pathetic forelock-tugging, but otherwise are of little use. Their main dramatic role is to emphasize that the wizard is wicked through and through. You should play up their wretchedness as much as possible, but then move on as soon as the Heroes have had a chance to express their anger and sympathy.

3. The Sword Blades

More steps, another corner, and another corridor. On either side of this passageway are giant stone hands; each clasps a huge scimitar, which it swings back and forth across the passage in a murderous arc! Anyone trying to walk down the passage will be sliced in two!

The Swords

Initially the Heroes may be shocked and frightened by the hands. But again there are several ways past this trap. Anyone with the *Climb* Special Skill could, following a successful roll, move along the wall above the hands where there is a space free of the blades; he could also knock a blade out of the hand while up there. Rangor could attempt to *Levitate* up and achieve the same object. A well-aimed bow shot (requires the successful roll of a *Bow* Special Skill) will knock the sword out of a hand. A boulder fetched from the cavern could jam a blade. The Heroes could try running past (test against *Dodge* skill) but, if they fail, the penalty is a savage cut and 4 points deducted from the Hero's STAMINA.

The Griffin

4. The Griffin

After the next set of stairs is yet another passage, this time with one door set in the side. The door is locked and barred on the outside. A Hero listening at the door will hear noises suggestive of a large, clawed beast; he will also smell the scent of a large animal and feel a draught coming from under the door.

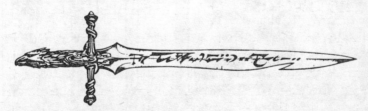

This is the lair of the Griffin. The far end of the room lacks a wall and is open to the air, but is barred by huge iron gates which can be opened to allow the creature to fly out. (This is the reason for the draught.) If the door is opened, the Griffin will rear up on its hind legs and screech. It is a very ferocious sight, especially startling to someone who has never seen a Griffin before (probably everyone present!).

If the Heroes decide to open the door to the room, they should be told what is inside and quickly asked to declare what they do next. If they say something like 'immediately slam the door and bar it!', let them do that. If they hesitate, the Griffin will bound across the room and they will have to fight. Although a trained riding beast, the Griffin is intelligent, vicious and loyal. It will try to kill anyone who is not its master. Its master is Xortan Throg.

Up to three Heroes can attack the Griffin at once (unless they opt to fight it in the doorway, in which case only one can get at it). The Griffin has two attacks. This means it can fight two opponents simultaneously; so two Heroes fight the Griffin as usual (rolling two dice plus Special Skill or *Initial* SKILL, as before). A third Hero can also fight as usual, but if the Griffin wins a round it does no damage to this Hero, merely fending off the blows. If only one Hero is fighting the Griffin from the doorway, the beast has only one attack, and combat continues in a normal fashion. The Griffin cannot get through the door into the corridor.

If anyone wishes to try a spell, their *Magic* Special Skill must be reduced temporarily by 3 points (so that someone with a *Magic* Skill score of 10 must roll 7 or less to succeed in casting a spell), because a creature the size of the Griffin isn't as easy to affect as someone of human size. As usual, a failed roll will result in something unexpected happening instead.

It is possible that a Hero will be killed here, but that is his own fault – the Heroes didn't have to fight, and the Griffin is an innocent creature. The Griffin has no treasure (would you give your pets gold and jewellery to play with? Well, the sorcerer hasn't). Its skin may be valuable in the markets of somewhere like Salamonis or Port Blacksand, but no one is going to stay and skin the beast right now, are they? Good. When everyone is ready (and after a spell-caster has tried to dish out some healing by means of a *Stamina* spell, perhaps), they may move on up the corridor.

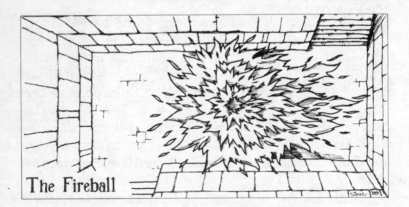

The Fireball

5. The Fireball
Beyond the Griffin's lair the passage ends in more stairs. As soon as the Heroes turn the corner at the top of the stairs, they see a long passage with a huge ball of spitting flame rolling slowly towards them. This object fills the entire passage; there is no way round it.

The Heroes can retreat back round the corner, but if they so much as poke their heads around, they see the fireball advancing upon them again, exactly as it was doing before; it doesn't seem to have got any closer. Strangely, it does not pursue them round the corner. This is because it is not really there – it is just an illusion to scare the Goblins and cannot harm anything – but the Heroes have to work this out for themselves. If they seem to be having trouble, suggest to them that despite the great ball of fire near by, they don't seem to be feeling any heat. The illusion cannot be dispelled by anything, but anyone walking through it will simply pass through into the passageway beyond.

6. The Giant Lizard
Beyond the fireball is another locked and barred door. Once again, noises and smells from the room beyond are suggestive of a large, clawed animal. This is the Giant Lizard – one of the large, trained beasts suitable for riding. A saddle and bridle hanging from pegs in the room should give the game away here. The Heroes can avoid a messy encounter by slamming the door, just as they should have done for the Griffin. Alternatively, they could just be firm with it as they would with any

Giant Lizard

other trained mount. If they do get to fight, it should be handled in the same way as with the Griffin. The beast has only one attack; anyone else fighting acts in the normal way, but if the Lizard wins a round against this second assailant, it does no damage in that instance.

The creature is worth far more alive than dead and could be taken by the Heroes. However, it is not trained as a cavalry animal and will refuse to enter a fight with a rider. It could be ridden elsewhere after a successful roll of a *Ride* skill (but deduct 2 from the Skill score for this roll, because the mount is not a horse).

Problems?

These traps should not pose too much of a problem for the Heroes, but if it is necessary to prompt them, then do so (especially if your players are beginners). Rather than just give them a clue, we recommend instead that you take one Hero aside and say something that uses that Hero's abilities or background. For example, confronted by the fireball, tell a spell-caster like Rangor or Darkfire: 'This immediately strikes you as very odd, being well

versed in the ways of magic. A huge permanent fireball like this requires a colossal amount of magical energy and no one would use such a thing to guard a passage. Besides, the air should be scalding hot anywhere close to it.' Or, for the Lizard, perhaps tell Brondwyn or Wolfric: 'On your extensive travels through Allansia you have seen such beasts being ridden, and it surprised you how docile they become when trained – like this one could be.'

Turn To . . .

Past the Lizard's room are yet more stone stairs. At the top of these is a large set of double doors, closed. If the Heroes listen, they will hear grunting sounds and dice being rolled. When they open these doors go to *Scene 4 – The Guardroom.*

Scene 4 – The Guardroom

Location

The guardroom is a largish room which covers both entrances to the upper parts of the castle. As the floorplan here shows, one set of doors lead to the stairway and down into the crag, one set leads to the main courtyard, and the third leads to the wizard's chambers. The room is sparsely furnished – just a few rough chairs and a table. In the third wall is a fireplace, and over the fire are the remains of a recently roasted something . . . quite possibly a Goblin?

FIREPLACE

TO THE
SORCERER

HEROES

COURTYARD

The Guardroom

Plot Summary

The Heroes somehow try to make their way past the wizard's brutish and inhuman guards.

Cast List

This scene features a number of Orcs (one per Hero, but a minimum of two) and Grudthak the Ogre. Orcs are like larger, more devious and better-organized Goblins, while Ogres appear to be even larger and broader versions of Orcs – with all the increases in nastiness that that implies. The Orcs, while knowing themselves to be superior to the Goblin hordes, are still minor lackeys; they grumble all the time but leap into combat as soon as they are told to – because the only other alternative is fighting Grudthak. When the Heroes arrive, the Orcs are playing dice to decide who gets the final leg of the Goblin. This is in fact a waste of time, because they all know that Grudthak will want it – but there's nothing else for them to do until the Heroes arrive.

The Ogre is leaning back in a rickety chair by the fire sucking on the remains of the Goblin's other leg. He is a lazy fellow who prefers not to fight unless he has to. Most of his fighting therefore involves keeping his subordinates in order – a task which, for someone of his size, is quite easy. As a result, he is not very fit and is therefore not quite as fearsome as he looks (he looks *very* fearsome).

ORCS each SKILL 5 STAMINA 6

Sword

GRUDTHAK THE OGRE SKILL 8 STAMINA 10
2 attacks Heavy club (damage as Sword +1 point),
Strength *Special Skill 10*

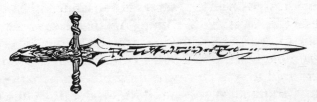

Props

During the fight Grudthak periodically flings half-chewed Goblin bones at the Heroes. If you want to simulate this for your players, a few of the toy bones that pet shops sell for dogs to chew on will come in useful here. If you want to be really authentic, a batch of week-old fried chicken drumsticks would be more suitable – but we don't see why you should behave as disgustingly as the Ogre.

If there are more than three Heroes in the party, things may prove rather confused once the fighting starts. To get the best results out of this fight, it will be helpful for you to use miniatures and a playing board (which you can draw on a piece of paper, laid out according to the map). This means that both you and the Heroes will be able to see exactly where each fighter and each piece of furniture is. Don't draw the furniture on the map; use a die or square of thin card to depict each item as it could well move about quite a bit. If you don't have any miniatures, you could use counters from a boardgame or pieces of paper to represent the protagonists.

Action!

When the Heroes first come through the door, the Orc guards will look up from their game, grab their swords and grin. A single grinning Orc is not a pretty sight; since there is an Orc for every Hero, this scene of multiple grinning Orcs could rank as quite X-certificate! Grudthak, meanwhile, puts down the piece of bone he was gnawing, and grunts out the following speech. The Ogre has a very deep, guttural voice and sneers unpleasantly as he speaks:

''Ere, you took yer time, didn't yer? I hope you ain't hurt none of the master's pets – or we might just have to take you alive, which won't be at all nice for you now, will it? No, it won't; no, not nice at all!'

Hopefully the Heroes will see fit to boast a bit in return, in a vain attempt to scare off the Orcs or perturb Grudthak. You should encourage them to do so, though it does no good. Orcs and Ogres never listen to what humans say if they can help it; there are always more important things to be done, like killing them.

If they think about it, the Heroes may gather from Grudthak's comments that they were expected, and can ask about this:

78

'Oh aye!' replies the Ogre. 'We been lookin' forward to your arrival fer ages and ages. Blinkin' borin' it were, too! Ain't that so, lads?'

'Grunt, snarl, yooman scum! Huk huk!' comment the Orcs with a widening of fanged grins.

More information than this cannot be obtained. Indeed, none of the guards actually knows how their sorcerous master knew that the Heroes were coming. Like all the other things he knows, it was somehow mysterious, uncanny and best not thought about. After all, thinking is a tiring business when you are an Orc.

The plan for the fight – and there seems little doubt that there will be one now – is that each Hero should fight one Orc (you will doubtless have noticed that we cunningly provided one each for this purpose) and then afterwards everyone can gang up on the Ogre.

During the first part of the fight, therefore, Grudthak will remain slouched in his chair, chewing idly on the roast leg and tossing bits of bone and what he considers to be witty and sarcastic comments into the fray. The bones don't hurt or distract anyone enough to make any difference. He will make no effort to fight until all the Orcs are dead – but if one Hero finishes his Orc off quickly, he may be able to force combat, especially if he makes a move to enter the wizard's chambers through the door.

This should be the most entertaining incident of the adventure, and you should take every opportunity to liven it up and play it for laughs. As well as the Ogre's sarcastic running commentary – and whatever oaths and grunts you care to give the Orcs – you have some furniture to play with, perhaps even a burning brand out of the fire or that one remaining Goblin leg.

Everyone will move towards one another and initiate combat. Combat is as before, with each round consisting of dice-rolls plus SKILL on either side, the higher roll indicating an injury to the other, which is then rolled on the weapons table given earlier (see page 56). Only close-up weapons and magic may be used (no bows or spears). This time you should run the combat on a round-by-round basis, with everyone getting to do something before the action moves on to the next round. If a character is free, he may move towards another opponent, if one is available. A character (Hero, Orc or Ogre) may move one square of the map per round of combat. Whenever there is more than one character free, the Bad Guys get to declare what they are going to do before the Heroes do, though everyone then makes his move at the same time.

In order to swap weapons (to pick up a flaming brand, say), a character needs to spend one round performing this action. A successful roll against the *Strength* Special Skill is needed to lift the table if a character wishes to use it as a weapon (so Grudthak or Axel Wolfric can perhaps try this). A flaming torch or roast leg can be thrown; a character must roll his SKILL or less on two dice in order to hit. If the roll is higher, the item just misses; but, on a roll of 12 exactly, the item has hit the next nearest person, whether Orc or Hero. The leg inflicts 1 point of damage to a character's STAMINA if it hits; a flaming brand does 2 points; the table will do 4, but it can't be thrown without a *Strength* roll, only pushed!

Magic works as normal, with a successful roll against the *Magic* Skill needed for it to work properly, and with the usual hilarious consequences resulting from failure. This time, a roll of 12 means something *extremely* odd happens. Casting a spell at Grudthak is slightly harder than zapping the Orcs: reduce *Magic* Skill by 1 if casting something at the Ogre so as to reflect this more difficult attempt.

When the fight is under way, you may find that two or more Heroes are fighting one enemy (or vice versa!). Run this combat using the normal procedure for multiple combat, with the outnumbered character fighting back against the two but able to wound only one opponent. Don't allow more than three people to gang up on one enemy. If the Heroes question this ruling, you may explain that, as experienced swordsmen, they know not to crowd an opponent too much for fear of hitting their friends as they swing. Besides, it isn't very Heroic, is it, and these are meant to be the Good Guys.

In some circumstances a Hero (or an Orc) may manage to creep up behind an enemy who is already fighting someone else. If you see this happen, allow the fellow at the back an unopposed strike – don't roll for combat, just for damage to the victim's STAMINA. Once he has been hit, the victim will be aware of the person behind him and will be able to fight back normally (unless he's also fighting someone in front of him, in which case the rules for fighting two opponents apply). Don't allow a free strike against the back of an unengaged enemy – experienced fighters are always looking around warily when in the middle of a pitched battle.

Once the Orcs have been killed, Grudthak will do his best to position himself between the Heroes and the door to the wizard's chambers, always trying to keep his back to a wall. His club is very heavy, and any Hero successfully hit by it will be sent sprawling backwards one square and will have to spend the next round out of combat, getting up again. Roll for the club's damage as if it were a Sword on the table on page 56, and then add 1 further point of damage. What is more, Grudthak enjoys two Attacks. These can be used only against two separate opponents. If he is attacking one opponent, he has just the usual one attack.

Problems?

It is quite possible that a Hero will die in this scene. That is all right, if unfortunate. Sad scenes are allowed in movies as long as someone survives to beat the Bad Guys in the end. Furthermore, it adds a poignant note to the combat which can counterpoint the hilarity of the actual fighting. Good Directors do this all the time in the movies, so why shouldn't you?

If things really go awry, with the Heroes making bad dice-rolls and stupid decisions, you may use your Director's powers to ensure that someone gets through, but don't make it too obvious or the Heroes will suspect that something odd is happening to them. If the Heroes are *very* badly wounded when they arrive in the guardroom, it may be a good idea to reduce the number of Orcs by one so that the sickest of them doesn't have to fight one. Don't forget that a spell-caster may have STAMINA spells to help heal injured characters.

It is unlikely that any of the Heroes will run out into the courtyard during the fight – they are Heroes, not cowards – but if they do, this is what it looks like:

There is a large open space. To either side are some wooden storerooms. The whole area is surrounded by a small wall, and at the far side there is a gate. From this, a drawbridge leads across a chasm to the main wall of the castle. The chasm surrounds the entire tower which the Heroes have just climbed. The drawbridge is up.

Having seen this; they will probably lose interest in the area and get back to the fight – and a good thing, too.

Turn To . . .

As Grudthak crumples to the floor dead (or, more probably topples like a felled tree in a thunderstorm) the doors that he was defending swing open of their own accord and a quiet, commanding male voice says, 'Welcome!' The camera swings dramatically to look in through the gap in the doors and we all go straight into *Scene 5 . . .*

Scene 5 – The Wizard's Chamber

Location

Everyone sees a large, well-furnished room. To one side is a fireplace. Immediately in front of us, the evil Xortan Throg sits on a splendid throne, flanked by incense-burners. To either side of him are two doors. Unless a miracle happens, a fight will take place here, so a map is provided in case you wish to use miniatures or counters.

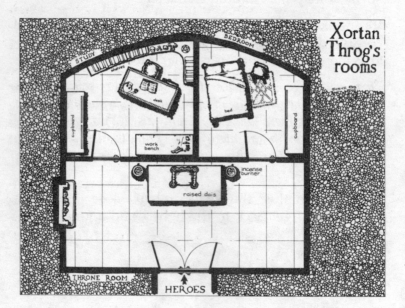

Xortan Throg's rooms

Cast List

Xortan Throg is an old, nearly bald man who wears ornate but rather old-fashioned, toga-like robes and the skull-cap so beloved of evil wizards everywhere. He speaks slowly and quietly but with considerable power and presence; clearly he is used to being obeyed, immediately and totally. He has no need of props such as magic wands and the like, but the incense-burners to either side of him seem to flare up whenever he casts a spell.

The wizard knows a vast array of spells but will call upon only a few of them; these will be detailed in the *Action!* segment when he uses them. If any of the Heroes have especially good senses (such as the Elf's *Awareness* Special Skill, for example) they may well notice, when the fight begins, that he moves rather slowly and woodenly. The reason for this will be revealed in a short while.

Also in this scene, nasty Prince Barinjhar reveals his true nature. He is an ambitious schemer who sneers rather unpleasantly when explaining his wickedness to people he has duped. When called upon to fight, he proves a capable swordsman and a match for all but the very best fighters among the Heroes, but he knows no spells.

If the Heroes make a mess of things, the beautiful Princess Sarissa may well make a brief appearance in this scene. She is described more fully in scene 6, where she is currently scheduled to make her proper appearance.

XORTAN THROG SKILL 2 STAMINA 6
Fingernails (as dagger)
Magic *Special Skill 20. The spells he uses are detailed below*

PRINCE BARINJHAR SKILL 11 STAMINA 14
Sword

Plot Summary

Xortan Throg and Prince Barinjhar reveal a scheme of quite sinister proportions. The Heroes teach them a lesson (we hope!).

Props

None needed, though miniatures will once again prove useful for the fight scene.

Action!

It is customary in all movies for the major Bad Guys to be given a long, dramatic speech in which they both explain their evil plot in great detail and gloat about how easily the Heroes have been tricked. That happens at the beginning of this scene. Hopefully, the Heroes will enter into the spirit of things and listen patiently; but if they are rude and try to attack in the middle of a speech, Xortan Throg will erect a *Barrier* spell across the middle of the room which will prevent them from approaching him. The barrier is invisible except for little bursts of light whenever anyone touches it. As he does this, Throg will say something like, 'Do not interrupt me when I am speaking. Be grateful that I have allowed you to live long enough to appreciate the sheer depth of my cunning!' (or

87

whatever is appropriate on the part of Barinjhar, if he happens to be speaking at the time.)

1. The Kidnap Plot

The scene commences with Xortan Throg welcoming the Heroes to his castle. Carrying on the speech he began at the end of scene 4, he says the following, which you should act out in high dramatic fashion, according to the notes about the evil sorcerer's character given above:

'Welcome to my castle, goodly fools! I trust you have enjoyed your stay thus far, though I must admit I am surprised to see so many of you still alive after the excellent entertainment I laid on especially for you. I can only apologize for that, but I hope to correct matters shortly. Before you die, however, I thought that you should know a little about the affair that your greed and arrogance have got you involved in. I'd like to introduce a friend of mine who will explain.'

At this, the door to the left of the wizard opens – and Prince Barinjhar enters the room!

You should leave a few moments for the players to retrieve their jaws from where they have dropped, before continuing as the foppish prince:

'Ah, my old adventuring friends,' he says. 'I am so glad to see you here. Father was right when he said he was hiring the best adventurers in all Allansia. Unfortunately, your famed abilities will do you little good here. You see, I cannot allow Princess Sarissa to be rescued. It was very thoughtful of my father to arrange such a prestigious marriage for me. She is both pretty and wise, a highly suitable match for my noble self.

'But were it to go ahead, it would not be long before Chalice would be full of "advisers" and "ministers" from Salamonis. Within two shakes of a roc's tail we would be nothing but a puppet of that vile city. I have no intention of so subjugating myself or my people, so I made a deal with my learned friend here. He has even more reason to hate King Salamon than I.

'Naturally, we had to make a show of rescuing the poor girl; but once the best adventurers in Allansia had tried and failed, it would be obvious that nothing more could be done. I must admit I am surprised to see you have evaded the little traps we laid for you on your way here, with a little help from those foolish priests whose secret passage was nothing but the entrance to the Goblin caverns, but you will understand that we simply cannot allow you to live any longer!'

With this, the Prince draws his sword and advances on the Heroes. If the magical barrier was present, it will now be dropped. There seems nothing to do but give battle.

2. The Fight

Prince Barinjhar will tackle one of the Heroes. Being an evil sort, he will try to pick one of the less capable fighters, but he will probably have to settle for the character nearest to him at the time. He will fight to the death rather than surrender, initially through over-confidence but later in desperation if he starts to lose (as hopefully he ultimately should). The Heroes, if they have any sense, will be trying to get to the wizard.

Once you get close to wizards, they are often easy to kill – but of course getting close is another matter. Xortan Throg will not re-erect the magical barrier because while it is there he cannot cast spells through it at the Heroes. Instead, he will pick one Hero (preferably not the one fighting Prince Barinjhar) and try to kill him. His priorities will be as follows:

(i) If the Hero fires a bow, casts a spell or throws a weapon at him, he will deflect it with a wave of his hand. He is a powerful sorcerer and can counter any spells the Heroes throw at him. You should make it obvious to the players that Throg doesn't need to have any dice rolled for him.

(ii) If the Hero advances towards him, Throg will cast a *Force Bolt*. The Hero has a chance to avoid this by *Testing his Luck* or successfully using a *Dodge* skill; but if it hits, it does 4 points of damage to the Hero's STAMINA and has a kick like Grudthak's club, sending the Hero (even one with *Strength* Skill like Wolfric) head-over-heels backwards, so that he ends up back where he started at the beginning of the round! *Testing One's Luck* is done by rolling one's LUCK or less on two dice; this attempt reduces the Hero's LUCK by 1 point, whether it succeeds or not.

(iii) If a second Hero succeeds in striking the wizard or knocking over an incense-burner, from then on Throg will concentrate on him until distracted again. He can never attack or defend against more than one Hero at once. (The reason for all this will soon be made clear; for now, it is sufficient that the Heroes begin to realize that this is so, though you shouldn't simply point this out to them unless they are failing terribly.)

Incidentally, don't worry about keeping track of STAMINA points for the sorcerer when he casts his spells. He is getting them from elsewhere.

If you are not using miniatures to control the combat, you will need some other means of knowing when the Heroes are close enough to do something. It takes *four* successful dodges against *Force Bolts* to be in a position to strike the wizard. If Throg is ignoring a Hero, the latter can get next to the villain, or to an incense-burner, in four combat rounds. It takes one round of free movement (or one successful *Dodge*) to move from an incense-burner to the wizard.

Remember to mention to the Heroes that the incense-burners flare up each time the wizard casts a spell. The Heroes may soon get the idea that they are somehow connected with his sorcerous powers. If one is knocked over (by an arrow, a kick or a thrown object), then Xortan Throg's powers are reduced: he can no longer deflect spells, and his *Force Bolts* no longer do any damage, though they do still knock Heroes back.

If both incense-burners are knocked down, Throg will not be able to cast spells at all and must fight hand to hand. He is armed with only long, claw-like fingernails (these do damage equal to that caused by a dagger). The wizard can deflect missiles aimed at himself, not those aimed at incense-burners.

Problems?

If three or more Heroes have survived thus far, they should have little trouble in overcoming the Bad Guys. Two Heroes should be enough to take out the wizard; they can improve their chances by one of them simply engaging the wizard in discussion while his colleague deals with the over-eager Prince Barinjhar. If only one Hero is left, Xortan Throg will wait until Barinjhar is dead before attacking, but a single Hero will have trouble against him unless he is very good at dodging (or extremely lucky!). If it looks as if the Hero is going to die, you will have to take matters in hand to make sure that the good guys win the day after all: your film can't end here! If there is a risk of the last Hero dying, this is what happens next:

As the lone Hero inches his way towards the wizard, the door to the left of the villain's throne opens quietly. A pretty young girl in tattered robes sneaks in. Princess Sarissa has managed to free herself from her bonds, and she creeps into the room carrying a large vase. Putting her finger to her lips as a signal to the Hero to keep quiet, she moves up behind Xortan Throg and brings the vase down upon his head with a tremendous crash! While the wizard is dazed, the Hero has a chance to leap at him and thrust a sword through his bony, sorcerous ribs.

Turn To . . .

Once Xortan Throg dies, you must move immediately to the closing *Scene 6*.

Scene 6 – The End?

Location

The closing scene of this movie takes place in the wizard's throne-room (detailed in the last scene) and in the two adjoining rooms. The door to the left of the wizard's throne leads to a bedroom. This is sparsely furnished with a chair and a four-poster bed. A small chest holds a perfectly ordinary (not magical) set of clothing, similar to the toga costume the sorcerer was wearing in the last scene. If Sarissa didn't escape in the last scene, there will be an ancient-looking vase standing in one corner. If she was not required to save the Heroes in the last scene, Princess Sarissa is lying on the bed, bound and gagged, her clothing in slight disarray but still completely covering her young body.

The door at the right of the throne leads to the wizard's study. Surprisingly, this contains little of interest. There are plenty of herbs and spices, stuffed crocodiles, odd little statues, animal and human skulls, and many other mysterious bits and pieces. There are also a few small gems in a leather pouch – worth about 20 Gold Pieces – but there is no sorcerer's spell book and no proper money.

Plot Summary

The Princess is rescued (if necessary) but, in a surprising twist to the story, the Heroes learn that Xortan Throg is more cunning than they had thought.

Princess Sarissa is sixteen years old, with long blonde hair, and is very pretty, just what one might expect a captive princess to be. She is also clever and brave. Rather than dissolving into tears and helpless wailing, she has been trying to escape and deciding how she is going to get even with her captors when she manages to free herself.

Having been brought up properly by her father, the wise and renowned King Salamon, she will be duly grateful to her rescuers, but not to such an extent that she falls in love with one of them or agrees to a marriage or other arrangement. Princesses are brought up to expect a rich and powerful prince for a husband, not a rough, ill-mannered adventurer, especially if they are princesses of one of the most prosperous city-states in Allansia. Being a person of noble birth and good upbringing, Sarissa naturally assumes that she is now in charge and that the Heroes will do what they are told. If they are uncooperative with her, she may become just a little petulant.

Oh, and Xortan Throg makes a surprise reappearance, though only from the neck upwards. Yes, we realize that this comes as a bit of a shock, but read on . . .

Props

If you can find a beautiful sixteen-year-old blonde girl willing to play the part of Sarissa, all well and good – but do remember to ask her permission first before tying her up or there may be problems later (only joking!).

You could also profitably use something to simulate the booming, echoing voice needed for the sorcerer's final cryptic pronouncement. If you don't actually have access to a megaphone or a 200-watt P.A. system with built-in echo unit, try rolling up a piece of paper and intoning through that.

Action!

Depending on their personalities (and the players controlling them), the Heroes will have one or another thing in mind. Most of them will be keen to rescue the princess and remove her from this dangerous place as rapidly as possible. Brondwyn the Thief and Grimbold Tornhelm will be just as keen to search for portable loot to stuff into their pockets, and the young wizard – Rangor – may well be after Xortan Throg's spell book (you should alert him to the possibility of there being one, full of lots more juicy spells to learn!). As they don't know which door is which, the first two *Action!* segments could happen in either order. If Sarissa has already rescued herself, just use her speech from segment 1, and then go straight into segment 3.

1. The Princess
Sarissa is bound and gagged, and will need to be released by the Heroes. If they are somewhat slow in doing this,

she will writhe about and try to plead with them through her gag. When finally released, she will admonish the Heroes for taking their time, and then take the situation in hand. Having expressed her extreme gratitude to the Heroes – and perhaps given each of them a quick peck on the cheek or a firm-but-gentle regal handshake – she will explain a few points that the Heroes may not have considered (you may have to paraphrase or omit some things from the following speech if the Heroes have already discussed them):

'Well, you can hardly go back to Chalice and claim your reward, having just killed King Pindar's only son, now can you, even if he was a right royal creep? Don't suppose for one moment that the King will believe any tales of wicked plots. Kings are no different from anyone else – they think their children can do no wrong. Fortunately for you, though, I expect my father will reward you just as lavishly as Pindar promised to – maybe better, indeed, because Salamonis is the richest city in all Allansia.

'Of course, we still have to escape from here. I heard that slimy Barinjhar telling old Throg-face that his men were on guard outside and would catch you if you tried to escape; but we can probably get out the same way you came in. That means I'll have to walk back through the forest, which will ruin my dress even more, but I'm sure Daddy will forgive me once he knows the circumstances. Shall we go?'

If the Heroes have the trained Giant Lizard with them, they may suggest that Sarissa ride on that. She will not be very impressed:

'Urgh! Oh no, I simply couldn't! Is it clean? And safe? It doesn't look very friendly, or very comfortable. I think on the whole I'd rather walk, thank you.'

All suggestions leading to marriage and the like will be greeted with disdainful comments in the order of:

'Sir, grateful as I am to you, I should point out that you are getting ideas a little above your station!'

2. The Study

The greedier Heroes will want to spend some time searching here and doubtless becoming very frustrated that there is no treasure. If Sarissa gets a look inside, she will comment on some of the pots: 'Ooh look, there are more vases like that one in the bedroom,' (which she may have ruined by smashing over Xortan Throg's head). 'They're smaller, but clearly the same design. They're ever so old, you know. I remember my tutor showing me a picture of one once and saying that they were made in a place called Carsepolis that doesn't exist any more. History is terribly boring, don't you think?' There is probably no answer to this, as the Heroes are unlikely to have studied any history at all, and certainly don't know anything about anywhere called Carsep-wherever-it-was. Sarissa then wanders back into the throne-room.

3. Xortan Throg Returns!

Once you can get everyone, including Princess Sarissa, gathered back in the throne-room, a miraculous event will occur. With a strange sucking sound the body of the dead wizard will suddenly collapse in on itself, leaving only his robes on the floor. A fire suddenly flares up in the fireplace, from nowhere, and in the flames can be seen the all-too-familiar head of Xortan Throg. He speaks, in a mocking and arrogant tone, his voice

booming; now's the time for the improvised mega-phone, if you have one to hand:

'Aah,' he booms in a loud, echoing voice, 'I have made contact again. It seems, good sirs, that your reputations are not false, you are as brave as I had heard. I hadn't thought that old fool Pindar could have afforded anyone as good as you. Heh-heh, perhaps he couldn't and was hoping you'd take pity on him – or he even thought to trick you out of your reward. I'll bet you didn't think to get anything in advance, eh? Never mind.

'Still, my brave boobies, it seems I was wise to take precautions. As soon as I heard who was coming after me, I decided to absent myself from the scene of the action. Sorry about that, but I've been leagues away all along. That poor creature you killed was a mere simulacrum, an artificial being animated by the force of my powerful sorcery. I am safe in my secret sanctum from which I will take my revenge upon you . . . one by one . . . slowly and hideously. Heh-heh-heh!

'And you, my pretty, don't think I have forgotten you! Return and tell your wise and good father that Xortan Throg lives still, and while he does no one in Salamonis can afford to sleep easy in their beds. Ahahahahah . . . !!'

The wizard's face fades out amid cackling laughter, leaving the startled Heroes and the white-faced princess alone in the tower. The closing titles roll.

The End

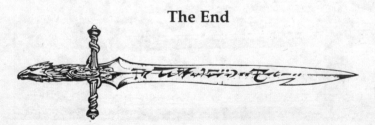

Problems?

If the Heroes manage to mess this up (if they somehow manage to kill the princess or do something equally daft), you obviously hired the wrong actors to play them, and there's not very much that we can do to remedy the situation. Sorry.

They may, of course, wish to search the rest of the castle for loot. Tell them they are welcome to do so, but also that there is nothing there and you are not going to waste your time filming such boring action. As far as everyone is concerned, the adventure is now effectively over and if they wish to continue, they must wait for the sequel!

Turn To . . .

Quite obviously there are several loose ends left which the players may harass you to clear up. Will Xortan Throg get even with the Heroes, or will they get to him first? Why does he hate Salamonis? All this and much, much more will hopefully be revealed in the main adventure detailed a little later in this book.

We intend to start filming again when the Heroes have reached the court of King Salamon, for nothing dramatically interesting will happen in the meantime. However, if you are feeling really keen, or if your players nag at you so much that you feel you can't leave out the journey, you might like to try your hand at writing a simple script for a separate adventure, telling how the Heroes and Princess Sarissa escape from the castle and flee through the wolf-strewn wilds to Salamonis, pursued by Xortan Throg, his Goblins and Prince Barinjhar's bodyguards. However, we still think you'd do better waiting!

Therefore you can now relax, recover your voice, turn all the lights back on, untie the girl, and so on. We hope you all had a good time, especially if this was everyone's first experience at role-playing. For now there's nothing much more to do but clean up the mess, collect the character sheets, and reflect on (we sincerely hope!) what fun everyone had. You might also care to arrange a date for the next instalment in this thrilling fantasy adventure series!

Coming Soon!

DUNGEONEER
ADVENTURE II;
'REVENGE OF THE
SORCERER'

3. THE RULES OF THE GAME

Now that you have played a *Dungeoneer* Fighting Fantasy adventure with your friends and have experienced some of the few simple rules we use to govern it, we can move on to slightly more complicated characters and situations. Before you play *Dungeoneer* Adventure II: 'Return of the Sorcerer', though, we recommend you read through this whole chapter in which we summarize all the rules which go together to make up the Advanced Fighting Fantasy game-system.

As we progress we shall show you how to create your own personalized Hero characters, how to kit them out in their adventuring equipment, and then how to use them to struggle against ravening monsters, swing from chandeliers, climb steep cliffs, swim mighty rivers, and generally do all the things that will make them famous throughout the length and breadth of mythical Allansia!

This whole chapter can be read by Director and players alike and may be consulted at any time before, during or after an adventure. It's likely that, for your first few adventures, this chapter will become very well-thumbed. Try not to spend too much time looking up every last little rule if it's going to destroy the flow of play, however.

Following the rules, we've provided a short section (starting on page 215), intended for the Director's eyes only, which gives some pointers on running and controlling an adventure so that everyone can enjoy the game to the fullest extent. In case you were wondering, the rules and guidelines on actually designing and running your very own custom-built *Dungeoneer* adventure will start straight after *Dungeoneer* Adventure II, on page 227.

As you read through this chapter for the first time, it may prove useful to have a few dice, a pencil and some blank paper handy. As we run through the examples, try rolling up a Hero of your own so that you will appreciate just what is going on.

One final point: in *Dungeoneer* Adventure I we detailed some of the rules as we went along. To make things easier for you and the players, we simplified some of these rules; you will therefore discover that some of the rules we now present are slightly more complicated versions of the ones you know already. From now on, we recommend that you use the new versions.

Right, let's start casting!

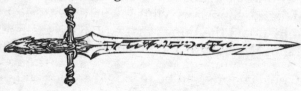

Creating a Hero

The single most important component of any *Dungeoneer* adventure is the Hero. Without a Hero to do all that daring stuff with his sword and his other skills, the princess would never get rescued, the evil necromancer would never be dispatched, the country would never be saved for good and loyal citizens everywhere!

Every Hero is defined in terms of two things. First, there are his *characteristics*; these are SKILL, STAMINA and LUCK. We shall always write them like that so that you will know we are referring to them. These characteristics are each assigned a numerical value which reveals – when we use the game rules – just how adept or not our Hero is at something – rather like knowing one's IQ score, for example.

Secondly, there are the *skills* and *spells* a Hero has. Just like anyone in the real world, each Hero is very experienced and practised at doing certain things, while he knows nothing at all about other things. These Skills are based on a combination of the *Initial* SKILL of a Hero together with any learning he may have received.

The *Adventure Sheet*

Over the page is an *Adventure Sheet*. This sheet will be familiar to you if you've played a Fighting Fantasy gamebook before – though this one has several modifications to it, to take into account the expanded skills and spells which some players possess. Every player should have a copy of this sheet, on which they will keep a record of all the numbers and skills relating to the specific Hero character they are playing. You have our permission to photocopy this sheet (for use in your own games only). If you can't get to a photocopier, you can always copy out the details on to a plain sheet of paper.

Now that you've played through the first adventure, you should have a fair idea as to what the various characteristics mean, but we'll go through them once more just to make sure. By the way, when you come to write the various scores on the *Adventure Sheet*, be sure to use a pencil rather than a permanent ink pen or ball-point, as scores can (and frequently do) change as the game progresses. Have an eraser handy for just such an occasion.

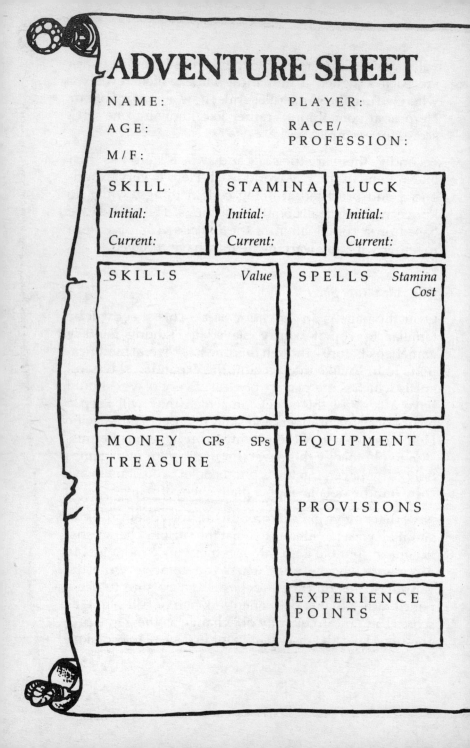

ADVENTURE SHEET

NAME:

AGE:

M/F:

PLAYER:

RACE/
PROFESSION:

SKILL	STAMINA	LUCK
Initial:	Initial:	Initial:
Current:	Current:	Current:

SKILLS *Value*

SPELLS *Stamina Cost*

MONEY GPs SPs
TREASURE

EQUIPMENT

PROVISIONS

EXPERIENCE POINTS

BACKGROUND:

PERSONALITY:

QUOTES:

NOTES:

PICTURE:

Skill

A Hero's SKILL *is found by rolling one die and adding 6 to the result.*

Unless you are going to learn how to cast spells, this is your *Initial* SKILL score. Either way, write it in the appropriate box on your sheet – but be prepared to rub it out or change it in a moment.

This SKILL score indicates a Hero's own superb skills in a range of areas: swordsmanship and general fighting abilities; strength and dexterity; intelligence, intuition and knowledge; and more besides. The SKILL score is also used as the basis for the individual Special Skills which we will discuss in a moment. Plainly, the higher the SKILL score the better, though Heroes with low SKILL scores have been known to defeat the most awesome opponents – for this game is about quick thinking and bravery just as much as it is about having a strong sword-arm!

Stamina

A Hero's STAMINA *score is determined by rolling two dice and adding 12 to the result.*

Your STAMINA is a measure of your Hero's fitness and good health, his will to survive, his determination and general constitution. Injury, hunger and exhaustion during an adventure may eat away at a Hero's STAMINA. Should it reach zero, the Hero may well die, according to rules we shall be covering in a later section. However, rest and recuperation, or the eating of some tasty Provisions, will replenish a certain amount of STAMINA.

Luck

A Hero's LUCK *score is found by rolling one die, and adding 6 to the result.*

LUCK is a very important fact of every adventurer's life; it shows how favoured by the gods he is, and how successful he is in his adventuring. The higher the LUCK score, the luckier the Hero is, and will be. At certain times during the course of an adventure, a Hero may be called upon to *Test his Luck* to determine whether a situation will go for or against him.

Sometimes an adventurer may choose to *Test his Luck* in an attempt to try and make a situation go more favourably for him. Of course, there is no guarantee that this will always happen; that's the way with luck and chance. Furthermore, each and every time a Hero *Tests his Luck*, whether or not he is successful, he must reduce his LUCK by 1 point. If he is not careful, his LUCK will run out altogether! We will explain how a Hero *Tests his Luck* in a moment.

Sample Hero:

To show how all this works, we'll create a Hero as we go along. Hero (as we shall call him for the moment) rolls a 3 and adds 6 for a SKILL of 9; rolls a 6 and a 2 and adds 12 for a STAMINA of 20; and finally rolls a 6 and adds 6 for a LUCK score of 12. This Hero is obviously going to have the nickname 'Lucky'!

Testing for Luck

At certain times during an adventure, a Hero may find himself in such a dire situation that there may be nothing he can do to escape certain injury or even death. At this point, however, the Director may allow you to *Test your Luck* and give you one last chance of avoiding whatever is about to happen.

The way you *Test your Luck* is as follows:

Roll two dice and add their scores together. If the result is equal to or less than your LUCK score, you have tested your LUCK successfully and avoided whatever it was that threatened you. If you roll higher than your LUCK score, however, you have been unlucky; whatever it is that threatens you is, we're sorry to say, going to get you after all.

Each time a Hero *Tests his Luck* this way, whether he is lucky or unlucky in the outcome, he must reduce his LUCK score by 1 point. Be careful that your luck doesn't run out entirely!

LUCK can also be used in combat to turn an opponent's blade away, or to use yours to wound him more gravely. We shall cover this in our section on *Fighting Battles* later (see page 147).

Special Skills

Everyone, everywhere, is better than the next person at doing some things and worse at doing others. For a Hero, the most important things to be better at include fighting with one's chosen weapon, the various adventuring skills (such as creeping silently about, climbing, sensing traps, seeing in the darkness, etc.) and even the ability to cast magic spells. In *Dungeoneer* we represent these abilities by allowing all the Heroes to choose several *Special Skills*.

Each Hero may assign the same number of points that he has in his *Initial* SKILL to any Special Skill of his choice, up to a maximum of 4 points per Special Skill. Each Special Skill then has a value equal to the Hero's current SKILL score, plus the number of points assigned to it. If more than 1 point is put into any Special Skill, this denotes even greater specialization; if players choose to put 1 point into lots of different Special Skills, this makes their Hero more of an all-rounder.

Special Skills can be increased further by training and practice later in the game. *Important:* if any Hero wishes to choose *Magic* as one of his Special Skills, consult the relevant section on this subject; it appears after the Special Skills list, below, on page 122. *Magic* is a quite different area of skill, and is a little more complicated than most Special Skills.

Sample Hero:
'Lucky' has a SKILL of 9; this gives him 9 points to spend. He decides he is going to be an expert warrior, and chooses to put 3 points into *Sword* and 3 into *Bow*, 2 points into *Sneak* and 1 into *Dodge*. Therefore he now has the following Special Skill scores: *Sword* 12, *Bow* 12, *Sneak* 11 and *Dodge* 10 (as well as his *Initial* SKILL of 9, which is unaffected). Let's hope he never has to climb on a horse or swim anywhere!

Special Skills List
These are the Special Skills which are available. We've divided them up into groups for easy reference, but these groups have no bearing on the rules. The Director might have invented some more Special Skills which are peculiar to the world which you adventure in; he will tell you if these are available for you to choose. Similarly, there may be some skills on this list which are not in use; if so, the Director will tell you.

One final point before you make your selection. It is assumed that most Heroes will be of human origin. However, you may choose to play a character who is a Dwarf or an Elf. Since there are a few rules about the Special Skills these races may choose, we recommend that anyone thinking of playing a non-human character should take a look at the section on *Non-Human Heroes*, below, on page 138.

The Special Skills available are as follows:

Combat
Axe
Dagger
Pole Arm
Spear
Sword
Two-handed Sword
Other Weapon (specify)

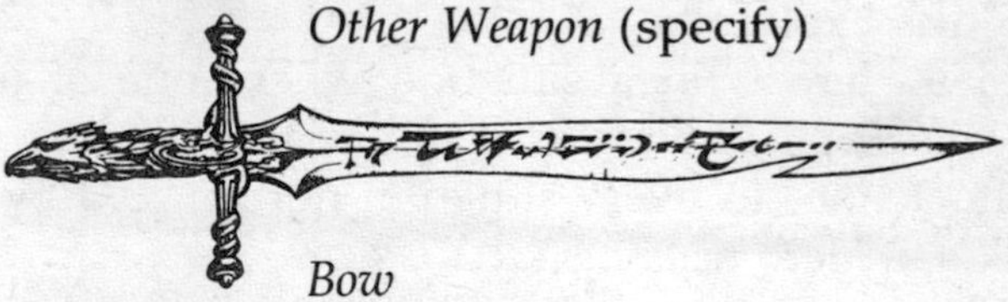

Bow
Crossbow
Javelin
Throwing Dagger
Strength
Unarmed Combat

Movement
Climb
Dodge
Jump
Ride
Swim

Stealth
Awareness
Dark Seeing
Hide
Lock Picking
Sleight of Hand
Sneak
Trap Knowledge

Learning	Con
	Etiquette
	Languages
	Magic
	Sea Lore
	Underground Lore
	Wood Lore
	World Lore

Special Skills Explained

Whenever a Hero is in a situation where one of his Special Skills applies, he uses his Special Skill score to resolve the action. In every situation not covered by a Special Skill, a Hero uses his SKILL score.

The individual Special Skills work as detailed below. It is not essential to learn every single aspect of the Special Skill at this time, but every Hero should know approximately what he now can and cannot do with his Special Skill. We'll go through them in alphabetical order:

Awareness – This gives the Hero a chance of spotting it when something is out of the ordinary or is otherwise 'wrong'. Depending on the situation, this could include hearing someone creeping up on you, smelling poison smeared on a lock, sensing the presence of a hidden trap, etc. This Special Skill will usually be checked for you by the Director: the Director will roll dice to see whether or not you are successful when using this skill.

Axe – The Hero is skilled at using a battle-axe in hand-to-hand combat. He also knows something about the care and maintenance of an axe to keep it shining and sharp.

Bow – The Hero with this Special Skill is well versed in archery and missile combat, and also in the care of his bow.

Climb – This Skill gives the Hero a better-than-average chance of scaling even the most daunting of slopes. Of course, there will always be some places where no one can venture, but this Hero is more skilled than most. Bear in mind, however, that the Director may, at his discretion, impose penalties on the chance of climbing a very steep or smooth slope.

Con – The Hero is sharp-tongued and quick-witted, and may very well be able to con someone into believing what he is saying, or into buying whatever rubbish the Hero is selling!

Crossbow – This simply endows a Hero with the skill of drawing and firing a crossbow, and also maintaining and repairing such a weapon.

Dagger – The Hero with this Special Skill is adept at fighting with a knife. This skill does not include throwing a dagger, which is a different skill – see *Throwing Dagger*, below.

Dark Seeing – The ability to see in near darkness, especially underground. The Director doesn't normally need to check this Special Skill with a roll of the dice, unless the Hero is trying to spot something specific which is hidden in the dark. This skill doesn't work where there is no light at all. Few characters will ever need more than 1 point in this Special Skill – unless they are going to spend their whole life underground! *Dark Seeing* cannot be learnt from scratch by experience, but it *can* be added to.

Dodge – This gives the Hero a chance of getting out of the way of anything or anyone moving quickly towards him; this could include a falling rock, a swinging sword or even (at higher skill levels) an arrow!

Etiquette – The Hero with this Special Skill is especially well versed in the ways of courtly behaviour. He knows just the right things to say to a king or prince – and, perhaps more importantly, when to shut up! This is an essential skill for anyone spending any length of time at a royal court.

Hide – The Hero is adept at finding somewhere to secrete either himself or something he wants to hide, so that others will not be able to spot him or it. Of course, no one can hide if there is nowhere to go, but, given sufficient material, this Hero can do better than most.

Javelin – This Special Skill allows the Hero who chooses it to throw a javelin with accuracy over a greater distance than his peers. He is also able to select and care for the best weapons.

Jump – This Hero is endowed with the ability to leap up, down or across greater distances than is usual without injuring himself in the process.

Languages – This Special Skill gives the Hero who possesses it a facility for speaking or reading a contemporary foreign (humanoid) tongue or script. It does not usually apply to the language of animals or magical beings.

Lock Picking – The Hero is more skilled than most at opening a tricky lock mechanism. This Special Skill is very important for any successful sneak thief!

Magic – The lore of spells and sorcery; a spell cannot be cast at all without this Special Skill, which also determines the likelihood of its being cast correctly and without the caster accidentally turning *himself* into a frog! See the special section on page 122 for many more details about magic and spell-casting.

Other Weapon – If your Director allows it, you can choose whichever weapon you want this Special Skill to apply to, whether it be a spiked ball on a chain, a war-boomerang or a ninja throwing-star. You must clear your choice of exotic weapon with your Director first, for it may not fit in with the background of the world your Hero lives in.

Pole Arm – This Special Skill allows a character to fight in close combat using a pole arm, usually a wide blade slotted into a long, spear-like shaft.

Ride – Simply, the ability to stay in the saddle while riding a horse. It also gives a (reduced) chance of being able to ride other, unfamiliar animals, be they elephants, riding lizards or giant eagles!

Sea Lore – Knowledge of the tides and currents, knots, sails and other aspects of sailing and the sea. The Special Skill's rating is a measure of how much the Hero knows.

Sleight of Hand – The Hero with this rather useful Special Skill has great dexterity in his hands. A Hero could use this skill to pick someone's pocket, palm a small item, do conjuring tricks, and so on.

Sneak – This Special Skill allows the Hero who possesses it to move about without being noticed. Implicit in this skill is the ability to go wherever you wish without being heard or seen.

Spear – Like *Pole Arm*, this Special Skill simply allows you to fight in close combat with a spear. It does not allow the spear to be thrown with any great skill.

Strength – The Hero with this Special Skill has trained himself and increased his physical strength to close to that of a Troll or Ogre. He can lift and throw heavy objects (and sometimes people, too!) and may add 1 point to damage done with a hand-held or thrown weapon or in unarmed combat.

Swim – This Hero is adept at swimming, both on the surface and under the water. Most sea-dwelling beings will have a very high rating in this Special Skill.

Sword – Our Hero has trained long and hard with his sword, and is on his way to becoming a master swordsman! This Special Skill also includes sword knowledge, including the care and maintenance of a sword, spotting a badly forged weapon, and more.

Throwing Dagger – This skill allows the Hero who has it to throw a throwing dagger with speed, strength and accuracy. It does not allow him to fight in close combat with any greater proficiency.

Trap Knowledge – The Hero has made a study of traps, and can spot, avoid or dismantle them with more skill than the average person. At higher levels, your Director may even allow you to design and construct your own devious mechanical traps.

Two-handed Sword – Fighting with a huge two-handed blade is very difficult and requires a combination of strength and dexterity, which this Special Skill bestows. The skill also includes knowledge concerning the care and upkeep of such weapons.

Unarmed Combat – This Special Skill gives a Hero a better chance at coming out the victor in any wrestling match or fight to the death, using only his bare hands. In Eastern lands this skill could include skill at some form of martial art, be it judo, karate, kung fu or whatever your Director allows in his game.

Underground Lore – This confers the ability to stay alive in a dungeon or cavern complex, not getting lost, noticing potential rock falls before they happen, finding one's way to the surface, and so on.

Wood Lore – The Hero is skilled at surviving in woodland, including the ability to find food, stay on a path, track someone, find shelter, and much more.

World Lore – This gives the Hero who possesses it a better chance of knowing a particular fact about an area's geography, history, legends, famous people and events, as well as the weather, the right route to somewhere, local personalities (whether to find, or stay away from, them), and so on.

Magic Special Skill

A Hero must have at least 1 point assigned to *Magic* Special Skill if he intends to cast any spells. Every time he wishes to cast a spell, he must succeed in rolling against his *Magic* Special Skill, otherwise the spell may well go wrong.

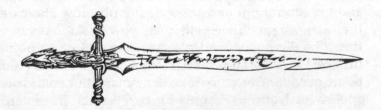

However, studying magic and the supernatural requires a very intensive effort, which is made partly at the cost of his other abilities. For every point put into *Magic* Skill, a Hero must reduce his SKILL score by a similar 1 point. This does not affect a Hero's first choice of Special Skills (he may allot as many points as he had in his very first SKILL score, as described above on page 113), but it *does* affect his SKILL and Special Skill scores and dice-rolls from now on. This new, reduced SKILL score is now counted as his *Initial* score, where necessary, and his SKILL may not be raised above it. So, all Special Skill points are spent on a range of Special Skills, and a Hero's SKILL is *then* reduced by the number of points put into his *Magic* Special Skill.

Every magic spell costs a certain number of STAMINA points to cast: casting magic requires a great deal of effort and concentration, and uses up the physical energy of the caster to give the spells their power. As a result of this, all spells are defined by how many STAMINA points they cost to cast; this is their Stamina Cost. For every skill point put into *Magic* Skill, a Hero may choose to learn spells worth a total Stamina Cost of 3 points.

Novice Heroes may choose only those spells which have a Stamina Cost of 1, 2 or 4 points. Spells costing 6 or more points to cast may not be learnt yet; they are reserved for more experienced – nay, legendary! – Heroes and especially nasty Bad Guys.

Sample Hero:
Our Hero, 'Lucky', has had a change of mind and now decides to become a sorcerer instead. From his SKILL of 9, he spends 2 points in learning to use a *Sword*, 2 on using a *Bow*, 1 on *Dodge*, and the remaining 4 on *Magic* (total: 9 points). He now has a SKILL of 5, *Sword* 7, *Bow* 7, *Dodge* 6 and *Magic* 9, and can choose spells with a total Stamina Cost of 12 points.

Spell List
Although Heroes may not choose spells with a Stamina Cost higher than 4, we have listed all the available spells here for the sake of completeness. The Director may have invented more spells exclusive to the particular world you are adventuring in, and he may allow you to choose them. He will inform you if any are available. Similarly, he may forbid certain spells from this list if they are incompatible with his game; if so, simply choose something else.

	Stamina Cost		Stamina Cost
Darkness	1	*All Heal*	4
Fear	1	*Arrow-Snake*	4
Fire Bolt	1	*Find*	4
Illusion	1	*Fly*	4
Light	1	*Grand Illusion*	4
Lock	1	*Grow*	4
Luck	1	*Invisibility*	4
Open	1	*Restrain*	4
Skill	1	*Shrink*	4
Stamina	1	*Speak to Animals*	4
Strength	1	*Wall*	4
Ward	1		
Weakness	1	*Banish Undead*	6
		Cockroach	6
Counter-Spell	2*	*Petrify*	6
ESP	2	*Raise Skeleton*	6
Farseeing	2	*Teleport*	6
Force Bolt	2		
Languages	2	*Death*	10
Levitate	2		
Mirror Selves	2		
Sleep	2		

* – See description below for more details.

❧

Spell Explanations
This is a list of what the spells can and cannot do. The effects of most of them cannot be avoided by their intended victim, and many last for a certain length of time (measured in real minutes). All spells of Stamina Cost 1, 2 or 4 can be cast and then forgotten about; the

higher-cost spells require full concentration in order to work.

Darkness (1) – This spell conjures up an area of murky darkness in a circular area, up to five metres round the caster, for up to three minutes. The darkness extinguishes all artificial light, and negates the *Dark Seeing* Skill.

Fear (1) – This spell terrifies one chosen person, sending him cowering as far away from the spell-caster as possible. The effects last for two minutes, after which time the victim recovers from his irrational fear.

Fire Bolt (1) – The spell hurls a short, stabbing blast of fire at one target from the pointed finger of the caster. Unless the target manages to *Dodge* the blast, or succeeds in *Testing his Luck*, the spell causes one die of damage to his STAMINA.

Illusion (1) – The spell-caster can use this spell to create an illusion that will convince one nominated person. For example, the caster may convince a pursuing monster that there is a bridge over a gaping chasm. The illusion will immediately be cancelled if anything happens to dispel the illusion (for example, if the monster steps out on to the 'bridge' – though in this case it may be too late for the monster!). Anyone wounded by an imaginary weapon will appear to take damage, even to the point of unconsciousness, but, when the illusion wears off, will reawaken and realize that it was all in the mind. The illusion lasts for a maximum of three minutes.

Light (1) – The spell creates a magical light which glows with the same intensity as a firebrand. It is usually cast upon the tip of a staff or torch. The light lasts for up to fifteen minutes, but can be snuffed out at will by the caster. A magical light of this sort is affected by *Darkness*.

Lock (1) – This spell simply locks a door, treasure chest or whatever by magic and stops it from being opened by unauthorized persons. The spell can be removed by an *Open* spell, or by the original caster casting another *Lock* spell on top of the first (so the original caster doesn't need to know *Open* in order to get back inside the chest!).

Luck (1) – When cast, this spell can restore an adventurer's LUCK score by up to 4 points. The LUCK score can never be raised above its *Initial* level; any additional points are lost. This spell cannot be cast while the spell-caster is in combat.

Open (1) – This one is used simply to open a lock, whether on a door, treasure chest, window, or anything else that is lockable. It also cancels out a *Lock* spell.

Skill (1) – As with the *Luck* spell, this simply restores an adventurer's SKILL by up to 4 points. The SKILL score cannot be raised above its *Initial* value; any extra points are lost. This spell cannot be used while the spell-caster is engaged in combat.

Stamina (1) – As in the case of the *Luck* spell, this simply restores an adventurer's STAMINA, but this time by up to 6 points. The STAMINA score can never be raised above its *Initial* level; any further points are lost. This spell cannot be cast while the spell-caster is in combat. If a Hero casts it upon himself, the Stamina Cost is deducted *after* the 6 points have been restored.

Strength (1) – This spell endows the caster (or another chosen recipient) with the strength of a Troll when it comes to lifting, carrying or battering. It can be very useful for getting heavy boulders out of the way, kicking open locked doors and so on. The Director should bear in mind that a Troll's strength may be just too great for a delicate task and judge the results accordingly. The spell lasts for a maximum of one minute or one major task (one locked door, one huge boulder, etc.).

Ward (1) – This spell may deflect one arrow, spear or other missile thrown at the caster. The missile whistles past and falls harmlessly to the ground.

Weakness (1) – This spell reduces a victim's SKILL score by 1–6 points (roll one die) for five minutes.

Counter-Spell (2 to choose, but read on) – This spell, which cancels out any other spell, works in quite a complicated way. When used, the spell will automatically cost the caster STAMINA points equal to the cost of the original spell being cancelled *plus* a further 1 STAMINA point, plus any special penalties which may affect the caster. Furthermore, for *Counter-Spell* to work successfully, the caster must reduce his *Magic* Skill by the Stamina Cost of the incoming spell before trying to cancel it. This spell works only on spells cast against the caster. The caster still pays the Stamina Cost even if the *Counter Spell* fails.

For example, cancelling a *Fire Bolt* cast at our Hero with his *Magic* Skill of 12 costs him 2 STAMINA points, if he can roll 11 or less on two dice. Cancelling out a *Death* spell, though, would cost him 11 STAMINA points (and, in that case, also cost him a year of his life) if he could somehow roll 2 or less on two dice.

ESP (2) – With this spell, the caster suddenly becomes able to tune in to a creature's thoughts. It won't allow him to read actual words or ideas, but can indicate a creature's emotions and general frame of mind. For example, it can reveal whether someone, who appears to be friendly, really is so. It cannot work on inanimate objects, unless they have some vestiges of intelligence. The power lasts for a maximum time of one minute.

Farseeing (2) – This spell simply endows the caster with the eyesight of an eagle, allowing him to see in minute detail for a distance of up to five kilometres, and, in less detail, even further. It should be remembered, though, that even eagles can't see *through* things like hills or walls. The effect lasts for ten minutes, but can be cancelled at will sooner.

Force Bolt (2) – This spell, similar to the *Fire Bolt*, delivers a lightning bolt which causes 1–6 points of STAMINA damage. There is no way of avoiding such a bolt, except by *Counter-Spell* or *Wall*.

Languages (2) – This spell temporarily gives the caster, or someone on whom the spell is cast, a *Languages* Skill of 12, and therefore a chance of being able to converse in (though not read) a specific language.

Levitate (2) – Anyone possessing this spell may cast it upon objects, opponents or himself. It frees the target from the effects of gravity and causes him to float freely up or down in the air under the caster's control. For more controlled movement – say forwards or backwards – one needs a *Fly* spell. The levitation lasts for a maximum of five minutes, but the spell can be recast in mid-flight (though, naturally, successful recasting requires another *Magic* roll!). If the levitation effect wears off, the object will glide slowly back to earth rather than dropping rapidly.

Mirror Selves (2) – This high-class illusion can convince one victim that the spell-caster is now three people! If fighting against the caster, the victim has only a one-in-three chance of choosing the right target. However, all three will attack him, and all three casters may wound the victim! The illusion lasts for a maximum of three minutes.

Sleep (2) – This spell, if it works, simply sends one victim to sleep for five minutes. If the victim is wounded while asleep, he will immediately waken (unless killed by the injury, of course). It is very bad form for Heroes to go around killing people while they sleep.

All Heal (4) – This powerful spell can restore a person's SKILL, STAMINA and LUCK to their *Initial* scores. It cannot be cast while the spell-caster is in the middle of a combat or otherwise engaged. If a Hero wishes to cast this spell upon himself, the STAMINA cost is removed *after* the scores have been restored.

Arrow-Snake (4) – This strange spell is a must for any sorcerer who likes giving people nasty surprises. What it does, quite simply, is to turn an arrow, when notched and ready for firing, into a poisonous snake (with SKILL 10 and STAMINA 4) which instantaneously bites and wounds the archer. The snake automatically inflicts 4 points of damage, before slithering away.

Find (4) – This spell may be used to find anything, from a seam of gold in a mine to the exit from a maze. It cannot detect emotions (find someone with evil thoughts, for example); and you should beware of looking for something too general (find metal, say, would probably lead you straight to your own sword). When this spell is cast and the appropriate subject is concentrated upon by the caster, he will suddenly know in which direction the sought object lies.

However, it should be remembered that the direction is suggested only in terms of a compass-point (north, south-west or whatever), and that no distance is specified. Knowing that a maze's exit lies to the south is of no help if one actually has to head north while finding the route to that exit. The sensation of knowing the correct direction stays in the mind for one minute.

Fly (4) – This spell is an advance on the *Levitate* spell, in that it allows the spell-caster (or whoever or whatever the spell is cast upon) to move in a sideways direction *as well as* up and down. The spell lasts for five minutes and can be recast while the sorcerer is still in the air. When the spell runs out, the flying person or object glides slowly down to the ground.

Grand Illusion (4) – Building on the *Illusion* spell, this more sophisticated spell allows for the fooling of as many people as the Hero's *Magic* score. Hence, someone with *Magic* 12 may fool up to twelve people with the same illusion. In all other respects the illusion works in exactly the same way as the *Illusion* spell, including a maximum length of three minutes. The spell can be recast before the spell runs out.

Grow (4) – When this spell is cast upon a person or an object, it will grow to half its size again, in all directions. Hence a shield a metre across will grow another half-metre, while a two-metre man will become three metres tall! Note that a person's clothing will not expand with him, and this could prove nasty in very tight armour! The effect will wear off after three minutes. Casting the spell again while the first is still working will cause the target to grow half its size again, and so on!

Invisibility (4) – This spell turns the caster (or someone or something else) completely invisible for three minutes. One should bear in mind, however, the following points: clothes and equipment are not affected by the spell, an invisible person is not necessarily a silent person, and invisible people still have to open doors, leave footprints in soft earth, and so on.

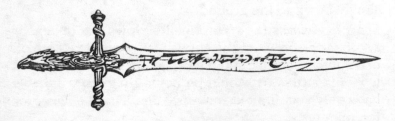

Restrain (4) – The nominated person or object upon whom this spell is cast will be held in magical bonds, rooted to the spot and unable to move, for up to three minutes. People restrained in this manner will still be able to breathe and move their eyes, but not to do much more. Objects measuring up to about three metres cubed can be held in place – so a boulder could be temporarily stopped from falling while a glacier could not.

Shrink (4) – This spell works in exactly the opposite way to *Grow*, shrinking a living being or an object down to half its size in all directions. The effect wears off again after three minutes. Casting the spell again while the first is still working will cause the target to shrink by half its current size again, and so on.

Speak to Animals (4) – This spell endows the caster, or another person, with the equivalent of a *Languages* Skill of 12 in the bizarre tongues used by the animals and lower creatures. It should be noted that many animals have only very limited conversations! The spell lasts for ten minutes.

Wall (4) – Casting this spell creates a wall round an area five metres in diameter, through which nothing can pass, for a maximum of five minutes. It can withstand arrows, sword blows, people, monsters and spells (though *Counter-Spell* may remove the wall). If anything from inside the wall touches it, it will immediately disappear. The wall need not be centred round the spell-caster – it could, for example, be placed round an important treasure to stop thieves getting at it.

Banish Undead (6) – This spell works in the opposite direction to *Raise Skeleton*, in that it returns an undead creature to the peaceful rest of true death. It will work on one creature, removing the magical life-force which had animated it. A banished corpse may not be resurrected again, so this spell may also be cast upon a corpse to stop it being raised again.

Cockroach (6) – This peculiarly named spell is in fact that classic of fairy tales and legends: the 'turn-you-into-a-funny-creature' spell. This spell will, if a *Test for Luck* is failed, turn its victim into the small, insignificant creature of the caster's choice. The victim retains its brain power, but is generally unable to communicate unless a *Speak to Animals* spell is employed. The effect is permanent, but a *Counter-Spell* (costing 7 STAMINA, remember) could remove it. Note that the spell doesn't turn a victim's clothes or possessions into anything – they simply remain where they were when the spell was cast.

Petrify (6) – Being turned to stone is very unpleasant indeed, but that's exactly what this spell does. A *Test for Luck* may be used to avoid this spell. The effect starts at the feet and slowly works its way up the poor victim's body, petrifying him and his clothes and equipment as it goes. The victim loses 1 STAMINA point every two rounds, and this will continue until he is turned completely to stone – that is, unless a *Counter-Spell* is used against it, or the sorcerer who cast it is killed, whereupon the effects will reverse until the victim has fully recovered again. If the victim dies before this can happen, he will not revert back to human again, and will remain a statue for ever.

Raise Skeleton (6) – This necromantic spell is used to breathe life back into a corpse, forcing it to return to life as a Skeleton under the control of the caster. The spell requires an hour-long ritual to work. While the corpse need not be complete, any missing features will not grow back when it is brought back to life. It should also be remembered that the undead do not really think for themselves, so any instructions given to a Skeleton must be very explicit if they are not to be misinterpreted.

If he doesn't much fancy the idea of all those bones walking about his domain, the caster can expend more effort and create various types of undead, which cost the following Stamina points: Crypt Stalker 7, Skeleton Warrior 7, Zombie 7, Decayer 8, Ghoul 8 (see *Out of the Pit* for further details of these undead beings).

Teleport (6) – To teleport is to hop from one place to another in the twinkling of an eye, setting off and arriving almost instantaneously. A sorcerer using this means of travel may go anywhere within ten kilometres radius in a single jump, and may take whatever he can carry in his hands (this can include another human being). The caster need not know the exact details of where he is going; the spell automatically stops him reappearing inside a mountain or at the bottom of the sea – but only, of course, if the spell works right!

Death (10) – This is the ultimate incantation in any evil sorcerer's spell book. It will almost never be used by a Hero, except in the direst of circumstances. If the *Magic* Skill roll succeeds, the victim dies, full stop. There is no *Test for Luck* to avoid its effects. It is little consolation to the victim to know that a sorcerer casting this spell and losing 10 points from his STAMINA in one horrific go will also age a full year in an instant.

Non-Human Races

Most heroes will be of human origin. After all, most of the population of Allansia are humans, and the other races generally try to keep themselves to themselves. However, occasionally there are Elf and Dwarf adventurers, so this is what you need to know in order to play one (if your Director will allow you to play one in his game):

Dwarf Characters
Dwarfs are, as their names implies, short humanoids, renowned for their great skills at mining, telling long tales, drinking and swinging battle-axes. They dress in

earth colours, have an earthy way of speaking, and mistrust just about everything. They loathe and despise those non-human races that practise evil (Orcs, Goblins, Trolls, etc.) and are liable to fly into a killing frenzy at the merest sight of one. Their favourite weapons are, as we said, battle-axes, and they hold all magic in great awe. Some Dwarfs don't get on with Elves too well, considering them too intellectual and weird, but there have been several notable adventuring partnerships between an Elf and a Dwarf.

There are few restrictions on Dwarf characters. However, a Dwarf character *must* have at least 1 Special Skill point in *Axe*, *Underground Lore* and *Dark Seeing*. A Dwarven sorcerer is very, very rare. They usually carry an axe as part of their equipment.

Elf Characters
Elves are notoriously shy about mixing with humans, whom they see as frivolous, chaotic and ignorant, rather like children allowed to run loose in the world. Most Elves, as you might guess, possess the very opposite of such qualities, being very learned, peaceful and serious. They spend most of their lives tending the trees of their forest enclaves, and occasionally warring with the Orcs who would burn their beloved plants down. The Elves are the keepers of wisdom on many subjects, including ancient history, the natural sciences and, above all, magic. Elven magic in its purest form is truly mind-boggling to behold, but these days it is seen only rarely in the world outside their forest retreats.

An Elven adventurer is likely to be a rarity, and he may be the object of surprise and curiosity in some remote areas. He is likely to be a bit of a rebel, having turned his back on Elven ways; but he will still retain many Elven qualities. Any Elf character *must* have at least 1 Special Skill point in *Bow*, *Wood Lore* and *Magic*. They usually carry a longbow as part of their equipment, along with their sword, and generally dress in shades of green.

Money and Equipment

One of the main reasons for setting out on an adventure is, of course, the acquisition of fame and wealth. Fame comes from brave exploits, from doing so many daring things that the minstrels can feel secure that, if they sing a song about you in some distant land, it will be heard through to the end without interruption. Wealth comes from much the same thing, and is often as hard to come by as fame.

The basic monetary unit in Allansia (and over much of the rest of Titan, too) is the Gold Piece (abbreviated to GP). There are also Silver Pieces, exchangeable in the ratio 10 SP = 1 GP. Different areas produce various coins in differing denominations to help with giving change and so on, but a Gold Piece is worth much the same everywhere.

Starting Characters

When he leaves his previous cosy life behind him and starts adventuring, a Hero will have only the barest minimum of equipment:

- a weapon, usually the one he has the highest Special Skill in using (probably a sword)
- clothing, not of the highest quality, plus some scraps of chainmail and plating which just about serve as armour
- a backpack, used for carrying supplies and any treasure that he may stumble across
- a small amount of food (known in game terms as Provisions)
- optionally, a horse, together with saddle and reins
- money, in the sum of 1–6 Gold Pieces (roll one die).

When the Heroes eventually acquire some money, they will be able to purchase more exotic items of equipment from the nearest town or settlement. An extensive list of items is to be found in the *Further Adventures* chapter, starting on page 371. The Director will tell all the players exactly what they can and cannot buy, and may even give some hints as to what the Heroes may need for their expedition.

Name and Sex

To personalize your Hero, you should decide whether the character is male or female, and give him/her an appropriate name. There are no advantages or disadvantages to be had in playing a female character in *Dungeoneer*.

Give some thought to naming your character; after a while you may not want to be stuck with a Hero called Fred or Kevin. Choose something a little more fantastical, and you could even add something personal, like a nickname based on some made-up exploit from his past or from his Special Skills. For example, a character with a high *Sleight of Hand* and who's previously made a career out of crime could be called Talgor the Dip or perhaps Vargas the Hand. Use your imagination, and your Hero will start to come to life before your very eyes!

Age

Although it has little bearing on a game, especially one recreating a violent medieval world where few people live beyond their twenties, knowing a character's age does help visualize his or her personality and appearance. This in turn will help in role-playing the character.

Most newly rolled Hero characters will be fairly young – though life will have already provided them with a few hard knocks – therefore, to ascertain a new character's age we recommend that you roll three dice and add 15 to the result. This will give an age somewhere between 18 and 33. For a (much rarer) older character, roll three dice and add 30, to give an age somewhere between 33 and 48. Very few characters will live beyond that age – and then probably only through the use of powerful youth-retaining magic and a whole host of mercenaries and other guards to do their fighting for them!

Experience Points, Treasure

These sections on the *Adventure Sheet* will be needed for noting these items either when they are awarded after a successful adventure (in the case of experience), or when found during an adventure (treasure). Leave them blank for now.

Personalizing Your Hero

Just a couple of things remain to be done in order to round off a Hero and make him or her ready for play. Since a large part of the fun of playing a game like *Dungeoneer* with your friends is pretending to be someone else and doing things you would never dream of doing in real life, the final step is to give your Hero a fully rounded personality. This is carried out in three simple steps.

Background

If you look at the pre-rolled Heroes from the first adventure, you will see that in this section of their *Adventure Sheets* we detail where they come from, what they were trained in before they became an adventurer, and so on. As to where they come from, either ask your Director for a suitable area or take a look at the map of Allansia on page 32 and choose somewhere.

As to their previous experience and past life, simply look at your Hero's Special Skills, and decide how he got them! Take a look at a pre-rolled character like Axel

Wolfric: he has *Wood Lore*, *Sneak* and *Strength* and a few common, not to say superstitious, spells (*Luck*, *Fear*, *Stamina*) – plainly someone who has spent many years out of doors. So, we made him a barbarian warrior from the northern plains.

Eventually, as you become more experienced at creating interesting Heroes who you think will be entertaining to play, you will be able to decide the personality and background of your character first, and *then* choose skills and spells to fit in with this.

Personality

This part of the background is a little trickier to set out at the beginning, and so we recommend that you think up a few ideas for this section and leave the rest blank for your first few adventures. For example, you may find that you have a character who has a very high STAMINA score but little in the way of SKILL. That might immediately suggest to you that he is large and a little clumsy – and you could then start playing him as such.

It's a good idea to have a few such ideas about who your Hero is and how he will react in particular situations; but do also allow new events in his adventuring career to shape his character as they happen. Anyhow, we predict that you will be too busy in your first few adventures merely trying to survive in this strange new world of monsters and magic to worry about pretending to be someone else! As you get more experienced and the rules and adventuring become second nature, you will then be able to have fun playing with different personalities.

Quotes

Finally, if you feel inspired, add a few choice oaths or favourite sayings for your Hero to mutter at vital points. These are great fun because, right from the start, they can become your Hero's catch-phrase; everyone will immediately know that when he says a certain thing he is annoyed, or happy, or thirsting for Orcish blood, or whatever. Take a look at what we invented for the pre-rolled starting Heroes, and do something similar.

If you are feeling really artistic, you may also care to draw a picture of your Hero in the space provided, though this is by no means essential to play.

Don't let yourself get too worried about all this talk about role-playing. While it can be great fun to escape into a new character, he or she will still have an awful lot of *you* in them. As you must know by now, for we've said it often enough, the ultimate object of all this is for everyone to have fun, not to recreate some form of high dramatic art. And talking of fun, we are now going to move on to the rules themselves, starting with that most thrilling of activities, *Combat!*

Fighting Battles

Combat is often the most exciting part of a *Dungeoneer* game, for it is where the Heroes come closest to failure and death. It is also where their most important skills and spells come into use, and where almost anything can happen (and often does!).

The Dice

As we have indicated, the six-sided dice are the most important tools we use to decide the outcome of battles. Usually, the Director will allow the players to roll the dice for their own Heroes. However, you should note that for certain skills (such as *Awareness*) the Director will be making secret rolls on your behalf. After all, he can't let you know that something is there for you to detect, if your roll then indicates that you don't detect anything – because he would already have given the game away!

If you have a Special Skill which requires secret rolls, your Director will tell you whether anything has come to your Hero's attention. Of course the Director won't be checking your particular skill every time he rolls the dice. Indeed, he may roll them every now and then just so that you won't know when he is checking and when he isn't!

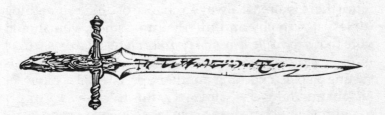

Dice can be used in the game to produce a wide range of numbers. The usual 1–6 or 2–12 rolls are simple. Occasionally the rules or an adventure will call for a number in the range of, say, 1–3 or 2–7. We list below some of the common rolls and how to determine them:

1–6: roll one die
2–12: roll two dice and add the totals together
3–18: roll three dice and add the totals together
1–3: roll one die; on a roll of 4, 5 or 6 deduct *three* from the result
2–7: roll one die and add one to the total
2–4: as for 1–3, but after rolling add *one* to the final result.

Very occasionally there will be no set rules for carrying out some specific activity (so don't try looking up the rules for swinging upside down from a chandelier by your ankles while juggling daggers and whistling a merry tune!). In such situations your Director will use his experience to assess the probability of your achieving this unusual manoeuvre; he will express it in terms, say, of 1 in 6, or 3 in 6. This simply means that, in the first example, you should roll one die and try to score a 1; in the second example, you will have to roll a 1, 2 or 3 to succeed.

Automatic Hits, Automatic Misses
Since there is almost always a chance of doing something (unless it is totally and utterly impossible), you should note that *a roll of double-1 on two dice always succeeds, except in the combat sequence*. This applies whether a Hero is casting a spell, checking another Special Skill, *Testing for Luck* or anything else. However, this rule does *not* apply to fighting which uses the combat sequence – see *Mighty Blows and Fumbles*, below, on page 156.

If there is quite a good chance of something happening, say a Hero having to roll 11 or less on two dice, a roll of 2 will indicate that something extra special has happened. Your Director will tell you exactly what has happened at the time, but it could include a spell sending someone to sleep for twice as long, an arrow catching someone right in the eye, or whatever the Director deems appropriate for the situation.

Conversely, of course, there is always the chance, however remote, of something going wrong. Therefore, you should also note that *a roll of double-6 always fails, except in the combat sequence*. Thus a Hero can have a *Dodge* Skill of 18 and still fail occasionally – and this is only right, since no one is that perfect!

Furthermore, if there is quite a high chance of failure, a roll of 12 will provide a quite spectacular failure! The exact nature of this bizarre quirk of fate will be decided by your Director, but it could range from the funny to the irritating or even to the downright dangerous! Extra-special care should, of course, be taken when casting spells, because there is already quite a high chance of their not working, and when they do go wrong they can *really* go wrong!

Note: these automatic hits and misses also apply to opponents.

Time

Time, like distance, is not all that important in *Dungeoneer*. If your Director wants your Heroes to get from A to B, he probably won't waste time shooting all that tedious footage of you actually travelling. More likely he'll say 'Cut!' and jump straight to the next scene. However, there are occasions, say when fighting or casting a spell, when time does matter.

Time is defined in two ways in these rules: first, in *minutes*. Yes, that's right, ordinary minutes, measurable on a watch or clock. Since these are real minutes, the players should be careful about time-wasting. There's little point in the party's spell-caster sending a bunch of Orcs to sleep for five minutes and the Heroes then spending so much time arguing about what to do next that the baddies wake up and leap to attack them again! After this has happened once or twice, everyone will get the message and learn how to keep such discussions short and to the point.

The second measurement of time is in terms of Combat Rounds; as the name implies, these are usually employed when a fight is going on. What they define is the time taken for everyone present to perform one round of combat, that is, one attempt to injure their opponent. These are abstract matters, however, and could last from two seconds to several minutes. In rules terms, a Combat

Round means one pass through the combat sequence, which we will detail in the next section.

Combat against One Opponent

The basic combat sequence presented here is used whenever one Hero is fighting one other being, be it another human or a huge drooling monster from beyond the depths of the infernal domain. We will deal with fighting more than one opponent in a later section, starting on page 168. Opponents with more than 1 Attack (usually those which are multi-limbed, very large or very dextrous) should be treated as multiple opponents.

Who Strikes First?

The combat sequence is so arranged that both Hero and opponent strike at each other at the same time, rather than one after the other. If both combatants are aware of the other's presence there is no need to work out who gets in the first blow. If opponents start off some distance away from each other, the order of moving is this: first the Bad Guys say what they are going to do, followed by the Heroes; then both parties move at the same time. This gives the Heroes the slight advantage of being able to respond to what their opponents are doing, but little else. Remember that missile fire (bows and other thrown weapons) and magic can be used effectively if the enemy is some distance away.

The Combat Sequence

First your Director will make a note of your opponent's SKILL and STAMINA scores, and any Special Skills, if relevant. The Director will be playing the part of your opponent in the battle. Each character will also need two dice. The sequence of combat is then as follows:

(1) The Director rolls both dice for the opponent. The result is added to the opponent's appropriate fighting Special Skill or – if none is available – to his current SKILL score. The Director checks to see whether any modifiers apply, for example fighting in an enclosed space or in darkness, and adds or subtracts them from the total (all modifiers are listed under appropriate headings following this sequence). The total finally arrived at is the opponent's Attack Strength. If a double-6 or double-1 is rolled, consult the section on *Mighty Blows and Fumbles*, below.

(2) The player rolls two dice for his Hero. The result is added to the Hero's appropriate fighting Special Skill or – if none is available – to his current SKILL score. Any modifiers for fighting conditions are added or subtracted from the total. This final total is the Hero's Attack Strength. If a double-6 or double-1 is rolled, consult the section on *Mighty Blows and Fumbles*, below. A Hero with *Dodge* may use it here – see below.

(3) The scores are compared. If the Hero's Attack Strength is higher than his opponent's, he has wounded it: turn to paragraph 4. If his opponent's Attack strength is higher, the Hero has been wounded: turn to paragraph 5. If both Attack Strength totals are the same, the blows have been blocked or avoided: return to paragraph 1 and start the next Combat Round.

(4) The Hero should roll one die on the Damage Table on page 155, cross-referencing it with the weapon he is using. LUCK or armour may adjust this figure (see page 158 and page 163). The number given in the Table

is deducted from his opponent's STAMINA. Turn to paragraph 6.

(5) When the adversary has wounded the Hero, the Director rolls one die and cross-references it against the opponent's weapon on the Damage Table below. The Hero's LUCK or armour may adjust this figure (see page 158 and page 163). The number given in the Table is the amount of damage the Hero must take, subtracting it from his STAMINA score.

(6) Everyone involved makes the appropriate adjustments to STAMINA and, if it was used, LUCK.

(7) If the opponent's STAMINA drops to zero or less, he is dead. Otherwise, the fight continues: return to paragraph 1 and start the next Combat Round. If the Hero's STAMINA drops to zero or less, he may be dead: see the section on *Unconsciousness and Death* on page 160. Otherwise, return to paragraph 1 and start the next Combat Round.

Damage

Quite clearly, smiting someone with a gigantic battle-axe will hurt him far more than hitting him with a feather pillow; the following table lists the number of points of damage to STAMINA various weapons will do.

Whichever combatant has wounded his opponent should roll one die and cross-reference the result with the weapon being used. The number given is the amount of damage the wounded character must deduct from his STAMINA score. *Note:* the die-roll may be adjusted up or down by using LUCK or wearing armour, and this is why scores of 7 or more can be rolled – see the footnotes below the table.

Note that a character may 'pull' a blow at any time in order to reduce the amount of damage it does to his opponent, usually as a prelude to asking him to surrender. The character need simply state that he is doing so; the damage delivered will be reduced to only 1 point.

Of course, missile weapons such as bows may not be used in close-up combat, but we have included them here for the sake of completeness; the section dealing with *Missile Weapons* comes shortly, beginning on page 172.

Damage Table

Weapon	up to 1	2	3	4	5	6	7 or more
Battle-axe	2	2	2	2	2	3	3
Club	1	2	2	2	2	2	3
Dagger	1	1	2	2	2	2	2
Pole Arm†	1	2	2	2	3	3	3
Spear	1	1	2	2	2	3	3
Staff	1	2	2	2	2	2	3
Sword	1	2	2	2	2	3	3
Two-handed Sword*	2	2	2	3	3	3	4
Arrow	1	1	2	2	2	3	3
Crossbow bolt	1	2	2	2	2	3	3
Javelin	1	2	2	2	2	3	3
Throwing dagger	1	2	2	2	2	2	3

Fist/kick, human size	1	1	1	2	2	2	3
Fist/kick, larger size	2	2	2	3	3	3	3
Bite/claw, small	1	1	2	2	2	2	3
Bite/claw, large	1	2	2	2	3	3	4
Bite/claw, very large	2	2	3	3	4	5	6

* – Two-handed swords are difficult to control in combat, and reduce the user's SKILL by 2, unless the Hero has a Special Skill in using the weapon.

† – Using any pole arm (guisarme, glaive, morning star, etc.) reduces the wielder's SKILL by 1, unless the Hero has a Special Skill in using the weapon.

More unorthodox weapons – tables, ale flagons, rocks, etc. – require special consideration and will therefore be covered in a separate section, below, on page 164, *Odd Weapons*.

Mighty Blows and Fumbles

In a similar vein to the automatic hits and misses described earlier, there are times when a Hero is able to swipe his opponent with a blow that is so strong or so accurate that the latter simply crumples to the ground stone dead! This is called a *Mighty Blow*.

A *Mighty Blow* occurs whenever a Hero, or his adversary, rolls a double-6 when determining his Attack Strength (see the combat squence, above). When this happens, the character on the receiving end is automatically reduced to STAMINA – 1: mortally wounded for a Hero, death for an opponent.

If *both* combatants roll a double-6, they both manage to block the other's blow, but their weapons break! Creatures using claws or bites are not affected by this, but lose 2 STAMINA points instead. A Hero with a broken weapon must find a new weapon or continue to fight unarmed (see the section on *Unarmed Combat*, below, on page 167).

Conversely, should a combatant roll a double-1 when determining his Attack Strength, he will *Fumble* his blow and fail to connect with his opponent, with one of the following results:

- If the Attack Strengths indicate that he would have struck his opponent (that is, even by rolling a 2 his total is greater than his opponent's), the result is changed to a draw, indicating a stand-off.
- If the result would have been a stand-off, the opponent is judged to have wounded the fumbling character – roll for damage as usual.
- If the result would have been an injury to the fumbling character, his opponent may add 1 to the die when rolling on the Damage Table.

157

Using LUCK *in Combat*

In combat, a Hero may, if he wishes, use his LUCK, either to inflict a more serious wound on his opponent or to minimize the effects of a wound inflicted upon him. *Note:* this modification does *not* apply to *Mighty Blows* or *Fumbles*.

If a Hero has just wounded an opponent, he may *Test for Luck* as described earlier. If he succeeds and is Lucky, he has inflicted a severe wound, and may add 2 to the die-roll when rolling on the Damage Table. If he is Unlucky, however, he must deduct 1 from his die-roll on the Damage Table.

If the Hero has just been wounded, he may *Test for Luck* in an attempt to minimize the damage. If he is Lucky, he may deduct 1 from his opponent's die-roll on the Damage Table. If he is Unlucky, however, his opponent may add 1 to his die-roll on the Damage Table.

Remember: a Hero must subtract 1 point from his LUCK score every time he *Tests for Luck.*

Using Dodge *in Combat*

Dodge Special Skill can be used in combat to avoid the blows of an opponent. The Hero must declare, *before* either character rolls to determine his Attack Strength, that he will attempt to *Dodge* his opponent's blows rather than fight him. The combat sequence then proceeds as normal, except that the Hero rolls two dice and adds them to his *Dodge* score rather than to his SKILL or weapon Special Skill. The scores are compared as usual. A roll of 2 by the Hero means he has definitely failed to dodge.

If the Hero's total is higher, he manages to avoid his opponent's blows, but doesn't himself inflict any damage. However, in the *next* Combat Round he has the option of either (i) escaping from combat and (if so skilled) casting a spell at his opponent in the next round, or (ii) adding a bonus of 1 point to his SKILL or weapon Special Skill if he wishes to attack.

If the opponent's total is higher, he hits and rolls for damage as usual, except that he must reduce his die-roll on the Damage Table by 1 point.

The *Dodge* Skill may also be employed to leap out of the way of a missile such as an arrow or crossbow bolt. The Hero must be aware that the missile is approaching, and then roll two dice whose total will be equal to or less than his *Dodge* score. However, since arrows travel so fast, there is a further handicap of 10 points if the arrow or bolt is fired from close range, of 8 points if from medium range, and of 6 points if from long range.

Note: it must be possible to roll a Hero's *Dodge* score, with these extra modifiers, on two dice for the dodge to succeed – the double-1-always-works rule does *not* apply in this special case; hence, for example, a Hero with a *Dodge* Skill of 9 could not evade an arrow fired from short or medium range.

Unconsciousness and Death
In the original solo gamebook rules, anyone whose STAMINA dropped to zero died. However, if there are comrades who can come to a Hero's aid, it is fairer to allow him a chance of survival, no matter how slim.

If a Hero's STAMINA is reduced to zero, he becomes unconscious. If his STAMINA is reduced to −1, he has been mortally wounded. If his STAMINA falls to −2 or less, he has been hacked to pieces and is quite irrefutably dead!

Unconscious characters will regain consciousness after between two and twelve minutes (roll two dice). When they awaken they will have 1 STAMINA point.

A *mortally wounded* hero requires assistance from others if he is ever to recover. After between one and six minutes (the Director rolls a die to discover how quickly) it will be too late. Potions or spells are the only ways to revive such a character; these must be used to raise the Hero's STAMINA above zero. If they are unsuccessful, the poor Hero bleeds to death where he lies.

Notes: (i) if everyone else is otherwise occupied, a severely wounded Hero's opponent could continue hacking at him as he lies prone, virtually guaranteeing his death.

(ii) If a character is alone, he will not recover from being mortally wounded.

(iii) These rules apply only to Heroes, not to their opponents.

Unopposed Strikes and Surprise

Occasions will occur when something leaps out of the shadows and startles the Heroes or, conversely, when they themselves leap into a room and catch a monster unawares. Your Director will therefore simply inform you that you have surprised an opponent, or perhaps that one has surprised you. However, a Hero with *Awareness* Skill can try to make a successful roll against his skill, which will then negate the latter result. If someone in one party is surprised, those on the other side may fire or throw missile weapons, or cast a spell, before closing for hand-to-hand combat. Depending on the distance between the parties and the speed at which they close, archers and sorcerers may be able to loose off a second volley.

There may also be occasions when an opponent is entirely incapacitated, or is unaware of his attacker's presence, and hitting him is little more than a formality. This is known as an *Unopposed Strike*. Delivering an *Unopposed Strike* is quite simple. If your Director rules that you are in a position to do this, you should try to roll two dice equal to or less than your SKILL or weapon Special Skill, with a bonus in either case of 3 points. A roll of double-6 is an automatic miss; a roll of double-2 has the same effect as a *Mighty Blow*. If the strike hits normally, the character has the option of either doing normal damage (rolled on the Damage Table) or simply delivering 1 point of damage to the opponent's STAMINA and knocking him out for 2–12 minutes.

Armour

The Damage Table has been carefully constructed with one factor already built in: it takes armour into account.

163

Every Hero wears some scraps of armour, usually just enough for some blows to glance off but not enough to slow him down when he needs to put on a burst of speed. In practice, this armour commonly takes the form of a mail jerkin, a helmet or strengthened leather cap, and perhaps some metal strips woven into a leather kilt. Few adventurers carry shields; while they may give a little extra protection, as any warrior will tell you, in the confines of a dungeon corridor, they are usually more of a hindrance than a help.

Most of the opponents facing a party of Heroes will also be protected, either by armour or by a thick, leathery hide – or (in the case of Orcs and Trolls) by both!

If a character, either Hero or adversary, removes his armour and fights unarmoured, all rolls on the Damage Table against him may add 2 to the die-roll. If a character uses a shield, he must reduce his SKILL or weapon Special Skill by 2 points, but may also reduce any roll on the Damage Table against him by 2.

Odd Weapons
Occasionally a character may find himself fighting, using an object which is not normally considered to be a weapon! This could include an item of furniture (especially handy in a bar-room brawl!), an ale flagon, a rock, or whatever comes to hand! Fighting with a weapon like this is done in the usual way, but the character's SKILL must be reduced by 2 points when an object which can be held in one hand is used, or 3 points if the object is larger.

A successful *Strength* Skill roll will normally be needed to fight with certain larger objects, such as tables, boulders, trees, etc. – the Director will advise!

The following list details the damage done after a successful hit using the most common unorthodox weapons. The Director will inform you what damage other items will do, based on these typical examples:

Hand-held
Bench – as Sword
Chair – as Club
Table – as Two-handed Sword
Tree – as very large Bite

Thrown
Ale flagon, plate – as Arrow
Rock, light – as Crossbow bolt
Rock, heavy – as Battle-axe
Boulder, huge – as Two-handed Sword
Tree – as very large Bite

Strange Locations and Conditions
While a great many fights will take place in spacious, brightly lit rooms and caverns, or out in the open air, there will be other times when the Heroes are hard pressed against opponents while waist deep in water, in pitch darkness, while drunk, in a corridor only just wide enough to squeeze through, and so on.

For each or all of the following conditions, apply the listed modifier which will reduce a character's SKILL or weapon Special Skill. The effects of these modifiers are cumulative (hence, for example, a Hero fighting while knee deep in water in a narrow corridor must reduce his SKILL temporarily by 4 points). *Remember:* any modifiers may well apply as much to opponents as they do to the Heroes.

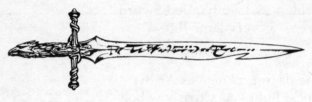

	Skill Modifier
Total darkness	−6*
Night-time darkness	−3**
Twilight	−1
Smoke/fog	−2
Torrential rain	−1
Knee deep in water	−2
Waist deep in water	−4
Up to the neck in water	−6
Swimming in water	−8
In snow or mud – as water of comparative depth	
Narrow corridor	−2
Very narrow corridor	−4
Steps (fighting down)	+1
Steps (fighting up)	−1
Narrow/spiral steps (down)	−1
Narrow/spiral steps (up)	−3
Mounted	−2†
Airborne	−5‡

Drunk	−2
Carrying Heavy weight	−2
Carrying Very Heavy weight	−4
Very large being attacking very small	+2
Very small being attacking very large	−1

---

* – *Reduced to* −4 *for characters with* Dark Seeing *and all underground dwelling creatures and beings (including Orcs and their ilk).*

** – *Reduced to* −1 *for characters with* Dark Seeing *and all underground dwelling creatures and beings (including Orcs and their ilk).*

† – *Applies to the unmounted opponent only.*

‡ – *Applies to both the airborne character and his grounded opponent. Furthermore, if the flying character is also on a mount, he must make a successful* Ride *Skill roll before every round, or he will spend that Combat Round out of action, recovering from nearly falling off.*

Unarmed Combat

Fighting without weapons is a specialized skill; but it may become a necessity if a character unfortunately breaks or loses his weapon. Many monsters and creatures, furthermore, are very used to fighting with tooth and claw. Of course, having *Unarmed Combat* or *Strength* Skill will help somewhat to redress the balance.

Fighting with one's bare hands uses exactly the same combat sequence as fighting with a weapon, and a character with *Unarmed Combat* Skill may use that score instead of his SKILL. Characters who are unused to fighting without a weapon must reduce their SKILL by 4 points for the purpose of the fight, unless they have *Strength* Skill or are currently under the effects of a *Strength* spell, in which case they need reduce their SKILL by only 2 points.

Any character whose STAMINA is reduced to 0 or 1 point by an opponent fighting with bare hands only will not die straight away; rather, he will fall unconscious for 2–12 minutes. A character reduced to −1 or less by an unarmed opponent will die or, in the case of a Hero, be mortally wounded. Plainly, none of this applies to beasts which use their claws and teeth to fight with; these creatures are considered to be armed!

Multiple Opponents

Some larger or more dextrous creatures are able to attack more than one opponent at a time. These creatures will, in the adventure text, be marked with a rating for the number of attacks they can make at once; if there is no rating, the creature has one attack.

Fighting more than one opponent or combining with an ally to attack a single opponent is carried out using the standard combat sequence, but with several notable differences.

If two characters are attacking one opponent (whether it be Heroes against a single Orc or several Orcs against one Hero), the usual combat sequence is used, just as if the lone combatants were retaliating against two adversaries. Before rolling, however, the outnumbered character must decide which of his opponents he is aiming for. He then conducts his fight *with that character*, injuring him or being injured according to the usual combat sequence, except that his SKILL is reduced by 1 point for every extra opponent he is having to fend off: hence, a Hero fighting four Orcs must engage all of them with his SKILL reduced by 3 points.

The sequence is then repeated for each *extra* opponent, again with the reduction applied for the number of opponents. However, if the outnumbered fighter wins an individual Attack Round, he doesn't injure his extra opponent. Since he is totally committed to fighting the original opponent, all he can do to any subsequent opponent is hold him at bay, by winning his round. If the outnumbered character loses a round to his second (or later) opponent, he must lose STAMINA points for an injury in a normal way. *Mighty Blows* and *Fumbles* do *not* apply in these multiple fights.

170

If a single creature with multiple attacks is fighting more than one opponent, it only delivers as many attacks as there are opponents. However, if it does not have enough attacks for every opponent, it must use the method described above to try and hold off all those it cannot attack! A creature with multiple attacks makes a *single* roll for its Attack Strength, which then applies to however many opponents it is facing.

If a creature with more than one attack is fighting just one opponent, it does not usually receive those extra attacks (except at the Director's discretion: he may rule the opposite to be the case, and in that instance the extra attacks will count to reduce the opponent's SKILL). More usually, the creature engages its single opponent using the normal one-to-one combat sequence.

Missile Weapons

Missile weapons include bows, javelins and throwing daggers. Missiles could also include just about anything that can be thrown – in a tight spot, all kinds of bizarre items may come to hand. Missiles are usually fired or thrown before characters close to engage in hand-to-hand combat, and are most suited to outdoor locations. Indeed, it is very difficult to loose off a missile at a target only a few paces away, and anyone attempting to use a weapon like a bow in hand-to-hand combat should be treated as being unarmed, with all the penalties that brings.

The first thing is to decide how far away the target is, as this affects the chance of hitting. Incidentally, it is worth mentioning here that a target must be at least partially visible in order to be hit. Look up the missile, or its equivalent, on the following Range Table:

Range Table

Weapon	Range (metres)		
	Short	Medium	Long
Bow	0–50	51–90	91–250
Crossbow	0–18	19–50	51–180
Javelin	0–10	11–20	21–40
Throwing dagger	0–8	9–18	19–24
Light object	0–10	11–20	21–30
Medium object	0–7	8–14	15–22
Heavy object	0–4	5–8	9–12

Firing

A bow or other missile weapon is fired accurately by rolling less than or equal to the appropriate weapon's Special Skill or the SKILL score, on two dice. However, there are modifiers which must be applied (see the table, below) – and they are cumulative! 'Very Small target' means one less than 30 centimetres across. 'Small target' means 30–90 centimetres (for comparison purposes, a Dwarf is typically around 110 centimetres tall). The rules concerning rolling double-6 (a *Mighty Blow*) and double-1 (a *Fumble*) also apply to this die-roll – which may lead to some spectacular accidents, or possibly to some real hawk-eyed shooting! Bow fire may be attempted in most situations; if in doubt, the Director will advise. However, certain situations will make the chance of actually hitting a chosen target very difficult. Firing a bow while engaged in hand-to-hand combat is not usually permissible. Shooting a bow into somebody else's combat is allowed, provided the firer is not himself engaged in combat; but note the heavy modifier and the chance of tragically hitting one's ally by mistake.

Modifier	
Medium range	−3
Long range	−6
Very small target	−4*
Small target	−2*
Moving target	−1
Firer moving	−1
Target obscured	−1**
Firing straight up	−1
Firing into combat	−5†
Throwing into combat	−3†

* – If three-quarters of, say, a human-sized target is obscured, the remaining portion must be judged to be the whole target so far as size is concerned. In this example, we would judge that the quarter of the human remaining visible would be a Small target (−2), three-quarters obscured (−3).

** – Per quarter of target obscured, up to −3.

† – If the shot misses its intended target, the character must roll again, as if firing or throwing at the next nearest target. If successful, this character is hit, whether they are the enemy or a member of the firer's own side.

Throwing

Throwing a missile works in exactly the same way as Firing, except that *Strength* is the Special Skill used, if it is available. All the modifiers listed above, with the exception of 'firing straight up', also apply to throwing a missile.

174

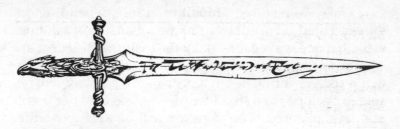

Magic in Combat

See the section on *Magic* in the following part of this chapter, beginning on page 198.

Healing and Restoring Characteristics

At various times during an adventure, a Hero's characteristics may be reduced, whether by injury, magic, curses, frequent bad luck or other causes. However, all is not lost, for there are many ways in which a Hero's scores may be restored to normal.

Skill

A Hero's SKILL score will not change much during the course of an adventure. The most that usually happens is that SKILL, or one particular Special Skill, is given a temporary addition or reduction for the duration of a specific fight or encounter. More permanently, an enchanted weapon (say, a Magic Sword) may add to a Hero's weapon skill whenever it is used. Of course it must be remembered that a Hero may use only one such weapon in any single battle, and hence can't receive the accumulated benefit of two such weapons! Very occasionally, a trap or some other special encounter may reduce a Hero's SKILL more permanently, thanks to an injury to the weapon-arm, for example.

SKILL may be restored (in part or in full, depending on the exact method used) by drinking a measure of a Potion of Skill, if one is available, or by the casting of a *Skill* or an *All Heal* spell. If such a spell is not available, it is possible that a sorcerer or healer in a nearby town or city will be able to cast one for a small fee of, say, 100 GPs per point of SKILL restored. The Director will be able to decide whether such an opportunity exists.

Stamina

This second characteristic will change constantly during an adventure, as monsters, exhaustion and various other penalties take their toll of a Hero. STAMINA may be restored quickly by consuming food and drink, expressed in game terms in the form of Provisions. Each batch of Provisions can restore 4 STAMINA points (up to the Hero's *Initial* level). A Hero may eat one batch per scene. Alternatively, a healing potion or a *Stamina* or an *All Heal* spell, if available, will quickly restore even more points.

Finally, STAMINA may also be recovered by resting between adventures and, if the Director expressly permits it, between scenes of an adventure where there is a lapse of time of three days or more. He will provide more information when this is an option.

Luck

A Hero's LUCK score is reduced by 1 point each and every time he *Tests for Luck*. A Hero could find things getting very fraught towards the end of an adventure with his LUCK running out very rapidly. The characteristic may be restored in a number of ways. A Potion of Luck, if discovered, will come in very useful, for it adds 1 permanent point to the Hero's *Initial* LUCK score, and then restores his current score to that level! Needless to say, Luck Potions are very rare and expensive items. LUCK may also be restored by employing a *Luck* or an *All Heal* spell, if one is available.

Additionally, in certain situations during an adventure when a Hero – or all the Heroes – have been especially fortunate, the Director may reward them with a bonus of up to 3 LUCK points. The Director will reveal such rewards as and when they are earned. *Remember:* LUCK cannot exceed its *Initial* level by this means.

Other Actions and Situations

As well as combat, a Hero will find himself in many other situations where he will have to apply his skills and cleverness if he is to avoid danger and win through to the end of his quest. This section covers each of these situations, based on the Special Skills typically needed to escape from them.

Carrying

Rather than enumerate specific weights in kilos throughout, we have found it easier to use four classes of weight: Light, Medium, Heavy and Very Heavy. To make matters even simpler, we suggest that you decide how much a strong Hero can carry by simply imagining how much a normal human can carry; if you then add to that all his weapons and armour, you should get an amount which isn't too unreasonable for your character.

As a simple rule of thumb, if one is really needed, each Hero can carry up to ten items. Light objects count as half-items, Heavy articles count as three items, Very Heavy objects count as between four and eight items, or even more (and may therefore have to be carried by more than one Hero). The amount being carried becomes important only if a Hero is carrying a Heavy or Very Heavy weight. Besides, only a character with *Strength* Special Skill (and perhaps making a roll against it, at the Director's discretion) could hope to push or carry most Very Heavy Items.

Light – a few coins, plate, ale-flagon, bow, dagger, cape, item of food, bird, domestic cat, etc.

Medium – a sword, bag of coins, small chest, saddle, shield, another creature (Dwarf- or Goblin-sized).

Heavy – a full treasure chest, sack of coins, table, bed, full suit of armour, another person of human size or greater.

Very Heavy – a stone idol, horse, stagecoach, small boat.

Climbing

Any Hero, whatever his strength and dexterity, is adequately equipped to clamber up a slope if there are sufficient handholds, or to climb up into a tree with low enough branches, provided he can make a SKILL or *Climb* Special Skill roll using the usual two dice.

The roll is made as follows: a Hero can typically ascend or descend one metre of sloping ground or a thickly branched tree every Combat Round. For every five metres covered, the Hero must make a SKILL or *Climb* roll; check the table, below, to see whether any modifiers apply. If the roll fails, the Hero simply stays where he is, unable to move on until another roll is made; if he rolls double 6, the Hero has fallen (look up the section on *Falling*, below, on page 187).

Our Hero can attempt to speed up his rate of travel by succeeding in making his SKILL roll with a −2 penalty for each extra metre of speed he seeks, alongside any other modifiers.

Scaling more difficult climbs – any slope of over 60 degrees, or of over 45 degrees without obvious handholds, or of a tree, like a pine, which has branches starting high above the ground – will require the application of one or more of these modifiers to the Hero's SKILL or *Climb* Skill. *Note:* the Director may impose more modifiers (plus or minus) according to the exact conditions of the location specified.

	Modifier
Vertical slope	−6
60°–85° slope	−4
45°–60° slope	−2
No handholds	−3
Unstable/slippery surface	−2
Overhang	−3
Smooth tree	−2
Few branches	−1
Using spikes/spiked boots	+2
Roped to another person	+2*
Under attack	−2
Carrying Heavy weight	−2†
Carrying Very Heavy weight	−4†

– This does not apply to climbing a tree. If the other person falls, the Hero must make a SKILL or Strength Skill roll to stay where he is, modified for handholds and/or spikes on the above table, or he too will fall – see Falling.

†– *See* Carrying, *above, for definitions of these terms.*

For example, a Hero with *Climb* 12 attempting to scale a pine tree in mid-winter, using spiked boots, while being shot at by pursuing Orc bowmen, modifies his dice-roll thus: −2 for the smooth tree, −2 for the icy tree trunk, −2 for being shot at, and +2 for his spikes. He must therefore roll 8 or less on two dice in order to climb up into the branches where he can remain hidden.

Detecting and Searching

The *Awareness* Special Skill is very useful, for it gives a Hero a sixth sense which can sometimes warn him of events before they happen. Because the Hero with this ability isn't usually aware that there is something around which *could* be detected or which is about to happen, a character's *Awareness* Skill is normally checked in secret by the Director.

Of course, a Hero can always specifically ask to check his senses at any time; but if there is nothing to be found, he plainly won't find anything, even if his *Awareness* roll appears to be successful. The Director will impose his own modifiers to the *Awareness* roll, according to how well an item or event is concealed.

Searching

In game terms, this refers to closely and deliberately scrutinizing an area in order to find a hidden item or person. This action could reveal secret passageways, traps, hidden panels in treasure chests, or whatever the Director has hidden. (This means that a secret doorway cannot be detected by someone with *Awareness* simply walking past where it is hidden!) *Note:* finding a secret doorway then poses the further problem of actually opening it – see *Doors and Locks*, below.

Deliberately searching requires a successful SKILL or *Awareness* roll (if searching in near-darkness, a *Dark Seeing* roll can be used instead). If the hidden object is a person using *Hide* Skill, the difference between the searcher's SKILL or *Awareness* and the target's *Hide* should be used as a modifier. Hence, for example, someone with a *Hide* of 9 imposes a 2-point penalty on a searcher using a SKILL of 7. The Director may add or remove similar modifiers to the roll if an item has been hidden by someone with a high *Hide* Skill.

Searching an area with sufficient care to find something takes one person one minute for an area measuring two metres by two metres. Finally, it cannot be stressed too highly that, just because a Hero doesn't find anything, this means that there is nothing to be found!

Dodging

The use of *Dodge* in combat has already been covered, on page 159. However, this skill can be used to duck out of the way of more than slashing blows and swooping arrows. Rock falls, suddenly sprung traps and other surprises can all be countered with a successful *Dodge* roll, as ever using two dice.

The following modifiers may need to be imposed, however, and the Director may have several more to add or subtract according to the specific situation. As usual, a roll of double-6 will mean something quite appalling has happened – quite possibly involving the flattening of one unfortunate Hero!

	Modifier
Dodging Large object	−1
Dodging Very Large object	−3
Unstable/slippery surface	−2
Carrying Heavy weight	−2
Carrying Very Heavy weight	−4

Doors and Locks

In the typical dungeon complex a great many doors will prove to be locked or barred, whether to keep ferocious monsters in or would-be treasure-stealers out. Other doors and locks will have peculiar ways of being opened, which may involve a secret catch, pulling a false candlestick, pressing the correct button, or whatever cryptic method its builder has devised to keep others out!

Listening

Listening may be done whenever a Hero requests that he do it, and not just at a door. If it is quiet enough to hear a distant noise, and if there is then anything to be heard, the Director will inform him of the details. If other Heroes are clattering about in their armour, fighting, arguing or generally making a racket, the listener is unlikely to be able to hear anything quieter than a shout or a roar.

Opening Doors

Unlocked doors can usually be opened by the simple method of turning the handle. Doors held shut by a *Lock* spell can usually be opened only by cancelling the spell with *Open* or *Counter-Spell*.

Locked doors can be opened if a Hero has the proper key or can pick the lock, or by being broken down. Usually, only one Hero at a time may charge a door, unless it is a very large door. The Hero must make a successful roll against his SKILL or *Strength* Special Skill. If the door is barred from behind, there is a −3 modifier; if the door is held shut with nails or spikes, there is a −6 modifier.

If the attempt fails, the door remains closed and the Hero must deduct 1 point from his STAMINA. Also, the next attempt must be made with a further modifier of −1. This modifier must be increased by 1 for every following attempt, so that on the fourth attempt there is a −3 modifier. Every attempt to batter down a door takes one Combat Round.

Thumping repeatedly against a stubborn locked door is a sure way of alerting every carnivorous denizen in the immediate vicinity that there are inquisitive adventurers in the area. Indeed, some may come to see what all the noise is about.

Locks
Locks turn up on a wide variety of objects other than doors, including treasure chests, cupboards, boxes and prisoners' shackles. Wherever the lock, it is probable that a very good reason exists for the lock being there – and that could mean a rich reward if it can be removed.

Magical locks will need to be countered by the casting of *Open* or *Counter-Spell*. Non-magical locks may be picked, using a successful *Lock Picking* roll, or wrenched off using *Strength*. The Director may impose modifiers for extremely difficult or weak locks. Heroes should note that some evil-minded Bad Guys take great pleasure in booby-trapping locks so that they fire poison darts or emit choking gas, and many other kinds of nasty devices abound.

If these Special Skills are unavailable, a pointed weapon such as a sword or dagger may be used to break or lever off a lock. A successful SKILL roll with a −2 modifier for a standard lock or a −4 modifier for a very tricky lock (determined by the Director) is required to do this. Using this method will slightly blunt the edge of the weapon used, reducing its effectiveness in combat by 1 SKILL point for every attempt made at breaking the lock. A weapon can be properly sharpened only between adventures.

Note: chests or boxes which have secret bases or compartments will need to be specifically searched by the Heroes to give up their secrets!

Drowning and Asphyxiation

The path of the adventurer is fraught with many dangers to be encountered and overcome on his way to the end of the quest. Among these hazards, there may be rivers to cross, clouds of poison gas and places with no air at all.

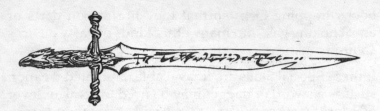

All situations in which a Hero is unable to take a breath are resolved in a similar way. For the first minute spent without air, whether under water or enveloped in gas, a Hero must roll his SKILL or less using two dice; for every extra minute, he must reduce this chance by 2 points. There may be other modifiers:

Under water	Modifier
Able to take a first breath	+1*
Has *Swim* Skill	+3
Under attack	−2
Carrying Heavy weight	−2
Carrying Very Heavy weight	−4
In full armour	−2
STAMINA 3 or less	−2

Gas, smoke, etc.	
Able to take a first breath	+1*
Under attack	−2
In full armour	−1
STAMINA 3 or less	−2

– Being able to draw a breath before being submerged depends on not being surprised by the sudden lack of air. A Hero already swimming will be able to take a gulp of air; a Hero suddenly submerged will be surprised and will not be able to take a breath on a roll of 1–3 on one die.

If a roll fails, the Hero will receive damage to his STAMINA from the hazard, according to its nature.

Water	1–6 points
Smoke	1 point
Dense smoke	1–3 points
Poison gas	2–7 points, plus any other optional effects designed by the Director, as appropriate.

Falling

Falling, obviously, is the opposite of climbing; unfortunately, some adventurers seem prone to doing rather a lot of it. Every Bad Guy since fantasy began has seen fit to fill his domain with spike-lined traps, stairs which turn into slopes, floors which give way, and countless devices designed to give amusement to him and pain to his victims.

Generally speaking, a human can fall two metres without any injury (unless falling on to something very sharp or pointed). Death is inevitable when falling from fifty metres or more – unless the Hero is very lucky indeed.

The extent of an injury is decided by the distance fallen and the LUCK of the Hero. When falling, the Hero must *Test for Luck*, his score being reduced by 1 point for every five metres of fall, but increased by 2 points if the Hero is able to slow his rate of descent significantly (by continually grabbing at bushes as he falls, for example). A character with *Jump* Skill will, on a successful Skill roll, reduce the amount of damage by 2 STAMINA points.

An Unlucky Hero must deduct 1 STAMINA point, plus or minus the following points:

	Loss of Stamina
For every 5 metres fallen	+1
On to sharpened spikes	+1–3
On to a soft surface	−2
Into deep water/snow/mud	−3*
In full armour	+1
Carrying Heavy weight	+1
Carrying Very Heavy weight	+3

* – *But see the* Drowning and Asphyxiation *rules above!*

Fire

Fire can be a deadly weapon in a confined space, and its use is still what sets man apart from the other creatures in many parts of the known and unknown world. In ancient Allansia, fire was seen as a blessing from the Fire God, Filash, and some out-of-the-way tribes still worship his fiery gifts. For the modern Hero, fire can be a very useful tool in discouraging unintelligent beings from approaching any closer – but it can also be dangerous.

Fire does damage according to how much of it there is and for how long a character is exposed to it:

Flame – A single flame (such as that of a candle or a torch, or in a lantern), will do 1 point of STAMINA damage per Combat Round. Extinguishing such a flame will require very little effort.

Small Fire – A fire of this size, such as a campfire, which gives out moderate heat, will deliver 1–3 points of damage per Combat Round. Extinguishing a small fire requires the equivalent of one or two buckets of water.

Large Fire – This blaze, equivalent perhaps to a large bonfire or a burning roof, will deliver 2–7 points of damage per Combat Round. Extinguishing such a fire will require the efforts of several people making a chain of bucket-carriers.

Intense Blaze – This inferno is far too strong to approach and is capable of melting lead. An intense blaze delivers 2–12 points of damage to one's STAMINA per Combat Round. Magical fire is typically as hot as this, though normally it is delivered in very short bursts (as in the spell, *Fire Bolt*). Creating a fire of this intensity by natural means typically requires a bellows-equipped hearth or a blacksmith's forge.

A typical blaze started on inflammable material will begin as a Flame for one Combat Round; then it will rise up as a Small fire (for three rounds); and then – if there is enough material around to fuel it – it will become a Large fire (for as long as it continues to be fed). Once everything inflammable has been burnt up, this sequence will be reversed as the fire slowly dies down and finally goes out. 'Inflammable material' unfortunately includes living things.

Note: a Large fire in a confined or unventilated place will fill the area with thick, choking smoke. Refer to the *Drowning and Asphyxiation* section on page 185 for more details concerning the sort of damage that smoke can do to a Hero.

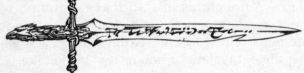

Flaming Arrows
These are made by wrapping cloth round the head of an arrow, dipping it in inflammable oil, and then setting it alight, immediately before dispatching it at an enemy. The cloth unbalances the arrow, imposing a -2 modifier to the chance of hitting the target. On hitting its target, a flaming arrow does normal arrow damage and it also starts the fire sequence described above, with the extra 1 point of damage for a 'Flame'.

Hiding

Hiding is a skill beloved of both thieves and other more cautious characters. Using it, a Hero can secrete himself away so that superior numbers go rushing past him; or he can use it in the course of spying, on enemy plans, for example. This skill can also be employed to hide a specific item so that it won't be found except after very diligent searching.

To hide himself, clearly a hero first needs somewhere to hide. Hiding in a totally empty room, or in the middle of a flat plain of short grass, is extremely difficult without a lot of preparation. The Director will rule on whether there is enough cover for the character to hide in. However, he will *not* reveal his decision – the Hero will discover soon enough whether he has been able to hide from his enemy!

When hiding from someone who is vaguely looking for him, therefore, a Hero's chance of success is rolled by the Director. The roll is made using *Hide* Skill, if available, or SKILL otherwise. If someone is actively searching for the Hero, modify the roll by the difference between the Hero's *Hide* Skill and the searcher's *Awareness* rating (see *Detecting and Searching*, above). There may also be other modifiers to the roll:

	Modifier
Hero/item invisible	+8
Hero/item very small	+5
Hero/item small	+2
Hero/item human-sized	—
Hero/item large	−2
Hero/item very large	−5
Hero/item camouflaged or hidden among similar items	+2
Item buried	+5
Hero in open country	−4
Hero in thick scrub/forest	+4
Hero moving	−2
Searchers looking from above	−3
Searchers using animals	−4

The Director makes the dice-roll in secret. If the roll is a clear failure, he should tell the Hero that he knows he isn't hidden. If the roll fails but comes close to the chance of success, the Director should let the Hero believe he has been successful – but of course anyone looking for him will find him. If the Hero's hiding roll is successful, he will discover the fact soon enough when the Bad Guys rush past.

Hiding an item works in exactly the same way; again it is rolled by the Director (though the results of failure will be less drastic). Heroes should be careful to remember just where they secrete items, especially those which are of value; we recommend the use of a treasure map for a really important cache of goodies!

Jumping

A successful *Jump* Skill or SKILL roll will allow any characters to leap twice their height horizontally, or up to their height vertically, provided they have a run-up. Jumping from a standing start will halve the distance covered. Carrying a heavy weight, or being in full plate armour, will also halve this distance; hence jumping from a standing start in full armour will quarter the distance jumped.

Jumping *down* comes under the category of 'controlled falling', and is therefore dealt with in the *Falling* section, above.

Languages

Most intelligent beings in Allansia are able to speak the native tongue, known as Allansian or Common Speech. Many can also read and write, though not with the same proficiency; this includes the Heroes. However, many other languages are employed by humans from distant regions and in all the various races.

194

Unlike most other skills, the study of languages is a very difficult and exclusive one; characters without the skill can attempt to translate something only with a 6-point penalty applied to their SKILL roll, unless they have had a *Languages* spell cast upon them. Characters with or without the *Languages* Skill must also apply the following modifiers to a roll on two dice for a successful translation:

	Spoken	Written
Other human	−1	−2
Dwarfish*	−1	−2
Dragon	−4	−5
Elemental	−4	−5
Elvish*	−1	−3
Giant	−3	n/a
Lizard Man	−2	−5
Orcish**	—	−4
Magical Script†	n/a	−5†
Ancient Allansian	−2	−4
Other ancient human	−4	−6

 * – *Penalty doesn't apply to Dwarfs and Elves respectively.*

 ** – *Orcish is the common language of all evil non-human races; though most races also have their own languages, usually further divided into obscure tribal dialects, one is unlikely to hear, say, Goblin or Trollish spoken outside the creatures' homes.*

 † – *Spell-casters have no penalty, but they still have to check with a dice-roll.*

 n/a – Not applicable: Magical Script is not spoken, Giant tongue is not written.

Light and Darkness

Deep under the ground there is very little light; unfortunately, deep under the ground is where many monsters and evil beings hide themselves away with their treasures. For most Heroes, venturing down into the darkness therefore requires some form of illumination. This typically comes from candles, burning torches, a lantern or *Dark Seeing*.

Candles

A candle will burn, in the game, for one (real) hour. It will illuminate an area one metre across with enough light to read or search by, but it can be seen from a much greater distance. For every three metres away from this central area, the chance of any skill which needs light being successful is reduced by 1 point.

If a candle is dropped, it will go out on a roll of 1–3 on one die. This roll should be repeated every round until it is picked up again or until it goes out.

Torches

Torches are simply bundles of sticks of wood, usually bound together and dipped into inflammable oil, which burn at one end. A torch will burn for thirty minutes. If held at shoulder height, a torch will light an area ten metres across with enough light to read or search by; if it lies on the floor, this distance will be reduced to an area three metres across. As with a candle, the chance of any skill which needs light being successful is reduced by 1 point for every three metres outside this area.

If a torch is dropped, it will go out on a roll of 6 on one die. This roll should be made every two rounds until the torch is extinguished or picked up again.

Lanterns

A lantern is basically a candle or an oil-powered wick set inside a small box, fitted with shutters to cut off the light and reflectors to boost it over a wide area. When the shutters are open, a lantern can light up an area four metres across, up to ten metres away (it doesn't illuminate the area immediately around its possessor), with enough light to read or search by. Outside this area, skills are reduced in the dimming light at the same rate as for a torch.

A lantern fitted with an ordinary candle will burn for thirty minutes. A lantern powered by oil will burn for one hour, and won't go out in anything under a raging hurricane. However, lanterns can be dangerous if dropped and broken. On a roll of 1–3, an oil-powered lantern will break, starting a Small fire (see *Fire*, above) that burns for three minutes.

Dark Seeing
This innate skill can be chosen only by a starting character. Since it is, in fact, a physical feature, it cannot be learnt by experience later. It operates in the same way as a cat's vision, needing some small glimmer of light to work, but then granting much clearer eyesight in such dim conditions than a human normally possesses. A *Dark Seeing* roll is usually needed only if a character is searching for something specific in the darkness.

Dark Seeing allows a character to see up to thirty metres, depending on just how dark it is. The Director will advise as to the exact distance that *Dark Seeing* is functioning at whenever he is asked in the adventure.

Magic

The use of magic has its advantages and disadvantages. The advantages – the effects that the spells deliver – are self-evident; the disadvantages become apparent on all those occasions when a *Magic* Skill roll fails and something completely untoward happens! Still, that's the price one pays for being able to do something miraculous every once in a while.

Provided only that he has enough STAMINA points to cover the cost, a spell-caster may cast a spell he already knows as many times as he likes. (Truly doomed Heroes may be allowed to cast a spell that will kill them, at the Director's discretion.)

As we have already stated, the chance of a spell working correctly is rolled against *Magic* Skill (characters without this skill may not cast a spell at all, so there is no SKILL check alternative to this procedure). There are, as one might expect, modifiers which should be applied:

	Modifier
Caster wearing full armour	−3
Stamina Cost of spell will reduce	
STAMINA to 2 or less	−2
Caster moving	−2
Caster drunk	−4
Caster restrained	−2
Caster under attack	−1
Caster actively in combat	−2
Caster otherwise disturbed	−1 or −2

If the dice-roll succeeds, the spell's listed effects occur. If the roll fails, the Director will decide what happens. Luckily, in some cases, the spell will simply fizzle out. In others, a missile spell (like *Fire Bolt*) may veer off course and zap the wrong person or *Sleep* may send its caster into a profound slumber! Depending on the urgency of the situation, the Director may allow a spell-caster to attempt a *Test for Luck* roll in order to stop a mis-cast spell affecting himself.

However – and this is where things start to get really tense – if a character rolls double-6 while casting a spell, he must then roll three dice and cross-reference the result to the appropriately nasty entry on the following Oops! Table:

Oops! Table

3   There's a flash, closely followed by an ominous croak – the caster has turned into a toad!

4   Twenty-five years of the caster's life drop away – now he may be a very small child.

5   A small shoal of herring materialize over the caster's head and for a five-metre area round him!

6   Suddenly the caster can communicate only in a totally weird and incomprehensible language that not even those with *Languages* Skill can understand!

7   The caster is suddenly inflicted with permanent hiccups (-4 to further spell-casting)!

8   The caster grows a not unattractive tail!

9   Every Gold Piece in the caster's possession turns into a butterfly – and flutters away!

10   A surprised-looked Orc (SKILL 7 STAMINA 8 Sword) has just materialized beside the caster!

11   The caster's hair turns bright blue!

12 The caster's footwear catches fire (Small fire)!

13 The caster suddenly grows a small pair of goat's horns on his forehead!

14 A dead Giant Squid materializes in the air directly over another member of the party.

15 The caster's hair starts to grow extra quickly and uncontrollably, and won't stop!

16 All the weapons of everyone in the room turn into flowers!

17 The caster changes sex, from male to female or vice versa!

18 The caster simply disappears in a puff of fragrant smoke, never to be seen again, leaving nothing but a pair of smoking boots!

Some of these curses may be lifted by a very powerful *Counter-Spell* or by the healing powers of a special character or item which the Heroes will have to seek out. (The Director is at liberty to replace any of the above entries with favourites of his own, if only to keep the players on their toes!)

Incidentally, learning further spells (if anyone dares to after that little lot!) is at the Director's discretion. He will inform the players if and when the opportunity exists.

Movement

The rate of a Hero's movement is usually important only in combat or when being chased by a ferocious opponent after an unresolved encounter! At other times, the Director most probably will cut quickly to the next scene and miss out all that tedious movement in between.

For combat we recommend the use of miniatures and a squared floorplan, with everyone moving one square per Combat Round, as is used in the guardroom scene in *Dungeoneer* Adventure I. If these are not available, assume that the Heroes move two metres per Combat Round on foot, or one metre if carrying a Heavy weight or worse.

Escaping

Escaping from a pursuer will involve either running as fast as possible, or getting far enough ahead and then hiding. Hiding is dealt with in the section of that name, above.

Escaping from pursuit requires a roll against the appropriate *Lore* Skill for the location (*Wood Lore* in a wood, etc.) or a *Test for Luck* if this Skill is not available. The following modifiers may also apply:

	Modifier*
Heroes on horseback	+4
Heroes flying	+7
Open terrain	−2
Carrying Heavy weight	−2
Carrying Very Heavy weight	−4
Wearing full armour	−2
Strength Skill	+2
Current STAMINA is within 3 of *Initial* score	+3

* – *Every modifier applies in reverse to the pursuers so that, if the pursuers are on horseback, there is a −4 modifier to the Heroes' chance of escaping.*

Swimming
Swimming requires a successful *Swim* or SKILL dice-roll every thirty metres. If the roll – adjusted by the modifiers below – fails, refer to the rules on *Drowning and Asphyxiation*, above. If the situation should arise, the modifiers for fighting in water are listed in the *Strange Locations* part of the Combat section on page 165.

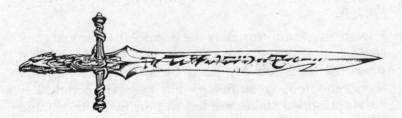

	Modifier
Calm water	+1
With the current	+1
Against the current	−2
Under attack	−2
Fully clothed	−1
Wearing armour	−2
Carrying Heavy weight	−2
Carrying Very Heavy weight	−4

Riding

Riding a horse doesn't usually require a *Ride* Skill or SKILL roll, provided the mount doesn't travel faster than a trot. If a horse moves up into a canter or a gallop, the rider must make such a roll successfully (− 1 modifier for a galloping horse), or fall from the horse and take 1–3 points of damage to his STAMINA.

A horse is capable of jumping obstacles up to two and a half metres high and five metres across. However, the horse's rider must successfully make a *Ride* Skill or SKILL roll with a −2 modifier, to stay in the saddle when the horse lands.

Poison

Poison may unfortunately be found in many places: contact poison is smeared on locks and handles; poisoned darts are triggered by an unwary hand or foot; venomous creatures are left to guard certain key areas; poisoned stakes are left in horrific pit-traps, and so on.

Damage from poison is usually delivered in addition to normal damage, from a bite, a pit-spike or whatever. The Director will inform the players as to the exact nature of the damage; this could range from as little as 1 or 2 points of damage to STAMINA, to complete paralysis and painful death within 1–6 minutes. Some situations may warrant a *Test for Luck* or a *Strength* Skill dice-roll to avoid the effects of the poison; others may be so toxic that no save is allowed. Once again, the Director will reveal just what happens in a particular situation, according to his adventure description.

Reactions and Persuasion

Each creature encountered by the Heroes will respond to them in a certain way. Most of these reactions will have been decided upon beforehand by the Director when he designed the adventure being played, and will be fundamental to the plot. The Director will reveal exactly how a being reacts, depending on what the Heroes do.

However, there may occasionally be encounters which could go either way, depending upon the reactions of the players. After all, not every monster need be hacked to death – many are quite willing to be bribed or can be talked into letting the Heroes past.

In the monster statistics given in the background section later in this book and, more importantly, in *Out of the Pit*, the Fighting Fantasy monster collection, each creature has a *Reaction* and an *Intelligence* score. The former appears as Friendly, Neutral, Unfriendly or Hostile, while the latter breaks down into None, Low, Average and High. These terms are self-explanatory.

Plainly, a creature's exact response to an encounter with the Heroes will depend upon these two ratings. Hostile beings are quite likely to attack immediately, whatever their intelligence, unless completely outnumbered. However, more friendly and intelligent beings may be bribable, while others can be conned into allowing the Heroes to do as they desire.

Distracting

Any animate creature of Low intelligence may be distracted by the Heroes. For example, tossing a huge, juicy steak at a watch-dog may well keep it happy for the several minutes a sneak thief needs to break into a house.

In such situations, a simple *Test for Luck* – modified by the Director according to the susceptibility of the creature to what is offered – is all that is required; or the Director may prefer to assess the chances of success as 1 in 3 or 1 in 6 or whatever, and roll dice accordingly.

Bribery and Conning

More intelligent creatures will need more substantial persuasion before they allow the Heroes to go past or take their precious golden idol, or whatever. The first thing that must be decided is how reasonable the request is (either Reasonable, Acceptable, Unreasonable or Impossible), bearing in mind the attitude of the creature being asked.

An example of a *Reasonable* request might be: asking a band of Dwarfs guarding a passageway for access to the tunnels beyond it. An *Acceptable* request might be: asking an Elven tribe for permission to make camp for the night in their area of the forest. An *Unreasonable* request would be: asking a band of Orcs guarding a corridor to allow the party safe passage to the tunnels beyond. An *Impossible* request might be: asking a band of Orcs to give the Heroes their fabulous gold-and-diamond-decorated idol of Halack, Father of Orcs!

There are two ways of persuading someone or something to cooperate with the Heroes. They can be *Bribed*: with money, goods, services, promises or whatever else the Heroes have to offer; or they may simply be talked into it, that is, *Conned*.

Either way, the procedure is for the Hero who is doing most of the talking to roll against one of the following: *Con* Special Skill, SKILL, or a *Test for Luck*.

Offering someone a bribe may tip the balance in the Heroes' favour. However, bribing someone can often be a risky business: one never knows quite what they will accept and what they will find insulting. In this game, it's the Director who has to decide in secret just what a creature's limit is. Offering a derisory bribe could be worse than not offering any!

Finally, the Director secretly rolls for the result of the Hero's approach, and then acts out the creature's apparent reaction accordingly. The creature may let the party pass; it may give them some vague clue in answer to their query; or it may suddenly turn around and attack them ferociously!

Why roll in secret? For the good reason that the players shouldn't be made aware of the bribe modifier of the creatures, and because more intelligent and cunning beings may only be pretending to be nice to the Heroes, before running them through when a better opportunity presents itself!

	Modifier
Bribe offered	$+1/-3^*$
Amount far too low	-4
Amount too low	-2
Amount high	$+2$
Amount excessively high	$+4$
Unsuitable bribe	-3
More than one person to be bribed	-1 per person
Heroes outnumber being(s)	$+2†$
Heroes outnumbered	$-2†$
Friendly being	$+2$
Neutral being	-1
Unfriendly being	-3
Hostile being	-5
Reasonable request	$+3$
Unreasonable request	-3
Impossible request	-6

* – *Some morally upstanding characters will be deeply offended at being offered a bribe; if so, use the -3 modifier.*

† – *'Outnumbered' in this case means there are at least twice as many on one side as on the other.*

Sleight of Hand

Whenever a Hero wishes to use his increased manual dexterity for some nefarious deed – whether it be picking someone's pocket, switching a fabulous diamond for a piece of glass, palming a joker at cards or snaffling a choice item from a sleeping Dragon's treasure hoard – the *Sleight of Hand* Skill will prove useful. If this is not available, an ordinary roll against the Hero's SKILL score will have to do.

If the victim, or someone watching, has *Awareness* Skill, a further modifier has to be applied: the difference between the Hero's *Sleight of Hand* Skill and the other's *Awareness*. Hence, if the Hero has *Sleight* 8 but the victim has *Awareness* 14, the Hero must suffer a penalty of 6 to his roll. Other modifiers are as follows:

	Modifier
Darkness	+3
Twilight	+1
Item is very small	+2
Item is medium-sized	−2
Item is large	−4
Item in plain view	−3
Item liable to make a noise	−3
Victim is unintelligent	+2
For every two extra people in the vicinity	−1

If the roll fails, it is likely that some form of outcry will ensue. The Director, playing the parts of the Extras involved, will decide the exact form this will take!

Sneaking

Being able to creep about without being noticed can sometimes prove an invaluable gift. The chance of moving silently or in an otherwise unnoticed fashion is represented by the *Sneak* Skill. A Hero should roll this score or less, or his SKILL or less, or *Test for Luck* successfully, in order to sneak about somewhere and not get caught.

If a character with *Awareness* Skill is on guard in the vicinity, the difference between that skill and the Hero's *Sneak* should be used as a positive or negative modifier. If the character with *Awareness* is not actively expecting someone or something, the modifier is reduced to −1. There may be other modifiers:

	Modifier
Hero invisible	+8
Hero very small	+5
Hero small	+2
Hero large	−2
Hero very large	−5
In full armour	−2
Carrying Heavy weight	−2
Carrying Very Heavy weight	−4
Open area	−2
Night	+4
Twilight	+2

Traps

Traps are the ultimate proof of the sheer deviousness of many Bad Guys. Some traps the Heroes encounter will be nothing more than simple stake-lined pits; others will be fiendishly complicated mechanisms designed to frustrate, torture and eventually dispatch their hapless victims.

Traps designed by the Director for a specific location in an adventure will have their own rules. Such traps will also be given their own Lethality score, ranging from 0 to 5.

As a rule, only a successful *Test for Luck* or *Dodge* Skill roll, modified by the degree of Lethality of the trap, will allow a Hero to avoid a trap he doesn't know is there. A trap may be detected by a Hero with *Awareness* if a successful roll is made (see *Detecting and Searching*, above).

Once a trap has been found, there is a chance that a Hero with *Trap Knowledge* will be able to deactivate the device. This requires a successful roll against *Trap Knowledge*, minus the Lethality of the trap. Characters without such a Special Skill must roll against their SKILL, deducting 2 points and the trap's Lethality rating. If the roll fails, the trap will be sprung.

At higher *Trap Knowledge* levels, a Hero may be able to design and build his own traps, but that will happen only in very advanced games.

Hunting Traps
Traps that are set by the Heroes and designed to catch an animal for food work in a different way. The chance of success of any trap catching something edible is equal to the character's *Lore* Skill for that area (whether it be in a wood, at sea, underground, in the mountains, or wherever). A character setting a trap in an area in which he has no special knowledge should roll against his SKILL score, with a −2 penalty.

The Director will impose further modifiers, where appropriate, according to the availability of food animals in the area trapped, the climate, time of year, and so on. The trap may be reset and tried again every four hours.

Playing Well

Our final concern in this section is to provide those players who feel they need them with a few pointers concerning the best ways to play.

Competition versus Cooperation

As a player, the first and most important object is to have plenty of fun. However, the second is to ensure that everyone else enjoys himself or herself too! For this reason, we cannot stress too highly the value of cooperation. Some players may feel that it is great fun to be one of those nasty characters who spends all his time stabbing the other members of the party while they sleep and running off with their treasure. This may well be great fun for him, but is a lousy way for the other players to spend an afternoon.

Far better, we believe, is for everyone to join together and share the adventure. Everyone should be caught up in the collective spirit of adventure and the unknown. After all, six people's imaginations are far better than one – and six Heroes can venture where one would fear to tread!

In *Dungeoneer*, as in all role-playing games, the object is for the Heroes to win by successfully completing the quest, defeating the Bad Guys and generally succeeding at their chosen task. It is not a question of fighting against and defeating the Director himself, but the situation he has created and is presenting. However, so far as the *players* are concerned, well, if everyone has had fun playing – regardless of how successful their Heroes have been – then *everyone* has won!

Life, Death and Heroism

Danger is one of the main facts of a Hero's life. That's what makes many games so thrilling to play! Even though the risk is imaginary, there's every likelihood that you will take pleasure in your Hero's successes and be saddened when the character finally dies. No matter what happens, though, it's all imaginary, it's only a game.

Our advice, then, is to play your Hero as you would want him to live, with courage and heroism. Don't hold back on being heroic just because there's possibly danger or some threat to the character. Treat him like a Hero and he'll turn into one on the tabletop in front of you!

TEN WAYS TO BETTER PLAY

(1) Know what your skills and spells do . . .

(2) . . . and use them – there's more to being a Hero than swinging a sword!

(3) Try to think like your character, make him come to life.

(4) Trust the Director.

(5) Don't ever trust a smiling Orc!

(6) Cooperation is the best way to succeed.

(7) Be careful when you make that Magic roll!

(8) Act like a Hero, brave and courageous!

(9) Even Heroes negotiate or run away sometimes!

(10) Have fun!

Director's Shooting Notes

In a few pages' time we shall present the second of our tabletop fantasy adventure movies, *Dungeoneer* Adventure II – 'Revenge of the Sorcerer'. It's a direct sequel to *Dungeoneer* Adventure I, but it contains some notable differences. In the first adventure we introduced what few rules were used as and when they were needed. In this new episode, though, we have simply presented the situation and the statistics for the Extras; after all, we've just spent the last hundred pages or so going through the complete rules to the game, so we're not going to tell you them all over again!

The other major difference to be found in this second adventure lies in its length and complexity. Quite plainly, *Dungeoneer* Adventure I was designed to be as simple and as straightforward as possible, its purpose being simply to introduce players to the concept of role-playing, while at the same time giving them some fun. Now that everyone knows a little more about what they are supposed to be doing, we can concentrate on making this new adventure more realistic and intricate.

As Director, you will have more to do in *Dungeoneer* Adventure II, from keeping track of everyone to perhaps inventing a few encounters to fill in an unexpected gap in the game. Don't worry, we know you can do it! Before you start, though, you may care to read through the next few pages, in which we'll explain a little more clearly what you should be doing.

Incidentally, we haven't yet mentioned one important tool of your noble profession – the screen. You will need a place where you can roll your dice and read from the adventure description and where your players cannot see what you are doing. If they can see everything you are up to, they will be able to cheat. To that end, we recommend you sit at one end of the table, with the players at the other end, a few feet away from you, and if possible keep all your bits and pieces hidden behind a screen. This divider could be made from a sheet of card folded to stand up, a couple of large books standing open, or anything else that comes to hand. Secret die-rolls and Director's-eyes-only notes must be protected from prying eyes!

The Director's Role

Your role falls into two distinct parts: before the adventure, and during the adventure.

216

Before a game, the Director must prepare his adventure. If you're using a prepared script, such as *Dungeoneer* Adventure II which follows, all you need to do is read through the full text while visualizing what happens, assemble any props you may be using, and invite everyone round for some heroic tabletop derring-do!

If a pre-written adventure isn't available, you'll have to write your own. At the close of *Dungeoneer* Adventure II there are half a dozen suggestions for further sequels, which you may care to assemble and expand into *Dungeoneer* Adventure III. Alternatively, there are more suggestions for aventure plots in the section on *Designing Adventures*, after the adventure, on page 359. This section also provides some handy hints on how to design your own plots and expand them into full epic adventures, complete with Extras and monsters.

During the game itself, it is the Director's job to inform the players about everything that is going on around their Heroes. To this end, three distinct questions must be borne in mind at all times.

What's Where?
The Director is, quite simply, the eyes and ears of the players – and, on occasions, their other three senses too. You must describe, in as much detail as the players require, the fantasy world through which their Heroes are adventuring. You present the players with the range of choices from which their Heroes have to choose the one which they believe will lead them to the end of their mission or quest. Of course, only some of this information will be important, while much of it will be merely scene-setting, designed to add to the spooky atmosphere of the location.

Whatever you are revealing, try to be as descriptive as possible. Remember that the Heroes can see colours, can smell peculiar scents, can feel if a room has a draught, can hear peculiar echoes away in the distance, and so on. The more relevant information the players have, the more their imaginations will be able to convince them that they are really there! On the other hand, of course, don't go on so long that your players never get to do anything – this is an interactive game, not a monologue!

On occasions, the players will ask for further information about some trivial topic, for which you are not prepared. To keep the game flowing, you will have to invent the relevant details. This is perfectly acceptable; after all, if you could predict perfectly everything the players were going to do in a game, you'd be a world-famous psychic, not a fantasy adventure Director! When improvising information, try not to stress the important clues at the expense of the trivial details. You're there to present the adventure as it happens, not to guide the Heroes safely through it without a scratch.

Who's There?

Sooner or later, the Heroes will run into other beings. They may be fanatically hostile enemies, more friendly creatures, or sometimes even other adventurers! You get to play each and every one!

Playing an Extra or a Bad Guy is quite demanding, for you have got to think your way into his, her or its personality, without drawing on your own knowledge as a Director. For example, if you (the Director) know that the Heroes are waiting to ambush a pair of Orc guard Extras, you will still have to send the Orcs round the corner into the trap.

As you become more experienced at being a Director, you will find your Extras starting to develop their own personalities. You will start using a special voice and certain catch-phrases for playing, say, an Orc or a Goblin or an evil sorcerer. Keep this up! Furthermore, don't be afraid of looking silly when you act out their speeches. After all, you're playing a game among friends, so it'll be fun!

What Happens?

The players will decide for themselves what they want their Heroes to do – or, at least, attempt to do! Your job is to determine, using the rules and your knowledge of the situation, whether they are successful. If there isn't a rule for the specific action being attempted, base the roll on SKILL or LUCK, or choose odds along the lines of 1 in 6, 3 in 6 or whatever.

Secret dice-rolls are also your responsibility. A Hero with *Awareness*, for example, cannot be informed that there may just be something around which he should try to detect. Instead, you must make the roll for him and inform him only if there really is something there and you have determined that he really has detected it. We recommend that you roll a pair of dice behind your screen every few minutes or so, whether there is anything to be detected or not, so that your players won't get suspicious when they hear that familiar clacking sound at some crucial moment. Plainly, in order to make a secret roll for a Hero, you will need to know what numbers you are rolling against; make a note of everyone's relevant characteristics and skills on a piece of scrap paper before play starts and update them when they change.

There will be occasions when players completely miss a wonderful set-piece encounter you have spent ages working on, or hack their way through it and leave it looking like a butcher's shop. When this happens, grit your teeth and move on. It's not your job to dictate what the players do or do not do. And remember, when set-pieces and climaxes do actually come together properly as you envisaged them, they can prove to be so thrilling that they effectively wipe away the memory of the occasional messed-up scene!

It's your responsibility to keep the game moving along. If the players are taking too long to finish something, cut the scene there and then and move on to the next location. Also, keep everyone involved – don't address all your remarks to one player, even if he thinks he is the leader of the party. Not everyone wants to leap about and yell all the time, but try to ensure that no one feels left out.

When talking about what happens, try to use what we call 'dramatic speech' rather than 'game speech'. This means, quite simply, don't refer to game rules and terms unless you have to; speak as a normal person would speak at the time, and you won't ruin the atmosphere.

For example, notice the difference between 'An Ogre leaps out at you, SKILL 9 STAMINA 19, carrying a sword . . . rolls a 4, giving him Attack Strength 13, roll your dice . . .' on the one hand, and the following: 'A brutish mud-coloured humanoid, fang-toothed and wild-eyed, leaps out at you from the shadows; he looks mean and fit as he swings his sword above his head to strike at you. His blow falls confidently, a 13 . . . what's your response?' The difference is plain. Try to use dramatic speech as much as you can, and encourage the players to use it as well.

If you're a really dedicated Director, ask everyone what they thought of the game when the adventure is over. Try to include more of the things they really enjoyed, and cut down on the bits they felt were boring. That way, your game will be even more enjoyable, and the players will keep coming back for more!

Other Concerns

Using the rules of the game together with the guidelines in the above notes, you should be able to handle anything that the Heroes do. Players, of course, are a law unto themselves. If you have a really dreadful player, or a really rude and disruptive one, grit your teeth and finish the adventure with good grace – but don't invite them back again. Part of the entertainment of a role-playing game lies in discovering what your friends are really like under pressure (no matter how imaginary).

Missing Players

If you all gather together to play the second part of an adventure, only to discover that one of the Heroes' players is unavailable, you have the choice of two courses of action. You can remove the Hero from the adventure, and make believe that he was never there. Alternatively, you can take over his role for this adventure only, and play him for the missing player. When playing a missing player's Hero, keep him in the background as much as possible, and do try not to kill him!

Heroes from Other Games

If more than one of you in the group is a Director who runs games of *Dungeoneer*, there is a strong possibility that regular players will want to use their favourite Heroes from other games in yours, too.

Before simply allowing Heroes to transfer over and start adventuring, have a look at their *Adventure Sheets*. Some Directors seem to run their games rather like Father Christmas, giving out magic swords and awesomely powerful potions as if they were Provisions. Take a look at the Hero's characteristics; if he's claiming to have SKILL 12, STAMINA 24 and LUCK 12, you shouldn't allow such a gross character into your game. A Hero like this can seriously unbalance your game! If in doubt, make a player roll up a new character under your supervision, and play that one instead.

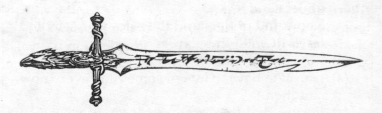

Heroes from Fighting Fantasy Books

Many people will start playing *Dungeoneer* having already played a selection of Fighting Fantasy solo gamebooks. Some of these people, as well as having immaculate taste, may want to continue in your game playing a Hero whom they first rolled up for a book. This is usually acceptable, provided the Hero isn't equipped with superhuman characteristics (the fabled 12/24/12 formation mentioned earlier) and isn't weighed down with 10,000 Gold Pieces and a +3 sword the size of a tree. Such characters are guaranteed to unbalance a game – unless every other Hero is similarly equipped and the adventures are especially designed for such awesome powers!

If the Hero *is* acceptable, simply treat the character as though he has rolled up his characteristics but not yet chosen his skills. Proceed by choosing Special Skills appropriate to the Hero, add a name if necessary, and start playing! Talking of which, it's time for the next adventure . . .

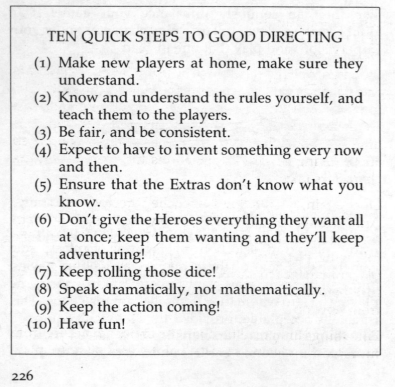

TEN QUICK STEPS TO GOOD DIRECTING

(1) Make new players at home, make sure they understand.
(2) Know and understand the rules yourself, and teach them to the players.
(3) Be fair, and be consistent.
(4) Expect to have to invent something every now and then.
(5) Ensure that the Extras don't know what you know.
(6) Don't give the Heroes everything they want all at once; keep them wanting and they'll keep adventuring!
(7) Keep rolling those dice!
(8) Speak dramatically, not mathematically.
(9) Keep the action coming!
(10) Have fun!

DUNGEONEER ADVENTURE II:

'Revenge of the Sorcerer'

Introduction

This second *Dungeoneer* adventure movie is set in (and underneath!) the city-states of Salamonis and Port Blacksand, and features the search for – and eventual dispatch of – the wizard Xortan Throg. It is much longer than *Dungeoneer* Adventure I 'Tower of the Sorcerer', although not all the scenes will be used. Some are optional and depend upon which route the Heroes choose to take to reach their ultimate goal. The adventure should last about twice as long as the first one did – though this time we hope that you won't be quite so concerned about giving lengthy explanations for every action the characters take.

Once again, what follows is for the Director's eyes only. Although we're quite happy for anyone to read and learn the game rules and hints given on the preceding and the following pages, it will only spoil everyone's fun if a player manages to sneak a look at the plot of this adventure before play begins. So, Mr Director, it's all yours from now on.

First things first: read through the entire adventure from here to the closing credits before you start to play.

Although you could just about get away with playing this by reading it scene by scene (as you may have done with *Dungeoneer* Adventure I), there are several more subtle sections which will work better if you know what is due to happen.

Also, unlike the first adventure, we won't be detailing all the new rules as we go along. After your experiences with that first story, and now having read the rules, you should be in a position to run the game without too much trouble. Don't worry about remembering every rule; just flick back to the appropriate section earlier and read what it says, as and when you need to. If you can't find one particular modifier, make up one of your own that sounds right; keep play moving.

When running this adventure it would be useful, though not totally essential, if you had access to a copy of *Titan* and *City of Thieves*. We mentioned *Titan* earlier in this book; it's the complete guide to the world of Fighting Fantasy. It contains information about the cities of Salamonis, Carsepolis and Port Blacksand (including a

highly detailed map of the latter, which we've repro-
duced in a much smaller version for this adventure), and
about the good wizard Nicodemus who also features in
this adventure. *City of Thieves* is a Fighting Fantasy solo
gamebook set in Port Blacksand, and it also features
Nicodemus; you may well have played it yourself. The
information in these books will enable you to expand this
adventure and increase the enjoyment you and the
players get out of playing it.

Don't worry if your players have already read *Titan* or
City of Thieves, or both. None of the information in the
books is secret and most of the Heroes are sufficiently
well travelled to have picked up any information they
can actually remember during their adventures. Having
this knowledge may well increase their enjoyment of the
story. The only problem you may encounter is that only
one of the Heroes can be the man who killed the Night
Prince, Zanbar Bone, in the City of Thieves. There will be
some hints on using a character from *City of Thieves* as a
Hero in a moment.

This adventure continues straight on from the events in
the one that ended on page 103; in movie terms, of
course, it's the inevitable sequel. Unlike most sequels,
though, this adventure is longer and much more interesting than the original!

It may well be that some of your players' Heroes died in *Dungeoneer* Adventure I; or perhaps you have some new or different friends who wish to play. If any of the prepared Heroes are still unused, players can choose to play them. Alternatively, the players could create their own Heroes using the rules given earlier in this book. They may even want to play specific characters, such as King Salamon's champion or Princess Sarissa. This is acceptable; but if a well-known character is being used, the player should be very careful to role-play him or her properly and stay in character. Players who did use a pre-rolled Hero in the first adventure are also at liberty to create and use a new character.

Using Previous Heroes

Any prepared Heroes used in *Dungeoneer* Adventure I will have recovered from all their wounds, and their LUCK will have been replenished too (this doesn't always happen – but for this adventure the Heroes will need every point they can lay their hands on). If they have any money, or the gems they may have found, they can buy some new equipment if they so desire. Salamonis is a large, well-connected city and just about everything they could think of will be available, at a price.

Using New Heroes

During the adventure, there are two moments when new Heroes can be introduced without disrupting the flow of the story. They may well be at the court of King Salamon in scene 1, and get signed up for the great adventure to help the other Heroes. Alternatively, they may meet the others at the Dragon's Tooth Inn in Port Blacksand (scene 3) and decide to tag along too. In that case, clearly they will have to come up with a convincing reason for wanting to join in, and impress the Heroes that they are of good character and can be trusted. Still, it's all role-playing and will be fun!

Using a Hero from City of Thieves

Tell the players before they sort out their characters that the adventure will involve a trip to Port Blacksand; if several of the players have played through and solved *City of Thieves*, ask one of them if he or she would like to play the Hero who starred in that adventure. If more than one begs for the role, they will have to toss a coin, roll dice or fight it out using their fists or wooden swords to decide who has the honour (we recommend that the first method be used). Treat the character just like any other new adventurer, created according to the rules given earlier; however, part of his background will obviously include a visit to Blacksand and the defeat of Zanbar Bone.

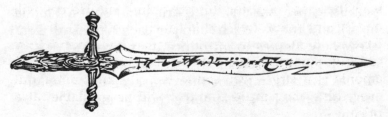

Remind the player of this Hero that his character has a white unicorn and a yellow sun tattooed on his forehead, and ask him whether he killed Sourbelly, the brutal Troll guard, during the course of his adventuring. *Don't* tell him that if he did kill Sourbelly he will be wanted for murder in Blacksand. Furthermore, the tattoo will make him easily recognizable – but leave him to find that out to his cost later. On the other hand, though, that Hero will already be an acquaintance of Nicodemus and will know his way round parts of the city. He can also tend to boast about his previous exploits there to his colleagues, and generally lord it over them.

Starting Play
Make sure everyone has the usual accessories (dice, pencils, paper, erasers, food, drink and optional minia-tures), and knows which character each is playing. Don't allow new Heroes to introduce themselves to one an-other in too much detail; this should be done when the Heroes actually meet in the course of the adventure itself, either at King Salamon's court or in the Dragon's Tooth Inn.

Sit yourself at the head of the table again, with this book kept away from the players' view and with some sort of screen hiding your secret dice-rolls. Make sure you've got all your own equipment ready too, including any Props you intend using in the course of the game, if any. We've gone to town with the Props for this adventure, but of course you don't have to use any of our suggestions (some of which, we must admit, are less than serious).

This adventure may well last over two playing sessions, depending on how much time you have to play in. If time is pressing and you find that you must break the adventure in the middle, we recommend that you take your interval after scene 8 – Captured! Of course, when you start play next time, you should give everyone a quick sequence of flashbacks to remind them where they are and what they are doing (you may even care to re-enact key moments with the players!).

And now, if you're ready for sound, cameras rolling, ready your boom, stand by studio, clack that clapperboard, and let's shoot it! Action!

Scene 1 – At the Court of King Salamon

Location

The adventure opens in a splendid hall in the royal palace at Salamonis. As befits the court of the most powerful king in this part of Allansia, it is decked out with beautiful and expensive hangings from all corners of Titan. There are no chairs except those for King Salamon and his family – everyone else must stand. As almost everyone should know, Salamonis is a very prosperous city-state of great antiquity, situated on the banks of the Whitewater River in the Vale of Willow. It is ruled over by the learned King Salamon the Fifty-Seventh, father to Princess Sarissa (from *Dungeoneer* Adventure I).

The Heroes have recently arrived in the city, fresh from their rescue of the princess from Xortan Throg's tower. News of their exploits has spread like wildfire. The court is full to overflowing with knights, noblemen and clergy all eager to hear the tale. These folk are all dressed in their best finery, making the Heroes – tired from the trail but doing their best to stand up straight in the presence of their betters – look poor, bedraggled and insignificant.

As we join the scene, Princess Sarissa herself has taken charge again and has already told most of the story, including her kidnap by Xortan Throg, the treachery of Prince Barinjhar, and her heroic rescue. The Heroes themselves will have been permitted to say a few words about how they fought their way through the wizard's castle, though they will have been quickly interrupted if they tried to glorify their role or were in any way overdramatic in its telling. (This city is an ancient seat of learning, and pompous boasting is looked down upon.)

Finally the princess tells how everyone discovered that Xortan Throg was not dead after all, and how he swore vengeance on the Heroes and on the city of Salamonis. At this alarming news, a frightened hush falls over the assembled courtiers and all eyes turn to look at the king, sitting upon his throne at the top end of the immense chamber, in order to hear what he has to say on this grave and worrying matter.

Plot Summary

King Salamon gives his learned judgement and asks the Heroes to kill Xortan Throg. He suggests that they seek aid from Nicodemus in corrupt Port Blacksand, and promises to reward them handsomely if they succeed. Keep your fingers crossed that the Heroes will agree – otherwise you have no adventure.

Cast List

King Salamon LVII is getting on in years (Sarissa is by no means the oldest of his many children) but he still strikes a finely regal figure. After all, he can afford to eat well and he has the attentions of the best healers in the country. The king is noted for his wisdom and fairness of judgement and does his best to appear considerate and kindly, no matter how aggravating the person he is faced with. He finds that this is a very effective way of keeping his subjects in order, since everyone not directly involved in a particular judgement usually tends to agree with his verdict. The greater his reputation for wisdom has grown over the years, the more people have come to agree with him for fear of seeming stupid!

Princess Sarissa is having the time of her life, since she has been firmly in the centre of attention ever since she got back. Being a royal princess (and thus immune to any hints of contradiction), she has been allowed to exaggerate her own part in the rescue somewhat. Her dishevelled attire caused her father to raise an eyebrow when he first saw it, but, after all these years bringing up precocious daughters, he has grown used to such things and has resolved merely to admonish her quietly later.

Prince Salamon is the king's eldest son, and thus heir to the throne. He has yet to learn the wisdom and evenhandedness of his father; if any of the Heroes says anything slightly disrespectful, rude or inappropriate, he will impatiently snap out a comment along the lines of, 'Father! Surely you are not going to allow this uncouth lout to get away with such insolence?'

Faced with such an outburst, King Salamon will reply soothingly along the lines of, 'I grant that our guests may be a little lacking in manners, but this is the way of adventurers such as these. All beings have their uses, and a wise king learns to make use of all objects, no matter how rough their edges. No one would criticize a horse for not being able to hold a sword or discourse on the manifold mysteries of Lord Logaan; it is a similar case here too.'

A murmur of approval always passes round the court when the king makes these wise pronouncements – though, if truth were told, a goodly number of the courtiers and royal knights haven't the foggiest idea what the old man is talking about. Still, so long as it sounds wise, they will automatically nod their heads and murmur their approval.

Archbishop Kalivan is the senior clergyman in all Salamonis. He was enthroned archbishop not because of his wisdom, power or ability but because he was such a kindly old fellow that no one could find a word to say against him. Needless to say, he is not much use as a royal adviser, except perhaps as a counterweight to some of the more bloodthirsty nobles. However, his goodness has been observed by the gods and sometimes he achieves quite remarkable miracles, especially in healing and curing diseases. He should be portrayed as a kindly but somewhat bumbling old man, with a smile so sweet and uncomplicated it could probably transform a ravening werewolf into a household pet.

A large supporting cast of courtiers is required, but they say little and do even less. They should murmur with approval whenever King Salamon says something which seems to be wise, gasp with horror at the mention of villainous acts or the threat of evil sorcery, and splutter with outrage if any of the Heroes says something out of place. Like most people who have achieved their position by virtue of someone else's qualities, they are terrible snobs who sway in the slightest breeze.

Props

If you fancy using some props, you will require some gold coins (but plastic ones will do if you can't get real gold) and some pieces of paper which have been drafted as Merchant Passes to the city of Port Blacksand (one per Hero). Also of use will be some small bottles containing liquid to act as healing potions. The liquid should preferably be green and pleasant-tasting if you can manage it; try a mix of water, sugar and edible food dye for that special effect. Don't, whatever you do, use something with a nasty taste, like washing-up liquid (or worse), if your players are actually going to drink the potions.

Action!

Many of the *Action!* segments described here take place only if the Heroes say or do particular things. Read through all of them before you start playing so that you know which one to go to when the Heroes respond to what they're told; but start with this one first:

1. The Judgement of Salamon

This is quite a long section, but it's essential so that the plot can be advanced. As usual, you can read the sections printed in *italic text like this* straight out to your players; everything else will have to be interpreted and revealed as the Heroes discover it. King Salamon talks in a gentle, measured tone which makes him sound intelligent and fully in control. As you read it, you may care to replace the gasps of the courtiers with real gasps for extra realism and atmosphere.

Having heard Princess Sarissa tell of Xortan Throg's survival and threats of revenge, King Salamon rises to his feet. The court falls silent in anticipation of yet more golden words from their sovereign.

'My beloved son and daughter, my lords, ladies, bishops and knights of Salamonis, Heroic adventurers, this is truly a most splendid tale we have heard, full of perfidious villainy and epic heroism. It is so full of excitements as to be worthy of the stage of our city's own theatrical arena. If it were just a story, we could rejoice that good has triumphed in the end!'

There are murmurs of approval from the court.

'But, alas, it is no mere tale, to frighten us during a few hours of light entertainment. The villainy we have heard described is all too real and threatens us still!' (Gasps of horror echo round the hall.) 'We must be on our guard until the evil of Xortan Throg is banished for ever from the land of Allansia!

'In the case of the people of Chalice, and of King Pindar in particular, I feel that it would be impossible to prove any evil intent on their part, were anyone compelled to attempt so to do. Besides which, as my daughter relates, the wickedness was Prince Barinjhar's alone. Since he is now dead, and given that the loss of their king's only child is a sore burden for any city to bear, I resolve to bear no further grudge against King Pindar or the people of Chalice.'

Murmurs of approval echo round the court once again, although the Heroes might not look so well pleased. If it appears that anyone is about to protest, Salamon will raise his hand to forestall him, before continuing with his speech.

'However, there is the important matter of the reward promised to these gallant adventurers. They have rescued my daughter as they agreed to do, and clearly they should receive just payment.'

There will probably be murmurs of approval from the Heroes at this point.

'As it is unlikely that they will be welcome in poor Chalice in the near future, however, and as a sign of immense gratitude for the safe return of my beloved daughter, I will pay the reward myself.'

At this point the king pauses so that this generosity can be noted, and then adds, to general laughter from the courtiers, 'And send the bill to King Pindar in due course! Chancellor, you will arrange for each of these gentlemen to be paid five hundred Gold Pieces before they leave the city.

'I must now turn to the grave matter of the sorcerer, Xortan Throg.' (More gasps from the court, who know an evil sorcerer's name when they hear one.) 'I, and my learned advisers, are totally mystified as to the nature of the grudge this creature bears against our fair city, for it is the first we have heard of the fellow. Of the threat he poses, however, there is no doubt!' (More gasps.) 'Fortunately, we have in our midst some of the bravest and most able Heroes in all Allansia, men – and women – for whom killing a wizard is a welcome relaxation after the hard work of Dragon slaying!' At this point, many of the knights at court begin shuffling their feet and trying to look inconspicuous.

'I refer, of course, to the brave heroes who so recently rescued my daughter from that self-same wizard. Who better to turn to, in order to aid us in our hour of need? Should they succeed in this quest, I will match King Pindar's reward with money from my own coffers!'

At this point, Prince Salamon leaps dramatically to his feet.

'Father! You don't seriously intend to waste yet more money on these boorish oafs? Why, all they did was kill a few Goblins and a magical simulacrum – and that only with my sister's help.'

'My boy,' replies the king, 'one day you will learn, a willing servant is always better than an unwilling one. These brave people are already the sworn enemies of Xortan Throg, and will doubtless set off to confront and kill him, no matter what we do. Since they are doing us a favour as well, it is only right that we reward them. If the worst happens and they fail, they will have no need of gold – and, of course, if any of the bold knights of my court can bring me the head of Xortan Throg before these fellows do, then I shall have no hesitation in giving the reward to him instead.'

The king pauses, and a heavy silence falls upon the court.

'I thought not!' he continues, with a stern look on his face. 'Now, as I said earlier, we have no idea who this wizard is or where he may be found. However, there is one man in Allansia whose knowledge seems almost unbounded, especially on magical subjects. I refer, of course, to my childhood tutor, the great sage Nicodemus. It is therefore my suggestion – and I think you will find I possess a talent for prejudging matters such as these – that you seek his aid in tracking down your elusive quarry.

'For reasons best known to himself – and surely none here are wise enough to fathom their subtle intricacies – Nicodemus has made his home in that odious hotbed of villainy called Port

Blacksand.' (*A whole host of gasps runs round the court, perhaps echoed by those of any Hero who has been to Blacksand!*) '*It is well known that the wicked Lord Azzur places strict controls on all who enter his foul city and, being no lover of Salamonis, he may well seek to foil your mission.*

'*In view of this, and knowing also that you will unhesitatingly accept this prestigious mission on my behalf, I have provided suitable disguises and paperwork to carry, to get you safely within the town gates. However, from that point on, I fear, you will be on your own. Are there any questions?*'

The Heroes may well have a few things to say for themselves during this speech. Remember, while all this is going on, that the court does not take kindly to the king being interrupted, let alone questioned. You should take note of what the Heroes say and decide whether they have behaved properly or not. In some cases their personalities may cause them to be a little rude (especially someone unused to civilized finery, like Grimbold Tornhelm or Axel Wolfric). This is acting in character and should be encouraged; but equally there are penalties for upsetting such a powerful king. If the other Heroes don't take immediate steps to shut their impolite colleagues up, King Salamon will be a lot less helpful than he could be.

2. Questions

If the Heroes do have questions to ask, you will have to think of appropriate replies for Salamon to give. Here are some suggestions for replies to the most likely queries:

Magical Assistance: If the Heroes ask for any magical assistance, the king will reply: 'Nicodemus is the greatest sage in the land, far greater than any here present in Salamonis. That is why I have suggested that you seek him out.'

Money/Promises of Marriage!: If the Heroes ask for more money than has already been offered (albeit vaguely), or for Princess Sarissa's hand in marriage, there will be general outrage, in the latter case not least from the princess herself. The king will remain calm, but will inform the Heroes thus: 'I have already given you my terms for this quest. I suggest you set about your preparations before I change my mind.'

Look in the Great Library: If there is a devoted sorcerer or other spell-caster among the party (such as Baradas Rangor), he or she may ask to be allowed to consult the famous Great Library of Salamonis. The king will say, 'If it is information about the quest you seek, my advisers have already been hard at work in the library ever since your arrival in our great city, but have found nothing of use to you. If mere scholarship is your purpose, there are many excellent schools in the city which will doubtless be more than happy to admit you as a pupil, once you have completed your quest. Learning is to be admired, but there is a time and a place for everything!'

Vases from Carsepolis: It may dawn on very smart players to ask about the ancient vases that they found in Xortan Throg's chambers. The king is well acquainted with such antiquities: 'Ah yes, from the description my daughter gave us, they seem to be relics of ancient Carsepolis, a seat of great learning and civilization on the coast. Wizards are known to have strange fancies, and a collector's love of old-fashioned pottery may be one of Xortan Throg's foibles. Carsepolis was destroyed three hundred years ago and no one, not even a wizard, has ever been known to live that long.'

Entering Blacksand: The Heroes may ask for more information about their disguises or for help in finding Nicodemus once they get to Azzur's perilous city. Salamon tells them that they will be provided with a wagon full of rich goods, which they are to take into Port Blacksand and sell to a certain man whose name will be revealed to them later. That man is in fact a spy in the pay of King Salamon, and he will advise them from there.

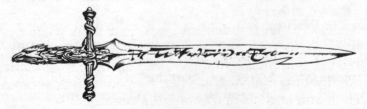

3. A Miraculous Removal

Finally, the Hero who killed Zanbar Bone in *City of Thieves* may think to ask for assistance with the concealing of his tattoo, especially if he is wanted for the murder of Sourbelly. (Let the character inquire about this without being prompted; after all, it will be entertaining – for you – later if the tattoo is still there!) King Salamon looks concerned, and then replies: 'I am sure that somewhere among our clergy you could find someone skilled in the removal of such marks. Archbishop?'

Kalivan shuffles his feet and murmurs respectfully, 'Well, your majesty, it isn't really the sort of thing we have much knowledge of. Not much call for it, er, you see.'

The king flashes him an exasperated look which seems to say 'Stop babbling, you old fool, and do something.' Had he been thinking out loud, he might also have added, 'It doesn't matter if it doesn't work; just show willing and then, if nothing happens, blame the gods!' Perhaps recognizing the slight impatience his liege is exhibiting, Archbishop Kalivan advances upon the appropriate Hero and lays his hands on his forehead.

'Oh mighty and lovely Asrel,' intones the Archbishop in a quavering voice. 'You who are the fount of all that is beautiful in this world! Have pity on this poor mortal. Though he is a reaver who wades through blood in search of gold, yet his cause is that of Good, his quest noble, and our need of him great. Lovely Asrel, we beg of you, remove this blemish from his face.'

The Archbishop lifts his hands . . . and the Hero's forehead is clear: there is not even a wrinkle on it. An astonished whispering breaks out among the courtiers: 'A miracle, a miracle, surely the gods are on our side. It is the will of Asrel! Xortan Throg will be destroyed!' Meanwhile several of the older ladies of the court can be observed sidling up to the Archbishop and whispering in a pleading fashion to him.

If this little scene does take place, the order of the court will be somewhat disrupted. The king walks down to the Heroes and says, 'I think this would be an appropriate moment at which to take your leave. Come now!' The Heroes should follow him out; but they may still ask him questions as they go. If the miracle does not occur, however, after the Heroes have asked all their questions, the king will instruct his chamberlain to have the Heroes taken away and suitably equipped for their quest.

Inform the Hero who was the beneficiary of the miracle that he has had a great honour bestowed upon him. Divine intervention is rare on Titan these days (except, as everyone knows, on the first day of Sowing, when the trickster Lord Logaan wanders the world playing tricks upon his creations to celebrate his birthday). The Hero should be made to feel that the Goddess Asrel is looking after him in particular; he may even consider doing something for Her in return; and this should be encouraged.

Turn To . . .

If the Heroes haven't yet been told how they are getting into Port Blacksand, tell them now about the wagon load of goods. In any case, you should tell them that the man they are to meet is called Halim Thrumbar (they should make a note of this in case they forget) and that he can be found in the Dragon's Tooth Inn. They should enter Blacksand by the main gate and walk due north to the market square. The Dragon's Tooth Inn is in the northeast corner of the square, at the corner of River Street.

Any weapons and armour that the Heroes require (other than magical ones) will be given to them, as will sufficient food to get them to Port Blacksand and the reward money for rescuing Princess Sarissa. They will also be given 300 Gold Pieces between them, as a sign of good faith that Salamon trusts them (they'll need no reminder of how they failed to get an advance from Chalice!)

If the Heroes have behaved well at court (and not interrupted or upset anyone), each of them is given a bottle of clear green liquid (or whatever colour your liquid is, if you are using Props). This, they are told, has been drawn from the sacred Healing Well of the White Goddess in Salamonis. Explain to the Heroes that drinking from a bottle will cure all their wounds, but that there is only enough for one draught in each bottle, so they should choose carefully when to use it. (For your part, you should note that if a character drinks the contents of a vial it will restore his STAMINA to its *Initial* level. Wounds received *after* the vial has been drunk will affect the Hero in the normal way.)

The Heroes then set off for Port Blacksand, disguised as merchants. The journey is uneventful, except that if you have a new player who wishes to take the role of Princess Sarissa, the Heroes will discover the girl hidden in the wagon during the journey. Since she will have had to run away from home to join them, the other Heroes may not be too excited upon discovering her. However, since their quest is urgent and Halim Thrumbar is expecting them, they haven't time to turn back now. They must press on . . . to Blacksand!

Scene 2 – The Gates of Port Blacksand

Location

From a distance, Port Blacksand looks much like any other coastal city. Behind high city walls, a jumbled collection of roofs and towers can be seen littering the skyline. In the bay, a collection of fine ships are riding at anchor, though the far-sighted may be disturbed to note that most of them are war-galleons flying the deadly Jolly Roger. The only strange object in sight is the occasional ruined building, well outside the walls. These ruins seem to be of considerable age.

As the Heroes approach the city, however, the true nature of the evil place, and the reason for its reputation, becomes apparent. To start with, there is the smell. In most cities there is a certain degree of stink because of the lazy housewives' habit of throwing their rubbish into the gutter in the middle of the street rather than carrying it to the sewers or the river. But in Blacksand the stench of ordinary, domestic rubbish seems almost swamped by a pungent and not at all pleasant aroma compounded of stale beer and rotting flesh. Even a Dwarf would turn his nose up at this stench – and that is saying something.

Small wonder about the smell of rotting flesh, incidentally, because lining the road to the city are many repulsive examples of Lord Azzur's famed and feared tyranny. Corpses hang from trees, severed heads impaled on poles line the way and, most disturbing of all, starving men crouch, suspended in small iron cages by the roadside, with dire warnings posted as to what will happen to anyone who dares to feed these convicted thieves and murderers.

Approaching the gate, the Heroes are hailed by eyeless and limbless beggars ejected from the city for thieving; desperate to get back inside and resume their trade, they plead with the Heroes for aid. Unfortunately for them, few can drag themselves far enough away to be out of the gaze of the tall, black-armoured guards who stand at the gate.

Accompanying their wagon laden down with fine cloth and other goods, the Heroes walk slowly towards the gate, Merchant Passes at the ready.

Plot Summary

The Heroes have some difficulty with the guards on the gate.

Cast List

Two Troll guards, Blackboil and Crackjaw, are on duty at the gate. Most Trolls are a pretty sour bunch, being descended from the same stock as Orcs and Ogres. Those depraved enough to work for Lord Azzur are doubly so, and greedy into the bargain. Naturally, their hatred for Dwarfs knows no bounds and, like all petty officials, they delight in throwing their weight around. There could be problems here. They wear black uniforms, marked with the insignia of Lord Azzur, and carry large, curved swords at their belts.

The *Captain of the City Guard* may also be needed in case of emergency. We shouldn't have to tell you how nasty and despicable a fellow he must be. He is human, and carries a large, black-barbed bull-whip with which to keep his slovenly inhuman troops in order.

BLACKBOIL   SKILL 9   STAMINA 9
2 Attacks Sword

CRACKJAW   SKILL 10   STAMINA 9
2 Attacks Sword

Props

Something pointed to prod the Heroes with; don't use anything too sharp – or you may have to postpone the game and go searching for bandages when they 'prod' you back! A blunt pencil should be sufficient.

Action!

It would be better for the Heroes to slip into Port Black-sand unnoticed; as far as you are concerned, however, it will be far more entertaining if there is a little action at the gate. To provide this, you need to engineer a quarrel between the Troll guards and the Heroes. Fortunately, Trolls are a pretty quarrelsome bunch and Heroes tend to be a little overbearing. We don't think you will find this confrontation very difficult to set up, especially if there is a Dwarf in the party, but here are a few ideas anyway.

If one of the Heroes still has a tattoo on his forehead, an immediate fight will result (especially if he was the one who killed Sourbelly). 'It's him!' the Trolls cry the moment they see the mark. 'The scum with the tattoo! Get him! Cut him down! Out of my way, fool! I saw him first!' They will fall over one another to get at the fiend who killed their old pal Sourbelly the last time he was here.

If one of the Heroes is a Dwarf, the Trolls will pick on him mercilessly. 'Never met a Dwarf cloth-merchant before, have you, Blackboil? Looks a limp kind of creature to me. Got a nice pair of scissors instead of an axe, have you, Dwarf?' Prod the person playing the Dwarf with your finger or something slightly more pointed. Press your face up close to his and sneer nastily at him through your teeth (imagine you are over two metres tall and have terribly bad breath when you do this). The Dwarf's player should soon get the idea of what is required of his character!

You may well be able to think up other excuses to start a ruckus, based on the particular Heroes you have, especially if they are given to what the Trolls will un-doubtedly call 'clever remarks'. If all else fails, simply have the Trolls invent a special new tax, for today only, of 50 Gold Pieces per wagon, or tell the Heroes that their Merchant Passes are invalid, or forgeries! Again, prod the Heroes with something and try hard to be really unpleasant to them. Make them really hate these Trolls.

The Heroes have several means by which they can avoid a fight. (Yes, we are trying to provoke them into one, but it would still be better for *them* to avoid getting injured. This is all part of the fun. Yes, wicked, we agree, but who says the Director can't have a little fun sometimes?) The Heroes could attempt to bribe the guards (50 GPs is an acceptable amount, because they look far too rich to offer anything less).

Alternatively a Hero could use his *Con* Special Skill with appropriate modifiers (saying something like, 'This is a special consignment for Lord Azzur, it's more than your hides are worth to delay us! You know that!'). Or they can use magic and simply zap the big lumps. If a fight does ensue, no one in Blacksand will take the blindest bit of notice, except perhaps the odd brave beggar or vagabond, who will tentatively cheer the Heroes and then dash off into a side-alley before the guards can recognize him and clap him in irons.

Problems?

We think it's rather unlikely that the Heroes will be unable to beat the Trolls. If they do seem to be in difficulty, have the Captain of the Guard come round on inspection. He will be furious with the Trolls for trying to kill merchants, and will immediately try to break up the fight, saying:

'What on Titan do you dummies think you are doing? How often do I have to tell you, Lord Azzur thinks highly of merchants? These fellows pay a lot of money in taxes over the years, far more than you scum will earn in a lifetime. If you want to kill somebody, go and find a few penniless adventurers to beat up. Jump to it, or you'll be feeding the plants in his Lordship's garden – the carnivorous ones!'

For a small consideration of just 200 Gold Pieces he will allow the Heroes into the city – and give the two now subservient Trolls a good whipping into the bargain.

Turn To . . .

The Heroes and their wagon enter Port Blacksand. Following their instructions (we sincerely hope!), they walk a short distance northwards until they reach the crowded market square. Pushing their way past the crowded stalls, buskers, stocks and pick-pockets, they park their wagon in the yard of the Dragon's Tooth (tipping the inn's stableboy 5 Gold Pieces to make sure it remains safe) and enter the building. Move straight on to Scene 3 – The Dragon's Tooth.

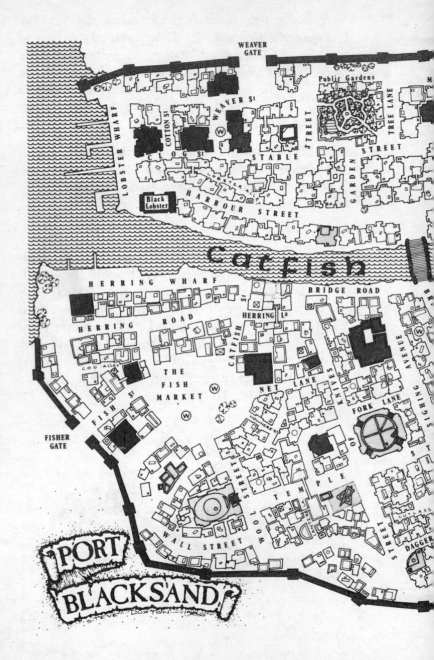

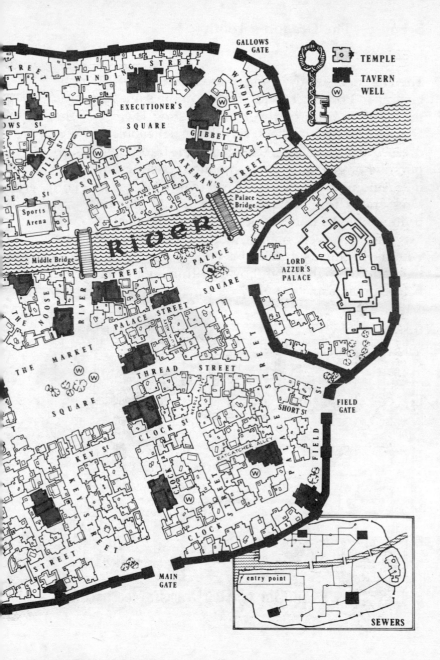

GALLOWS
GATE

TEMPLE
TAVERN
WELL

STREET
WINDING STREET
EXECUTIONER'S
SQUARE
WINDING St
GIBBET La
SQUARE
AXEMAN'S STREET
HILL St
OWS St
CUT-THROAT AV
Palace
Bridge
Sports
Arena
RIVER
PALACE
Middle Bridge
PALACE SQUARE
LORD
AZZUR'S
PALACE
THE NOOSE
RIVER STREET
PALACE STREET
CUTLASS St
PALACE STREET
THE MARKET
SQUARE
THREAD STREET
NEEDLE ALLEY
SHORT St
FIELD
GATE
CLOCK St
RATCATCHER ALLEY
PALACE STREET
FIELD St
KEY St
CLOCK St
KEY STREET
CLOCK STREET
MAIN
GATE
STREET
CLOCK STREET

entry point

SEWERS

Scene 3 – The Dragon's Tooth

Location

The Dragon's Tooth is one of the slightly less infamous taverns in Port Blacksand; it is not in the same league as the Black Lobster or the Hog and Frog. Even so, the Heroes will find it filled with the usual rabble of over-dressed scurvy knaves, engaged in the traditional tavern pursuits of guzzling ale, gambling, boasting and arguing. Among the clientele we can make out several Half-Orcs and a few Goblins lurking in the shadows and trying not to be noticed. Some of the humans look even less pleasant: every man jack of them is the sort of chap who'd pick his teeth with his cutlass, bite his own toe-nails and whip the cabin-boy to within an inch of his life before breakfast.

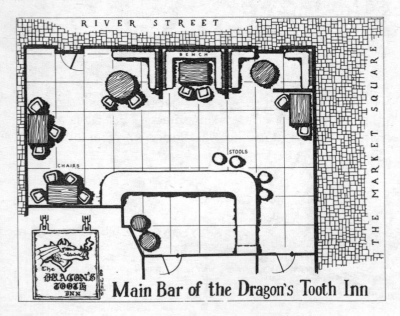

Main Bar of the Dragon's Tooth Inn

We've provided a plan of the main bar in case a fight breaks out (you may be surprised to learn that we don't mind either way this time; it'll be down to the players if one does occur here). There are plenty of chairs and tables to be thrown around, if necessary; if they run out, there are always the beer mugs or, at a push, the Goblins themselves to be hurled about.

Plot Summary

The Heroes meet up with their contact, Halim Thrumbar, and find out what to do next. New Heroes may be introduced to the party. The Heroes may very well indulge in the traditional pub games of gambling and brawling!

Cast List

Halim Thrumbar appears to be a typically overweight merchant, but there is a surprising amount of muscle beneath the fat. He is tough and fit – you have to be, to work as a spy in Port Blacksand. It may well be that he works for other people besides King Salamon – certainly he has a very wide range of contacts – but he is a good man at heart, and can be relied upon and trusted by the Heroes.

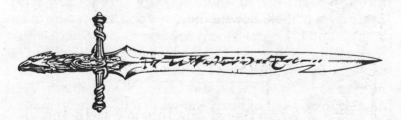

Of course, *they* don't know this; to them, he almost certainly looks like an overweight, greasy-haired, pompous slob with a terribly extravagant taste in fine clothes and scent. When Thrumbar speaks to the Heroes, lean close to them and talk in a low, earnest voice as if trying to avoid being overheard. While you talk, look around nervously every so often and give the general impression of being very afraid that everyone is going to be unmasked as a spy.

Gregor, the landlord of the Dragon's Tooth Inn, is a large, jolly chap, as befits an innkeeper. A former sailor, his body is covered in all sorts of exotic tattoos, and he is happy to entertain newcomers with long tales of his voyages to distant parts of Titan, including the Old World and distant Khul. The locals, who have heard these tales a great many times before, could tell you that the details change so often they are sure Gregor has made most of them up; but they are good tales, so no one really minds. Gregor's conversation is peppered with telling phrases like 'as happened to me one day in Khul', or, 'a little something that I picked up in Analand . . .' If he ever says 'By the way, did I ever tell you about . . .' anyone in any sort of hurry knows that it is time to make excuses and run for the door.

The Locals don't need to be described individually. They are all yobbish ruffians of one sort or another, and most of them would murder their own grandmothers for the price of a flagon of Catfish ale – if Granny didn't get them first, of course.

LOCALS   each SKILL 6   STAMINA 8
Sword or improvised weapon

Props

A pair of dice – preferably the weighted ones that you use for cheating in Fighting Fantasy battles. (Only joking!) Some money to gamble with. Toy money will do, as long as there is enough for everyone who wants to gamble, to have a stake.

If you're really into using props, why not provide some drinks to serve to the Heroes? We recommend that you don't serve Port Blacksand ale – anyone who's not used to it will be ill for a week.

Action!

The exact order of these Action segments will depend on just what the Heroes do. Apply them as necessary, or, in the event of something unexpected happening, improvise around the information we've provided.

1. Halim Thrumbar

If the Heroes go up to the bar and ask for Thrumbar, Gregor will point him out to them with a grunt. Otherwise, once they have sat around for a while, the merchant (and spy) will come and sit at their table and attempt to make conversation:

'I guess you fellows must be travelling merchants, for you look well enough and I've not seen you around here before. I'm in the business myself; perhaps we can be of use to each other.'

He won't reveal his name for a short while, as he's very careful just who he does business with, of whatever sort. Have fun watching the Heroes trying to get around to asking him if he's their man, before revealing his name as he introduces himself.

Halim will take charge of the Heroes' wagon, making it appear, if anyone is watching the little group, that he has bought the goods from the Heroes. He will also tell them how to find Nicodemus (assuming they need to know – the Hero who's been here before in *City of Thieves* should be able to find the wizard himself). His directions run as follows:

'The old fellow likes to keep himself to himself these days, I hear. Got fed up with people knocking on his door every two minutes to pay tuppence to have a wart removed, I expect. Leave here, go back into Market Square and leave by Bridge Street, the one that

leads out of the north-west corner. That will take you to the Singing Bridge. You can't miss it, it's the one with the skulls. Nicodemus lives in a hut under the bridge, on this side of the river. I must warn you to take care to be on your best behaviour, though. He's a bit testy these days and doesn't take kindly to visitors dropping in on him unannounced.'

The Heroes may wish to converse with Halim about Blacksand. He gives it to them straight:

'My advice, gentlemen, is to spend as little time here as possible. It's a foul place. Practically everyone you meet is out to cheat you somehow. Just do what you need to do and then get out.'

If asked about Xortan Throg, Halim (truthfully) says that he has never heard of the fellow, and inquires why they are asking. It's up to the Heroes whether they tell him the truth or not – if they tell him anything at all. Halim is honest, and is one of the few Blacksanders who doesn't fit into his own damning description of the place.

2. New Faces

If you still have some new Heroes to introduce to the group, this is the ideal time to do it. Just who they are is up to the combined creative powers of you and the players. Perhaps they are old adventuring comrades of the Heroes, warriors who have retired to Blacksand for a rest from the heroic life. Are they perhaps just passing through, having stepped off a boat on their way to somewhere else? Alternatively, they could just be locals, who get into conversation with the Heroes and seem to get on well with them, and who are prepared (if trusted) to help out.

3. Gambling Fever

If the characters Grimbold Tornhelm or Gordo Brond-wyn (or any other disreputable sneak thief or Dwarf) are with the party, there is a good chance that they will want to join in one of the games of dice. The other Heroes will probably be keen to get on their way; but gambling can get a hold on a man, especially when you are proud of your skill at cheating. At the first sign that one of the Heroes is interested, a group of three locals, all disreputable-looking types, invite the Heroes to join in their game.

The dice game is very simple. Each character decides how much money he is going to wager on the throw. Then each throws two dice – and the highest score wins all the money. Simplicity itself! If two or more players get the same high score, they share the winnings between them. If the money cannot be divided equally, the remainder is left in the pot for the next throw.

One point you perhaps should note: *everyone cheats*. To simulate this (if you don't have any crooked dice and can't fix rolls yourself), when making a cheating roll use four dice and count the best two. Each round of throws, the Heroes may try to spot the locals cheating. To do this, a Hero must make a successful *Awareness* roll.

If they wish to cheat themselves, the Heroes must make a successful *Sleight of Hand* roll, or may *Test their Luck* (with the usual deduction of 1 point from their LUCK per attempt). If a Hero spots a local cheating, he may decide to accuse him. This will start a fight, no two ways about it. Equally, if a Hero fails in an attempt to cheat, the locals may accuse him. This can happen at your discretion; we suggest that you let the Heroes get away with it once or twice before spoiling their fun! Besides, since the locals know this will start a fight, they only bother to accuse him if the cheating Hero would have won the throw; otherwise they pretend not to have noticed.

4. Bar-room Brawling!
Once a fight starts, the entire population of the inn joins in. Since the Heroes will have armour and good weapons, they will be much better off than the locals, so give each of them two locals to fight at the same time. If you have miniatures available, you can set up the fight and use the tables, chairs and mugs of ale as weapons as well. Remember that the tables need a *Strength* Skill roll to lift before they can be thrown.

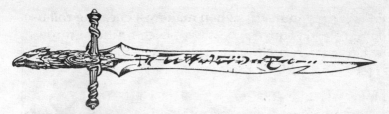

When everything has quietened down, the wreckage produced by the fight will look fairly serious. Gregor will pretend to be very angry with the Heroes (if they are still here) and demand payment for the damage. If they offer to pay without specifying an amount, he asks for 50 Gold Pieces; but if there is any problem over payment, Halim Thrumbar will intervene, saying that the Heroes are friends of his and promising to settle matters with the landlord. He then bundles the Heroes out through the door and tells them to get on with what they came for and not to waste any more time.

Problems?

If the Heroes are starting to get into trouble during the fight, have Gregor shout 'The Watch is coming!' at which point the pub will empty with amazing speed. The Heroes should take the hint and make their escape as well. If they are slow in leaving, have Halim Thrumbar drag them out.

Turn To . . .

It takes only a few minutes to walk round Market Square and along to the Singing Bridge where Nicodemus lives. If the Heroes decide to dawdle, use one of the brief time-wasting encounters detailed in Scene 5; otherwise, move straight on to Nicodemus and Scene 4.

Scene 4 – Under the Singing Bridge

Location

The Singing Bridge is one of the most stomach-turning sights in all Port Blacksand – and that is saying something. Its rickety wooden timbers, withered with age and heavily patched, seem to be on the point of giving way, to plunge the unwary traveller into the stinking waters of the Catfish river. From the water comes the putrid stench of the city's decomposing rubbish as it gurgles its slow way out into the bay, where diseased seagulls pick at 'choice' morsels.

Lining the walkway of the bridge stands an avenue of bleached skulls on long poles. Few of them are human; many more have hideous fangs and fierce horns. And, most horrible of all, the wind passing through the crumbling structure and its macabre ornaments makes a ghastly keening, whistling noise that, were it not quickly drowned out by the bustle of the city as you leave the bridge, would surely drive all sane folk from Blacksand within a day.

At the southern (nearest) end of the bridge, a set of rickety wooden steps leads down to a small hut built into the very foundations under the bridge. As the Heroes climb down, they are sure to notice the words 'KEEP OUT' scrawled in large red letters in several languages on the door. Nevertheless, they should knock and, after a short while and several muffled shouts of 'All right, all right, I'm coming!', the door opens, to reveal an old, white-bearded man and a surprisingly neat wizard's study.

Plot Summary

The Heroes meet Nicodemus and learn further information concerning Xortan Throg, Carsepolis and other subjects.

Cast List

Nicodemus is one of the greatest wizards in all Allansia, though you would never think it to look at him. (Some of his exploits are chronicled in *Titan*, if you need to know more.) He is a kindly old fellow at heart, but has grown sick and tired of being constantly pestered by people seeking to take advantage of him at all hours of the day.

As a result, he has taken to living where none but the most desperate or needy would seek him out. He has no patience with idle requests (people really wanting their warts cured or swords enchanted), but he will take an important request very seriously indeed. Play him as a slightly doddery old fellow who gets a little confused at times and has a habit of getting sidetracked in the middle of long explanations and forgetting what he was talking about. Beneath it all lurks a sharp mind, if only he could concentrate it on the matter at hand.

Props

You will be playing Nicodemus in this one scene, so get yourself a tall, pointy hat and a long white beard (a cone of rolled-up newspaper coloured black and some cotton wool will do). You may also care to have a few wizardly props scattered about, such as a wand, a shrunken head and a jar of live toads, but Nicodemus doesn't really need them.

Action!

Once again, this section is divided into segments which should cover the various options open to the Heroes.

1. Getting In

If the Hero who visited Blacksand in *City of Thieves* is with the party, getting in will be no problem. Nicodemus (you) will say:

'My dear young man! How good it is to see your face again. Welcome! Welcome! I know that you succeeded on your quest, for much evil went out of the magical ether with the destruction of that infernal Zanbar Bone. I'm awfully sorry about the mix-up with the powder, but I knew the gods would guide you in sorting it out. It always comes out in the wash, I always say. Come in, come in! How do you happen to be here again? More trouble, I'll warrant you. Tell me all about it . . . and who are these fine friends of yours?'

However, if Nicodemus does not know any of the Heroes, they will have a little more trouble:

'Who do you think you are, bothering a poor old man like this? As if I hadn't enough to do, keeping this foul river from seeping up through my floorboards, without having visitors as well. Still, you don't smell quite as bad as the river water, so plainly you can't be locals. State your business and be quick about it! If you've no good reason for disturbing me, so help me I'll turn the lot of you into sticklebacks and chuck you, lock, stock and barrel, into the river! I've always wanted to know how long a living creature can survive in that filthy water! Well, speak up!'

Fortunately, they only have to mention that they are on an urgent mission from King Salamon and they will be ushered in with great haste; the door will be shut and the latch pushed down. Even though the Heroes hadn't noticed any chairs besides Nicodemus's, there will now be enough for each of them to sit down.

2. Explaining the Quest

It's over to the Heroes for them to explain to Nicodemus what they are trying to do, and then to request whatever help they may desire. Some of the replies that he will possibly give are listed below. You may not need to use all of them, depending on what the Heroes say and ask for.

3. About Xortan Throg

'Well, I know of him, certainly. You can't be that good a wizard without coming to the attention of your fellow mages. It's the genies, you see, they really are the most terrible gossips, a real bunch of old fish-wives at times. And if you've never heard fish-wives gossip, then take yourselves down to the docks here one morning. I swear you'll not believe it until you've heard it with your own ears.

'Now, where was I? Oh yes, Xortan Throg. He seemed an innocuous enough fellow, at least until this affair with the princess. Kept himself to himself. But that's the trouble with wizards, you see. Some of the matters they dabble in can take years to sort out, so there they are, quiet as temple mice, then suddenly they find what they were looking for and they cause the most awful trouble for everyone! Shocking, I know, but that's wizards for you. My advice to anyone who asks is: always steer clear of them. They're an odd lot.'

4. Where's Throg?

'Ah, now that I can help you with. You see, he lives here. No not here – in the city, Blacksand! Well, not exactly in Blacksand itself, I suppose. More underneath it, to be totally accurate. As I understand it, he has a passion for old Carsepolis and he's been delving into its ruins. Of course he has to live in the sewers for that. Must be the only person in Allansia to have a more unpleasant home than I do! Still, serves him right. He's been doing some deals with the Fish People – that's the goggle-eyed lot with feet, not the Mermen who have tails. There's a small colony of them under the harbour somewhere, I'd hazard, though I haven't heard where exactly. Your best bet is probably to try some of the old sluice-gates by the docks, but you'll need to wait until dusk. The city guard are pretty hot on smugglers trying to avoid port taxes during the day, but at night old Azzur doesn't seem to mind them sneaking in watever takes their fancy. He's a rum one. You know, one year he . . . oh, there I go again! What was I talking about?'

5. About Carsepolis

'Yes, sorry tale, that. It was here, you see. The biggest and brightest city in all of Allansia. You may have seen some of its ruins as you approached Blacksand, though much of what lies above ground has long since been plundered for building materials. Not much left of it at all now. Then, let me see, oh, it must have been nearly three hundred years ago now. There was a great war, the War of the Wizards as I'm sure some of you must know, and Carsepolis was besieged by the Armies of Foul Chaos.

'Eventually it was relieved; but the city had been so badly damaged that it was abandoned by all but the lowest of its citizenry. They stayed on, and after a few generations they got themselves organized and built this place. Sometimes I think that the Forces of Chaos would be happier with it now than they were when they'd levelled the place. But then, that's often the way with us humans. We seem to fight hard to protect something, then only a few years later we let it turn into the very thing it was they were trying to stop it becoming! Typical! Ah well. Anything else?'

6. Can He Help?

'Hmm, let's see. One or two of you seem to have got yourselves a little scratched. I can certainly cure those nicks for you. But I don't carry stocks of potions or enchantments these days – they'd be too much of a temptation to my ruffian neighbours. Not that I have any trouble fighting them off – but I don't see why I should have to bother. If they know I've got nothing worth stealing, they leave well alone. I can still make such things, of course, but they take many days, weeks even. If I were you, I'd go after old Throg straight away. The more time you give him, the more likely he is to learn that you're here and take precautions to stop you ever curtailing his, erm, activities.'

7. How to Kill Xortan Throg

*'Good question, good question! You see, with some wizards –
like that old Zanbar Bone, for example – it is quite straightforward because they've so hedged themselves about with magical
protection that everyone knows about the few things left that
will kill them, and the Demons they've been using have probably fixed it so that anyone who has got the right bits will find his
task very easy indeed. Awkward little beggars they are, which is
why I've never gone in for all that nonsense.*

*'Now, Throg, though, being the matter in hand, is an ordinary
chap like you or me. A knife through the ribs will see him dead
enough. It's getting close enough to deliver the blow that's the
problem. He'll have a whole load of spells ready to use against
you. No, my friends, I'm afraid that's something you'll have to
sort out for yourselves. There are no easy answers there. Let us
pray that the gods see fit to grant you their protection and guide
your hands in their service. It's about time they were on our side
for a while.'*

Nicodemus will answer any other questions along similar lines (that is, very long-windedly). As long as the Heroes are polite, he remains quite friendly and he will cure their wounds if necessary (restore everyone's STAMINA to its *Initial* score), but he can offer them no other help beyond information. He will not accompany them into the sewers – he is far too old for that sort of thing.

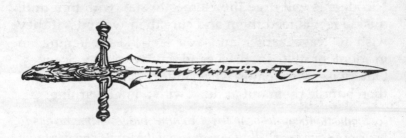

Problems?

If the Heroes are rude to Nicodemus, he can give them some minor affliction – warts or boils, perhaps, or an extra-long nose – to teach them some manners. Should they be daft enough to attack him, he'll carry out his threat: turn the lot of them into fish and drop them in the river to see how long they live (about five minutes). Anyone that stupid and ill-mannered deserves everything they get.

If there is a spell-caster like Rangor in the party, he may ask Nicodemus to teach him some spells. That is a fair request, at which Nicodemus will smile and answer thus:

'Well, very flattering of you to ask, young one, but I'm not a very good teacher. Far too tetchy, you see – at least that's what my old master used to say. You'd be far better off in one of those fine schools in Salamonis. After five years or so there, you should be good enough to work through stuff on your own. Come back to me then and, if I'm still alive, I'll show you a book or two. How's that for a deal?'

Turn to . . .

Nicodemus will urge the Heroes to stay with him until dusk. He will feed them and cure their wounds. If they wish to leave earlier and you feel like designing an incident or two in Blacksand, move on to Scene 5. Otherwise Nicodemus will natter on all afternoon and then bundle them out at dusk with a final warning:

'Remember, the quicker you get to him, the less time he has to prepare for your arrival. If you're lucky, he won't know yet that you are here, but don't waste any time! Good fortune to you.'

Following Nicodemus's instructions, the Heroes cross the Singing Bridge and turn left down Harbour Street. Eventually they pass the Black Lobster Tavern, where lights are blazing amid the sounds of breaking tables and shattering tankards, and arrive at Lobster Wharf (Scene 6).

Scene 5 – The Streets of Port Blacksand

Special Note

If you feel like trying your hand at inventing some scenes of your own, this is the ideal place to slot them in. The Heroes have a few hours to kill before dusk, and they could spend them exploring Port Blacksand. You will find *Titan* and *City of Thieves* useful aids in creating such scenes. Alternatively, you could use one or more of these incidents, filling in the details yourself:

1. Passes Please!

A couple of city guards, one human and one Half-Orc, both decked out in the usual black uniforms and each carrying a pole arm, stop one of the Heroes and demand a Holy Day pass. Actually, no such thing officially exists; the guards may sell him one for 200 Gold Pieces, if he's willing. If he's not, well, a punch-up will enliven the guards' rounds, and their arrest record is a little down today anyway.

2. Stop thief!

In a crowded market street, one of the Heroes (not one with *Awareness* skill), suddenly feels a hand dipping into his belt-purse. The scrawny young pickpocket takes to his heels, dodging in and out of the crowd until he disappears round a corner. If the Heroes try to give chase, they'll have tremendous trouble weaving in and out of the market-day crowds. If they overturn any stalls and spill any produce, they may have to pay out more cash to calm the crowd down. Incidentally, the pickpocket stole 8 Gold Pieces.

3. 'Ere, Mister!

As the party wanders the streets of Port Blacksand, one of the Heroes feels an insistent tugging at his belt. It's a small gutter-waif, either a boy or girl but difficult to tell which. There is a tiny, rat-like dog at its heels, and what it wants is a coin for some food, a fact indicated by its outstretched palm and the way its other hand is pointing to its mouth. If the Hero shoves it away, it'll immediately start to screech at high volume, accompanied by the frantic barking of its equally loud-voiced dog; and the local shopkeepers and stall-holders will have a few strong words to say to the Hero about treating children properly.

Of course, if the Hero gives the child a coin, he will soon be stopped by another, and then another, until a whole crowd of apparently starving children are trailing along behind him, palms outstretched for money! (On the stroke of tea-time, the children will suddenly disappear back into the alleys from where they came, as if they had never been there.)

4. Hey, Shorty!

Use this incident if there is a Dwarf in the party. As they round a street corner, a pair of very large, hulk-like humans leaning against a wall decide to abuse the Dwarf about his height, making jokes about needing stilts to scratch his head, about being hung on a chain and worn as a pendant, and so on. As long as no one threatens them, they'll continue to offer these and other frightfully hilarious jibes. Being unarmed, however, at the first sign of trouble they'll run for it! (This incident could also be used, with variations, for an Elf, a barbarian warrior or for just about anyone who's slightly different.)

5. Watch Out Below!

A pail full of unbelievably smelly, slimy stuff comes sloshing down, thrown from an upstairs window, just as one of the Heroes is walking by underneath. The man at the window will look down, snigger, then point out that he did shout out, honest, before slamming the window shut again. The Hero is absolutely covered with it, and its smell is extremely nasty. People will start giving him odd looks, and small children will avoid him in the streets. (Funnily enough, however, when the party descends into the sewers, this character need not reduce his SKILL by 1 point, as he's quite used to the noxious smell by now!)

Turn To . . .

At dusk, the Heroes must make their way to Lobster Wharf. Move straight on to Scene 6 now.

Scene 6 – Lobster Wharf

Location

The docks of Port Blacksand are a hive of activity during the day, with ships arriving from all corners of the world bearing goods and passengers. As night falls, however, the population disappears to their hammocks and bunks, or into the taverns, or curl up in a corner in an alleyway. The only people who move about after dark are either up to no good or are members of the city guard – or they are Heroes, looking for a way down into the sewers, on the trail of a troublemaking sorcerer.

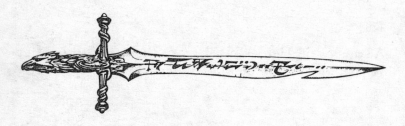

Huge, graceful pirate ships are tied up at the wharf. We see vessels such as *The Black Swan* and *The Swordfish*, names that are spoken with fear and dread throughout the twelve seas of Titan. And their villainous captains are not mentioned at all, for fear that the mere mention of their names will cause the evil buccaneers to appear!

Beside the ships stand piles of empty crates and barrels. Our Heroes slink between these, hoping to avoid the ever-watchful gaze of the city guard, should they appear, and looking for the sluice-gates that Nicodemus

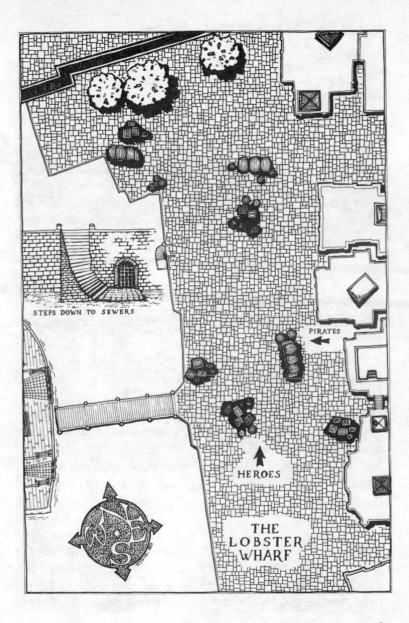

STEPS DOWN TO SEWERS

PIRATES

HEROES

THE
LOBSTER
WHARF

said would be their best method of entrance. Suddenly they stop, spying movement ahead. A small group of people, obviously pirates by their dress and gait, are sneaking along the wharf; between them, they are carrying two large chests. They make silently for a flight of steps at the edge of the dock.

Out in the water of the harbour, a scaly head with large, bulbous eyes breaks the surface and a scaly arm waves the men forward. The pirates head down the steps. There is a creak, as of a rusty iron gate opening, and they vanish from sight. Along an alleyway leading to the wharf, the Heroes can see a similar group of figures carrying two more chests.

Plot Summary

The Heroes spot some pirates entering the sewers guided by Fish Men. They have the choice of knocking out or killing the pirates and then impersonating them, or following them at a distance.

Cast List

A group of Pirates – exactly one per Hero. They won't have a chance to say anything, but they carry themselves with a swaggering, rolling gait as if recently returned from rough seas.

PIRATES each SKILL 8 STAMINA 10
Sword (cutlass)

A Fish Man. These creatures are half fish and half man – the result of rather grisly and warped experiments by an evil sorcerer many years previously – but unlike Mer-men, who are men down to the waist and fish from there to the tail, Fish Men have the head and body of a large fish, but with thin, spindly arms and legs; the entire body is covered in yellow-green scales, and fingers and feet are webbed.

Fish Men can breathe both air and water, but need to keep their skins moist. They speak in gurgling tones as if full of sea-water. Try speaking while gargling or blowing through a rubber tube that dips into a bowl of water, and you'll see what we mean. They are normally armed with tridents and are capable opponents, especially in water. This Fish Man will not be involved in any fight with the Pirates.

Props

Two large, heavy boxes, and a very strong smell of fish. We leave it entirely up to you how to represent the latter.

Action!

Use the segment or segments which apply to your Heroes' actions:

1. The Pirates
The Heroes cannot tackle the first group of pirates with-out the second group seeing them; once the first group

has disappeared, however, ambushing the others will prove easy. At this point, the Heroes have three clear options. (1) They can attack the second group of pirates and then impersonate them. (2) They can follow the second group, keeping them in sight. (3) They can wait until all the pirates have gone and then make their own way into the sewers.

If the Heroes choose to attack, there will be a fight. The pirates are caught by surprise and are still carrying the chest(s) when the Heroes spring the ambush. Because of this, the Heroes get an unopposed strike at the pirates before the latter can draw their swords. After this, run a normal fight with each Hero tackling one opponent, armed with a cutlass (treat it as a Sword on the weapon damage chart). Once everyone is disposed of, the Heroes may avail themselves of the odd hat, cutlass, headscarf or eye-patch to complete their rather hurriedly improvised disguises, before making for the sewers.

2. The Chests
Being curious and not a little greedy, the Heroes may wish to know what is inside the chests. (Plainly, they can open them up and look inside only when the fight is over.) The first contains various herbs, spices and dead animals: just the sorts of things that wizards use for their potions. The other contains weapons – swords and daggers; someone is obviously setting about equipping a small army.

3. The Fish Man
If the Heroes are impersonating the pirates, they will make their way down the steps carrying the chests. As they do so, a Fish Man will appear out of the water and wave them on. 'Follloww mee,' he gurgles at them.

'Pllaacce the chhesstss whherre I shooww youu and youu wwill bee paidd as prommissed!'

With this, the Fish Man wades through the gateway into the sewers, glancing back every so often to make sure that the Heroes are following close behind him.

Problems?

The Heroes may be daft enough to attack the first group of pirates. If they are, you should handle the fight like this: in the first round of combat, the Heroes catch the pirates by surprise and get an unopposed strike. In the second and third rounds, the first group of pirates fight the Heroes normally while the second group drop their chest and run forward. In the fourth round, the second group of pirates arrive, and each Hero must then fight two pirates at once (unless he has already killed his first opponent, in which case he just has to confront the new one).

Turn To . . .

The Heroes move down into the sewers, the Fish Man padding along ahead with a light slapping sound as his webbed feet patter on the wet stone. The smell becomes foul, a mixture of every nasty smell there is in the known world. From now on, everyone must deduct 1 point from his SKILL and hence from his Special Skills too (unless one of the Heroes has had an encounter with something nasty from the sky – see earlier!). As they proceed, more Fish Men appear as if from nowhere to escort them, and they are guided deep under Port Blacksand. Move on to the many-legged horrors of Scene 7!

Scene 7 – A Giant Centipede

Location

Down in the tunnel system beneath the city, the Heroes are walking along a well-paved walkway that runs alongside the sewer water. The Fish Men, if they are with the Heroes, keep to the water but with their heads in the air (no self-respecting fish breathes Port Blacksand sewer water unless absolutely necessary!). At first, the Heroes will think that the sewers of Port Blacksand are extremely well constructed, but anyone making a successful *World Lore* roll will realize that they are walking on the docks of ancient Carsepolis! The people of Port Blacksand have simply built over the old city, using its forgotten streets for their sewers.

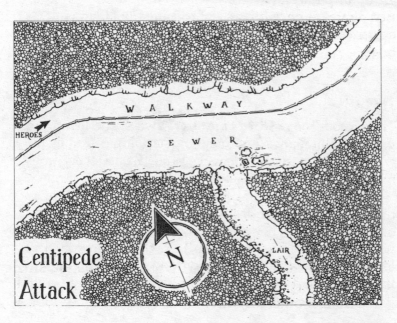

Though it is quite gloomy in the tunnel, there is enough light – from the entrance, the occasional shaft in the roof, and a species of luminous algae which decorate the walls – for the Heroes to see where they are going without recourse to lanterns. Characters with *Dark Seeing* will have no problems anyway.

Plot Summary

The Heroes encounter a Giant Centipede in the tunnels. What happens depends on the choices they made in the last scene.

Cast List

Five Fish Men. Don't bother to give them individual names or personalities – the Heroes won't be able to tell one from another anyway.

A Giant Centipede, about the size of a large stagecoach.

CENTIPEDE   SKILL 9   STAMINA 20

Large bite

The Centipede's skin is so tough that all damage done to it is reduced by 1 point (and so hits doing 1 point don't harm it at all!).

Props

Something to make a loud clattering noise to startle the players with; a wooden rattle of the kind waved at soccer matches would do very nicely.

Action!

The Heroes (and Fish Men, if present) are alerted by a loud clacking sound. Ahead of them is a side-tunnel, the first the Heroes have seen, which comes into the path on the far side of the tunnel. From that tunnel, a vast insect head appears. Many antennae search the tunnel, undulating and probing ahead of their owner: a Giant Centipede. The noise is made by the horny carapace of the massive insect. The centipede slowly lifts its huge body across the deep main channel, plants a few feet on the walkway, and turns into the tunnel – totally blocking the way forward.

Exactly what happens now depends on the choice made by the Heroes in the previous scene, whether to go with the Fish Men or to follow on at a distance. If they are following at some distance, they will have to fight the Centipede themselves before they can move on.

If the Heroes have an escort, the Fish Men will demonstrate how to get rid of the beast for them. As the Centipede approaches, they swim close to one another and clash the poles of their tridents together, making a noise very similar to that made by the Centipede. It should dawn on the Heroes eventually that the giant creature is almost blind; it hunts by sound and by feeling things with its long, undulating antennae. On hearing what appears to be the approach of another of its species, the monster elects not to risk a fight and slowly backs into the tunnel from which it had come.

If the Heroes are impersonating the pirates, they can pass freely with the Fish Men as the Centipede retreats. If they are following closely behind the Fish Men and the real pirates, they have more of a problem. With the 'other Centipede' now heading up the tunnel, the real one decides to move forward again (it finds going backwards very difficult, with all those legs to coordinate) and turn the other way – towards the Heroes!

The Heroes can choose either to fight it or to use their shields to make a rattling noise, as the Fish Men did. Either way, they will have to make quite a racket. By this time the Fish Men and pirates have turned a corner, but they may well have heard the commotion behind them and realized that they are being followed by intruders. Don't inform the players of this possibility; let them find out in a moment.

The Centipede fights by detecting victims with its antennae and then snapping at them with its huge mandibles. Each Combat Round, roll dice to see which of the Heroes fighting the creature is touched by an antenna (Heroes not in the front rank and using bows or spells are never touched) and have the Centipede take a bite at him. Despite its size, the slow-moving monster has only 1 Attack. (Don't forget that the smell of the sewers has reduced almost everyone's SKILL by 1 point.)

If a Hero wishes, he may forgo his attack and concentrate on dodging the antennae instead. To do this, he just opposes the Centipede's attack with his *Dodge* Skill score, adding the result of two dice and comparing it to the Centipede's attack score. This may help Heroes who have dropped their weapons and the wizard whose *Dodge* is better than his combat skills!

The Heroes may also try to chop off the antennae. There are four antennae altogether; to hit one requires a weapon Special Skill roll with a penalty of 3 points. This must be done when the Hero is unopposed, or he won't be able to defend himself. A hit on an antenna will automatically sever it, and the Centipede will screech in pain. Once two antennae are severed, the Centipede will take fright and retreat into its tunnel, and so away.

Problems?

If the Heroes kill the Centipede, they may elect to investigate its tunnel. To do this they must first swim across the main channel (no armour may be worn or they'd sink; it must be left on the path) and then wade up the side-channel (or swim again in the case of someone short like a Dwarf). After about 200 metres they reach a dead end – an open area which the Centipede uses as a nest and to turn around in. The only treasure to be gained here is a few tridents and a small pile of humanoid bones – all that remains of the Fish Men the Centipede has eaten in the past few weeks.

Turn To . . .

Once the danger is past, or overcome, the party can continue along the tunnel. If the Heroes are impersonating the pirates, turn straight to Scene 9; otherwise, move on to Scene 8.

Scene 8 – Captured!

Location

This scene takes place in tunnels very similar to those for Scene 7, the path continuing alongside the sewer water for many more paces, occasionally turning and twisting round corners as it heads deeper under the city.

Plot Summary

The Heroes get captured by the Fish Men.

Cast List

A large number of Fish Men – at least three per Hero, all of them armed with vicious-looking tridents.

FISH MEN   each SKILL 7   STAMINA 6

Trident (as Spear)

Props

Something to poke the players with: preferably a trident, but a fork will do (try not to be too boisterous with anything sharp, or you'll probably regret it).

Something slimy and horrid to smear on your fingers before touching the players, to simulate the feel of the Fish Men's skin when they have just emerged from the sewer water.

A large net to drop on the players. The plastic netting that is sold in garden centres to keep birds off vegetable plots should do nicely, though you may have some trouble keeping this hidden from your players until the moment you need it.

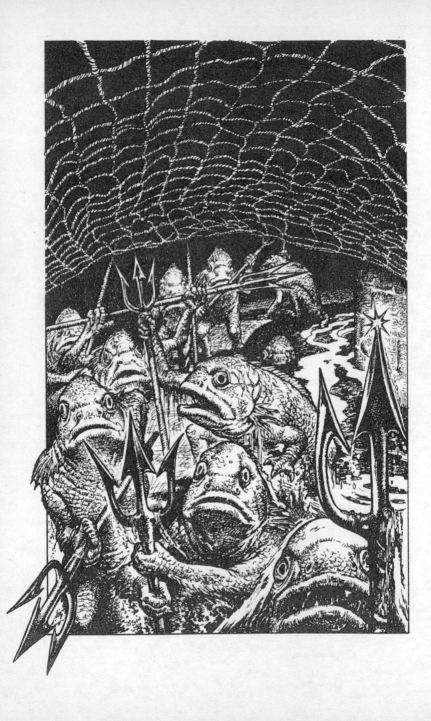

Action!

As the Heroes inch their way along the tunnel, a large net falls from the ceiling and envelops them. There is no chance of detecting it in advance or avoiding it. Immediately a large party of Fish Men emerges from the murky waters of the sewer. The Heroes are disarmed, tied with cord and prodded with the sharp ends of their tridents. The Fish Men have damp, scaly skin and their touch feels slimy and horrid.

Once they have the Heroes safely secured, the Fish Men urge their captives to their feet and herd them along the tunnel. Like most Bad Guys, they are happy to gloat and tell the Heroes just why they've been captured. Each Fish Man will chip in with one comment or another; there is no clear leader to the group. (Please add your own gurgles to their speech as you go along.)

'Ha! Got you now, we have. Urgle! Horrid, hated Dry Ones! Fry you in batter we will! That'll learn you! Heh, heh, heh!'

'No, no such luck for you! You go to wizard! Dry Ones deserve one another, yes they do! Gloop! Fight one another all the time. That's what we like! Dry ones kill one another off, then we kill what's left! Heh-heh-heh! No more Dry Ones! Good! Good!'

Not surprisingly, the Fish Men have immense difficulty pronouncing the name 'Xortan Throg', but the Heroes should be able to understand from their speech that he is the person they are being taken to. The Fish Men will try to answer any questions, using their answers to slip in yet more gurgling remarks about hated Dry Ones – and to boast a bit, too – but they know nothing of the wizard's plans except that he intends to conquer Port Blacksand. If asked where he lives, they will reply simply: 'You find out soon, Dry Ones, yes you will! We take you there, then you not be so eager to go! Urgle!'

Problems?

The Heroes may believe they have a chance to fight their way out of this situation. Ah, but don't forget they are all in a net. That means all their skills are *halved*. And they have to fight three Fish Men at once, numbers two and three getting unopposed automatic strikes because of the restraining net. They should soon think better of it, though let anyone who feels that reckless try it for just one round.

Turn To . . .

Bound and disarmed, the Heroes are herded along the tunnels. The Fish Men walk after them, prodding them with tridents as they go. The action moves straight on to Scene 9.

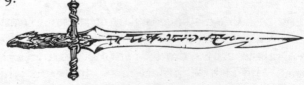

Scene 9 – An Offer of Help

Location

As the Heroes and their Fish Men guides or captors (depending on the situation) pass through the tunnels, they come upon an open area to the side of the path. The roof here is supported by pillars. It is as if the people who built this part of Port Blacksand intended to create a cellar here – or perhaps they just didn't want to build on this particular spot. Beyond the open area, the tunnel continues further into the darkness, deep under the city.

Sargon's Lair

Extending some distance back from the main tunnel, the open area is quite dark. Strangely, none of the fluorescent algae grows there or in the nearby portions of tunnel. The Fish Men nervously chatter in whispered gurgles as they approach this area (though if they have prisoners they don't let their attention waver for a moment).

Plot Summary

An ancient ghost appears, scaring off the Fish Men. It offers to help the Heroes.

Cast List

The Fish Men, as before.

Sargon, a long-dead priest from Carsepolis. Being a ghost, Sargon speaks in a rather hoarse whisper; but he seems friendly enough, perhaps even glad of their company. Other than that, his manner is proud and commanding, as might be expected of a man who once held high office in a great city like Carsepolis.

Props

A blast of cold air would come in useful here. If you are running this game during the winter, open all the windows for a moment when the ghost appears. Alternatively, turn on an electric fan and point it at the players for a few seconds (but watch out for scattering scraps of paper, etc.).

Action!

This scene is divided into segments again; use only the ones you need, starting with the first.

1. The Manifestation

As the party reaches the centre of the open area, they feel a cold blast of air and a dull glowing area of white light appears between the pillars. The Fish Men are quite terrified by this sudden apparition. They drop anything they are carrying except their tridents (so, if the Heroes were captured, they can get their weapons back in a moment) and flee, swimming off at great speed. They are so frightened they actually put their heads underwater. You must hope that the Heroes will prove to be made of sterner stuff.

Slowly the white light expands, dimming a little as it spreads out, and a shape forms. It is an old man, a priest of some sort from the look of him, but dressed in strange robes the like of which the Heroes have never seen before. (It looks rather like a cross between a Roman toga and an Aztec sacrificial robe.) 'Good evening,' the ghost says quite calmly, 'and whom do I have the honour of addressing?'

307

2. Conversation with a Ghost

Presumably the Heroes are polite enough to introduce themselves, if only through chattering teeth and the sound of knees knocking together. In return for their names, the ghost announces that he is Sargon, a high priest of that most glorious of cities, Carsepolis. He says that he was killed during the great siege by darkly sorcerous means, as a result of which his soul has been condemned to wander these dark and rather boring tunnels for many centuries.

'It is a pleasure,' he continues, 'to have live men to talk to once more rather than these foul and cowardly fish things. Pray, do me the honour of staying and conversing with me for a while. I am sure there must be some interesting reason for your presence in this blighted place, and it would give me exceptional pleasure to hear it told.'

The Heroes can discuss whatever they like with Sargon. In actual fact, he wants their help with something, so he will be open and friendly. However, there are a few topics he is a bit touchy about.

If the Heroes ask which god or goddess Sargon used to serve, he replies that he was the High Priest of Elim. It is unlikely that any of the Heroes will remember who this god is (*World Lore* Skill roll with a 5-point penalty), in which case Sargon bemoans the changes in the world these days but explains no further – if no one knows of the god these days, then obviously he has deserted Titan and there is little point in worshipping him any more. (Sargon is not being entirely truthful here – he doesn't really want to discuss his god. If pressed, he will use the old excuse of not being able to discuss the mysteries with non-initiates.)

If some of your players have been studying the ancient legends of Allansia very closely (that is, they succeed in making the roll!), they may remember that Elim was one of a trio of very ancient primal deities worshipped by a race of people who were wiped out during the War of the Wizards. Elim's name translates as 'Dark', which may make the Heroes suspicious of Sargon. And so they should be; but at the moment Sargon actually happens to be on their side. In any case, the priest will not discuss his religion with the Heroes and will go on trying to get them to talk about something else. See *Titan* for more information on Elim.

There are two things that Sargon *is* keen to discuss, the first, and most obvious, being how his soul may be allowed to rest properly. It seems that the Heroes may be able to help him. This is his explanation:

'One of the holy relics of Carsepolis was a Crystal of Power. This crystal was a force of great good and healing, but it was of little use in the siege, for our attackers knew of it and could counter its powers whenever we attempted to use it. When it seemed that the city was about to be taken, some of us priests, wishing to preserve the relics from the forces of Chaos, threw the crystal into the care of the seas of the Western Ocean.

'In the seemingly endless years during which I have lived here, I have learnt that it has been recovered. The Fish People discovered it and have taken it to the old Temple of Hydana, the sea god. In olden times, the temple was located on the dockside, so that mariners could make offerings there before setting out to sea. That temple is quite close to here, but I am unable to enter it. It is well guarded by the Fish People, but I know of a secret entrance. If you can take that crystal and bring it to me then my soul will be freed from its wanderings.'

Sargon will not reveal just why he is barred from entering the Temple of Hydana (it's because of the great difference between the goodness of Hydana and the evil of Elim). The Heroes may offer to help Sargon out of the goodness of their hearts, but they may well want to know what Sargon can do for them in return. Fortunately, once he learns of their quest, he is only too keen to tell them:

'Xortan Throg, eh? Oh I know of him, the young idiot! Do you know, he fully believes himself descended from the royal family of Carsepolis? And so he is in a way, if only via a chance liaison between the last king and a young serving-girl – which he doesn't know about. Needless to say, the royal blood-line has been further diluted over the centuries, but his family have kept alive the story of their origins, and now this upstart seeks to win back what he considers to be "his" city. Ha! He has grand enough plans – he's working hard on raising as many of the old royal guard as he can find corpses for and, with his skeleton army, thinks to storm Lord Azzur's palace from the sewers. Later, no doubt, he'll raise a real army and set off to conquer the world.

'Pah! Let a man get a few spells in his head and he thinks he can do anything! Oh he's a good enough wizard, but he'll never be able to hold together an undead army large enough to take on Lord Azzur. And now, of course, it seems he won't get the chance to try, as you bold fellows are going to finish him off. Of course, you might need a bit of help and advice. I can tell you how to beat him, and I will, if you will do something for me in return.'

The Heroes may ask Sargon why it is that Xortan Throg hates Salamonis; and this question will receive the answer:

'Humph, probably just jealousy. I gather that it is the most powerful city in the world these days, for all that it was a collection of mud huts with a wall round it when I was alive. It's the city he will have to beat if he intends to conquer Allansia and bring all under his evil sway, et cetera et cetera, so I'm not at all surprised he's busy doing ill to its people already.'

Problems?

Don't fret if the Heroes don't agree to the deal with Sargon. They'll change their minds once they've wandered round the sewers for a while (Scene 10). What they may want to do, however, is to go back to Nicodemus and ask whether they can trust the ghost. This is not a particularly Heroic thing to do, and there are a number of ways you can dissuade them.

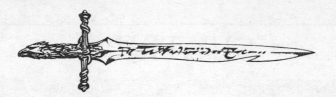

First, remind them what Nicodemus said about time being important – the longer they delay, the more time Xortan Throg has to prepare for their arrival, and hence the less chance they have of succeeding in their task. If they still want to go back, they may have to get past the Giant Centipede, and they will have to get out into Port Blacksand. Coincidentally, at this very moment a group of Troll city guardsmen is sitting on the dockside discussing the various merits of different parts of the Gnome anatomy and ways in which each can be cooked.

If the Heroes fight their way out (one Troll per Hero, SKILL 9 STAMINA 9, armed with Swords) or wait for the Trolls to go, you may as well let them go back to Nicodemus. He will not be pleased at being woken up; he knows nothing about Sargon (though he does know who Elim is) and will give the Heroes a lecture about the need to get a move on quickly. The ghost is the best opportunity they have – unless they have a better plan; why don't they get on and *do* something and stop depriving him of valuable sleep?

Turn To

If the Heroes fall in with Sargon's bargain, he will instruct them how to find the secret entrance to the Temple of Hydana (see the map in Scene 11). Move everyone on to Scene 11. If they decide they can deal with Xortan Throg themselves, move instead to Scene 10.

THE SEWERS (PART)

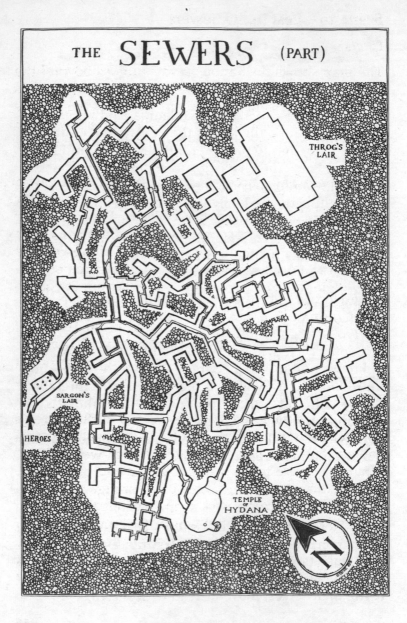

THROG'S LAIR

SARGON'S LAIR

HEROES

TEMPLE of HYDANA

N

Scene 10 – Lost in the Sewers

Location

The map shows the various sewer tunnels beyond the area haunted by Sargon. Note that not all the tunnels have a path, of course. For many of them, the Heroes have to wade, waist deep (or neck deep for a Dwarf!) in filthy stinking sewer water. Where a path ends, it simply slopes down into the water.

There are several places where the tunnels connect with the rest of Port Blacksand's sewer system. The reason for marking a dead-end is because the roof of the sewer becomes so low that it meets the water. The Heroes are welcome to try swimming through, but the sewers are not the most salubrious of water to be drowned in. You should emphasize strongly the maze-like quality of the tunnels, and also their quite horrid conditions.

Two special locations are marked. One is the Temple of Hydana (see Scene 11 for further information). There are two entrances, the secret one that Sargon knows of but which the Heroes cannot find without his help, and the main one, which leads to a room full of Fish Man guards.

The other special location is the route to Xortan Throg's domain. It is unlikely that the Heroes will find this without Sargon's help because it is very well hidden. What they have to do is to go off the end of the path beyond the entrance and come back through the water, which quickly becomes neck deep, to where the entrance is marked. This is a tunnel which goes under the path (which is why the Heroes can't see it from the path). Again, the water is neck deep (forehead deep for a Dwarf!), but the tunnel is passable by air-breathers at low tide.

315

Plot Summary

Having declined Sargon's offer, the Heroes wander round the sewers, trying to find Xortan Throg. They encounter various creatures that inhabit these dark and noisome tunnels. After a very short while, they begin to feel very miserable.

Cast List

Various wandering monsters are available. When you need one, simply roll 1 die and consult the following table, according to the result. All creatures may be encountered again and again, with the exception of the Tentacled Thing (if you roll a 6 a second time, roll again).

(1) GIANT RATS: Two per Hero, each SKILL 5 STAMINA 4

Small bite

(2) CROCODILES: One for every two Heroes, each SKILL 7 STAMINA 7

2 Attacks, Large bite

(3) FISH MAN patrol: Three Fish Men, each having SKILL 7 STAMINA 6

Trident (treat as Spear)

(4) RAT MEN: Four of these half-rat/half-human mutants, SKILL 5   STAMINA 6

Small bite

(5) GIANT TOADS: 1–3 Toads lurk in the sewer water, SKILL 5   STAMINA 7

poisoned tongue delivers 4 points of damage

(6) An Unknown TENTACLED THING: one of these rare nasties lurks just under the surface. It has SKILL 8 STAMINA 10

3 Attacks

Once it has hit someone, its tentacles will continue to deliver 1 point of damage until the creature is killed (it will still defend against attacks but, if successful, will only do another 1 point of crushing damage).

Props

If the Heroes decide to wade into the sewer water, you could always tell them to run a bath and stand in it with their clothes on. (Yes, we know it is messy. At least we didn't suggest you empty the dustbin into the bath or make them roll around in the garden first.) Of course they will refuse to do it (they'll probably ask for stunt men to stand in for them!), but it should get the point across as to how unpleasant the place is.

Action!

The Heroes will probably be fairly happy wandering for a while. When it begins to sound as if they are getting bored, introduce a wandering monster. At first you should make it easy by having the enemy come down the tunnel towards them; but the longer they delay, the nastier you should make the encounters. If they are being total pains and refusing to get on with the task at hand, wait until they are wading through the water, then have them surprised by a Tentacled Thing. That should end the game, or this scene at least.

Problems?

It is the Heroes who are in trouble, not you; they chose to do things this way. If they seem unhappy, remind them that Sargon did offer to help, and hope that they reconsider and return to him for help after all.

If the Heroes really get lost (because they can't map the tunnels correctly), suggest they walk towards the lighter areas (moonlight enters at the gate on the docks) and, when they ask for the direction, send them the right way to get back to Sargon.

Turn To . . .

There are two possible endings to this scene. First, the Heroes could finish up back with Sargon and ask him for directions. He will direct them to the secret entrance to the Temple of Hydana. Alternatively, they may stumble on the temple by accident. Unless the Heroes have already sorted out the denizens of the temple (in which case they are still lost!), go to Scene 11. If the Heroes have actually managed to sort out affairs at the temple, and gain the Crystal of Power, and they now wish to return to Sargon, move the action on to Scene 12.

Scene 11 – The Temple of Hydana

Location

The old Temple of Hydana in Carsepolis was built on the dockside so that mariners could make offerings to the god of the sea before setting sail into the fearsome northern reaches of the Western Ocean. Much of the temple has now been demolished and built over by the Blacksanders, but two rooms remain: the main hall and an ante-room.

The temple is now used by the Fish Men for whom Hydana is the supreme, if not the only, god. Most of the other gods they regard as evil because they all portray themselves as a 'Dry One'; and the Fish Men reserve a special loathing for Glantanka, the Sun Goddess, who they term Quuosshreeggaa, the Stealer of Water.

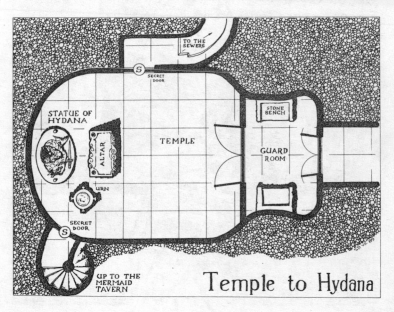

Temple to Hydana

The ante-room is bare of furnishings except for a pair of stone benches running along the walls; but it is nicely decorated, with tile mosaics showing dolphin and seaweed motifs. It is permanently occupied by a small force of Fish Man warriors whose duty it is to protect the temple and its priest from intruding outsiders and the nastier wandering creatures of the sewers. Because the temple is a very holy place to the Fish Men, these guards will fight with fanatical ferocity.

The main temple hall is also unfurnished, save for the great statue of Hydana at the far end and the altar in front of it on which rests the Crystal of Power. The statue is some two metres tall; it depicts Hydana in typical pose, perched upright with his tail curled beneath him and holding his net and trident. The crystal is made of an opaque, quartz-like substance and is about twenty centimetres high and ten centimetres across, cut and faceted like a first-water diamond. It is mounted in a special gold stand but is not fixed to it. Golden goblets stand at both ends of the altar and on either side of the statue. Beside the statue is a large urn containing clean sea-water.

At the base of the statue is a large, ornate sword, another relic of the temples of Carsepolis. This weapon is magical and confers a bonus of 2 points to the SKILL or *Sword* Special Skill of anyone who fights using it. Unfortunately it has lain underwater for many decades and is now a little brittle: the blade will snap in two the first time it is used unless something is done to repair it (see Scene 12). You may tell the Heroes that the blade is a little tarnished and flecked with rust. The blade's weakness will be noticed only if someone states that they are examining the sword carefully and makes a successful *Sword* or SKILL roll.

Although the Fish Men would much prefer to flood the temple rooms, they believe that it would be sacrilegious to defile Hydana's house with the filthy sewer water of Port Blacksand. Therefore they keep the temple dry, but wash the floors regularly with clean sea-water which they bring in from the deep ocean. Incidentally, during ceremonies in the temple the priest also anoints each worshipper with sea-water.

There are two more entrances to the temple. One is the secret entrance to which Sargon directs the Heroes. From the passage side, it appears to be a normal door but is in fact a plain stone slab which is hinged along one side. It cannot be detected from the temple side unless one knows it is there.

The other entrance, also hidden and unlikely to be found by the Heroes, leads to the cellars of the infamous Mermaid Tavern at Weaver Gate in Port Blacksand. The evil owners of this Inn have made a pact with the Fish Men: careless customers who fall asleep after too many pints of strong ale may very well wake up just in time to find themselves being sacrificed to Hydana.

Plot Summary

The Heroes enter the temple, possibly fight some Fish Men, and – we hope – acquire the Crystal of Power.

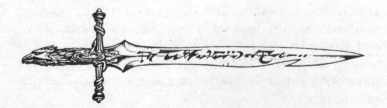

Cast List

Fish Man guards, two for each Hero. These are elite Fish Man troops and, as explained before, are fanatically brave, so they are slightly tougher than the average Fish Man warrior.

FISH MAN GUARDS each SKILL 8 STAMINA 7
Trident (as Spear)

The Fish Man priest is also present; he is a poor fighter but knows several magic spells which he will prefer to use:

FISH MAN PRIEST SKILL 4 STAMINA 6
Hands (as Dagger)
Magic *Skill 10*, spells: ESP, Fire Bolt, Sleep, Stamina, Weakness

Props

A few goblets (gold would be nice, brass will do, or use plastic if you are desperate). A large stone or lump of glass (a paperweight?). A sword, which can be plastic but should look splendid!

Action!

What happens in this scene depends to some extent on how the Heroes enter the temple area. If they come in through the main door, they will have no option but to fight with the Fish Man guards first. If they come in through the secret entrance, they will have a chance of killing the priest, snatching the crystal and getting out without alerting the guards.

1. The Priest

If the Heroes come in through the secret entrance, they will take the priest by surprise. He is busy, praying in front of the altar, at the time, decked out in a long linen robe decorated with seaweed and small shells. They have two rounds in which to do something before he alerts the guards. In the first round, he will look up, fishy eyes widened in surprise. In the second round, the priest will run and hide behind the urn of water. In the third round, he will start using his spells and will yell for the guards. In the fourth round, the main door will open and the guards will appear. As well as casting spells, the priest will call down all sorts of curses in the name of Hydana upon the Heroes: may their skins dry out, their water be choked with weed, their wives be taken by shark, and so on (we're sure you can invent even more blood-curdling oaths for him).

2. The Guards

This is a standard fight, with each Hero having to fight two Fish Men at once. If the priest is still alive, some Heroes may have to take on three Fish Men while one of their number finishes off the priest to stop him casting his spells (especially *Sleep*, which could be disastrous for them).

3. The Sword

Some bright spark may take it into his head to grab the sword and try using it. If he asks to examine it first, tell him that it looks rusty and a bit brittle. If he wades straight in with it, well, the first time he makes a success-ful hit, goodbye one magic sword – it simply snaps into several pieces!

4. The Crystal of Power

The crystal is a very powerful magical artefact, but none of the Heroes will know how to use it, so it won't be of much help to them. If they do try some experiments with it, you should note that details of its operation are explained by Sargon in Scene 12.

5. Ransacking the Temple

It will hopefully have occurred to some of the Heroes that stealing things from temples is not a very nice thing to do; they *are* supposed to be good guys, after all, and this is a temple to an ostensibly good deity. Well, of course, the crystal and sword don't really belong to Hydana, and anyway he knows that they are to be used for a good purpose, and so he doesn't mind them being taken. If the Heroes try to take the gold goblets as well, he will not be quite so pleased.

If a Hero picks up a goblet with the intention of stealing it, the eyes of the statue will start to glow red. Tell the Hero who is in the best position to notice this and let him warn the others. If the Heroes persist in trying to steal the gold, then three more things happen. First, the secret entrances all jam shut. Secondly, water starts to pour out of the urn by the statue at an alarming (and quite impossible) rate. Thirdly, the guards, or a similar group of Fish

Men if the guards are already dead, appear at the main door, ready for battle. If the Heroes put down the gold and make a run for a secret entrance, Hydana will unjam the door and allow them to escape. Otherwise they will have to fight the Fish Men.

Fighting in water is a problem for the Heroes. The first three rounds will be fought with the water swirling round their knees and they will have a penalty of 2 points deducted from their SKILL and all combat Special Skills. For the next three rounds, the water will be getting up to their waists and the penalty rises to 4 points. In the next three rounds, the water is up to their necks and the penalty is 6 points. From round 10 onwards, they are swimming and the penalty is 8 points; fighting while trying to swim is very difficult indeed. Remember that a Dwarf is much shorter than the others. When they are knee deep he is waist deep, when they are waist deep he is neck deep, and when they are neck deep he is swimming. The Fish Men are at home in water and on land, and suffer no penalties.

Problems?

The Heroes may manage to find the door to the cellars of the Mermaid Tavern. If they open it, tell them that there are dusty stone stairs leading up and faint sounds of revelry. The stairs lead up to a trapdoor and thence into the cellar – easily recognizable as a pub cellar from all the barrels of ale lying around, of course – and the sounds of revelry are much louder.

If the Heroes pursue their investigation and come up from the cellar, land them right in the middle of a pub brawl (use the one from Scene 3 again). If they are still on their feet after that, have the city watch arrive to investigate the disturbance. Any Heroes who survive all that deserve to be allowed back down into the sewers to continue their quest.

You may have gathered by now that there are ways in which the Heroes can fail in this quest. Getting badly lost in the sewers is one very distinct possibility; stealing Hydana's gold and entering the Mermaid Tavern are others. It is still the general intention that the Heroes should succeed, which is why they get every warning that things are going wrong; but if we make life too easy for them, they may feel that they can get away with anything. Your responsibility as Director is always to do everything possible (short, that is, of outright orders) to encourage them to behave sensibly and Heroically. If all your best efforts fail, then you may just have to abandon them to an ignoble death and hope that they will learn to be more Heroic next time.

Turn To . . .

Assuming that all is going according to the script, the Heroes should hasten straight back to Sargon with the crystal, in which case move on to Scene 12. If they are still being awkward and want to keep on wandering round the sewers, go back to Scene 10.

Scene 12 – Freeing the Spirit

Location

Sargon's area of the sewer tunnel again; see the description given in Scene 9 if anyone needs reminding.

Plot Summary

Sargon comes back to life, but he keeps his bargain with the Heroes and tells them how to find and kill Xortan Throg.

Cast List

Sargon, until recently a ghost, described earlier. He appears now as a more solid version of the transparent vision he used to be.

SARGON   SKILL 10   STAMINA 12
Magic *Skill 29, spells:* Cockroach, Counter-Spell, Darkness, Death, Teleport, Weakness
(and lots of others that he won't need)

Props

Use again whatever you used to represent the Crystal of Power in the last scene.

Action!

Sargon will not tell the Heroes anything until they allow him to touch the crystal. He promises that he will still be present afterwards to give them the information. When he touches the crystal, something unexpected happens:

his body solidifies and colours. In a few seconds a live Sargon is standing in front of the Heroes. He speaks, plainly pleased with his transformation:

'Ah, that's better. Nice to see it's still in working order after so many years!

'Hmm, I can see by your faces that you are somewhat surprised at my revival. I do confess that I told you a slight untruth, my friends, for I feared you might not bring me the crystal if you knew what it would do for me. Still, I've had my side of the bargain, so now you must get yours. Fair's fair. So, this is what you must do . . .'

First, Sargon gives the directions to the tunnel that leads to Xortan Throg's domain. (These are given in the location description for Scene 10.) He then goes on to tell them how to break through the wizard's magical defences:

'*That crystal that you are carrying is a very powerful artefact, as you have all just seen. One of its properties is the ability to reflect a spell back at its caster. Take the crystal with you, but keep it well hidden so that your enemy does not suspect you possess it – he may have heard of it and know of its powers. When you find him, goad him into casting his strongest spell at you. Tell him that you simply don't believe he can cast a Death Spell or something like that. Yes, yes, I know this is a very dangerous course of action, but it must be done if you are to defeat him.*

'*When he casts the spell at you, as he surely will, uncover the crystal and hold it in front of you. The spell will be reflected back at him and he will die. But beware! Like me, his shade will be condemned to wander the ruins of Carsepolis. You must guard the crystal with care, for, if the ghost is ever able to touch the crystal again, he will be restored to life just as I have been.*'

The Heroes may work out from this that Sargon must therefore at some time have cast a *Death* Spell of his own at someone carrying the crystal. If they tackle him on this point he will look rather disgruntled, and then say:

'*Very clever of you, and quite correct. However, that happened three hundred years ago and is of little interest to young fellows like you. I wouldn't pursue the matter if I were you.*'

If the Heroes have been reasonably polite to Sargon –
that is to say, not tried to attack him or get the information without freeing him – he will do them one more
favour (but only if the Heroes have the sword with
them):

*'I see you have had the good sense to rescue the sword from the
Temple of Hydana, too. I should have thought of that myself.
You know, it once belonged to Prince Erechion of the royal
house who ruled over Carsepolis at its height. It is in pretty poor
shape at the moment, but if you will let me touch it I can restore
its strength for you.'*

If Sargon is allowed to touch the sword, it magically
regains its strength and can be used to fight with in the
usual way, continuing to deliver its enchanted SKILL
bonus for many years to come.

The bargain having been completed, Sargon takes his
leave of the Heroes with these words:

*'It has been a pleasure dealing with you young fellows. You
have been fair with me, as far as I know, and I have been fair
with you. However, I have work to do, and after three hundred
years I am a little behind schedule, as you may imagine.
Farewell until we meet again! Farewell!' So saying, Sargon
raises his arms. As he brings them down again, an unnatural
darkness suddenly descends upon the tunnels. Slowly it clears,
like mist blown away by a breeze, and when you can see again
Sargon has vanished. There is no sign of his passing.*

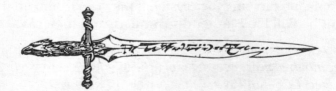

Problems?

The Heroes may try to attack Sargon. If he has not given them the information they need, he will try to dodge out of the way and talk them into stopping, but he will vanish if they are close enough to harm him. If he has given them the information, he vanishes as planned.

Turn To . . .

The Heroes follow Sargon's directions, wading through the sewer water again. By now their senses will just about have adjusted to the smell, and they need no longer deduct 1 point from their SKILL and Special Skills (restore it now). Eventually the tunnel they are walking through begins to climb a gentle slope and they come out on to dry land – and Scene 13.

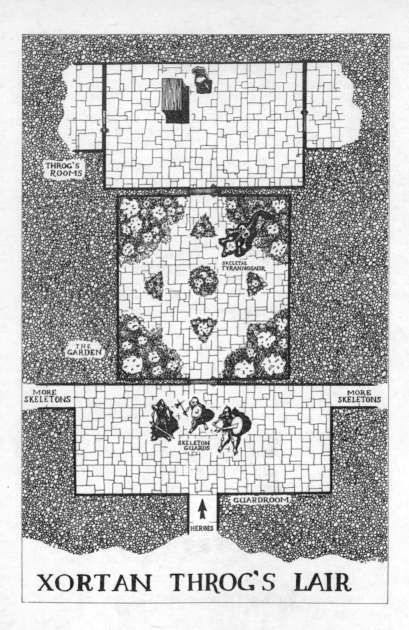

XORTAN THROG'S LAIR

Scene 13 – The Legions of Carsepolis

Location

Coming up the tunnel from the sewers, the Heroes arrive at an open area. To either side are open gateways, flanked by pillars, leading to other passages. In front of them is a splendid doorway, also flanked by pillars. Although there is no way the Heroes could know this, they are actually standing at the main gate of the military barracks of ancient Carsepolis. (The whole area, like much of Carsepolis, has a distinctly Roman feeling to its architecture and design, if you need to picture it in your head. Of course the Heroes have no idea what 'Roman' means, but your players may well have.)

Lined up in front of the doorway are the skeletons of several of the long-dead guards (there are two for every Hero present, less one). But how is it that the piles of bones are standing with every bone in its correct place? And how is it that, although their armour is old and rusty, their swords are shiny and new? Surely they aren't . . .

Plot Summary

The Heroes must fight their way past Xortan Throg's undead army.

Cast List

The Skeleton guards, freshly resurrected from long-dead Carsepolis. They wear metal helmets and breastplates, together with skirts made of strips of leather and more metal, and sandals. (They look very similar to Roman legionaries, if you need a comparison.)

SKELETONS each SKILL 9 STAMINA 7

Sword

Props

None are needed for this scene. Besides, your players won't want to be distracted while dealing with their skeletal enemies.

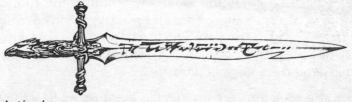

Action!

Although long dead, the soldiers of Carsepolis have lost none of the discipline and training which once made them feared throughout the continent of Allansia. As the Heroes advance nervously towards them, the guards come smartly to attention. Then, moving almost as one, they form into two ranks. Those in the front rank raise their shields and swords and advance. As they do so, the second rank clash their swords against their shields in unison. This makes quite a racket in the echoing cavern (indeed, they are doing it to sound the alarm to their fellows, a short distance away).

Run the fight as a standard one-to-one confrontation. The second rank of Skeletons will move forward to fill in only as their comrades fall – all that discipline has its disadvantages!

As was pointed out in *Out of the Pit* (the Fighting Fantasy monster book), attacking Skeletons with edged weapons such as swords and daggers is not very effective. This is because they don't have any flesh for the weapons to dig into; blades are always being deflected by bones. All edged weapons do only 1 point of damage if they manage to hit the Skeletons. If the Heroes specify that they are using the flats of their blades, or if they find something to use as a club, then they may do normal damage. Do not tell the players that using a blunt weapon will work better; let them find out for themselves – but remember that changing weapons requires one round during which they must take an unopposed strike from their opponent. (If present, the Dwarf's axe is so big, and is swung so enthusiastically, that it is not turned by the bones, and does normal damage.)

Also, the Skeletons are unaffected by most spells – they never *Sleep* anyway and *Weakness* has no effect; other spells which do not work include *Fear*, *ESP*, *Petrify* and *Death*. However, any spell-caster will be relieved to discover that they do burn, so the *Fire Bolt* spell works normally.

As the Heroes are (we hope) finishing off the last Skeleton, they hear a rattling noise. Looking to either side, they can see fresh units of skeletal warriors marching in from the side-passages to engage them. There is little choice but to dash through the door.

Problems?

The Heroes may think they can outfight the new batch of Skeletons. Point out to them that there appear to be columns of undead warriors as far as the eye can see down the passages. Did Sargon not say that Xortan Throg planned to raise the entire army of Carsepolis? Gulp!

Turn To . . .

There is only one thing for it – escape! And the only way to escape is through the doors, and straight into Scene 14.

Scene 14 – Something Nasty in the Garden

Location

The Heroes dash through the door, perhaps turning to bar it behind them (there is a bar for that purpose, interestingly enough). They find themselves in the atrium of the barracks. This is a small garden, once open to the sky but now deep below Port Blacksand. The grass has long since withered away, but the dead and petrified skeletons of trees and shrubs still decorate the area, giving it an uncanny atmosphere – it's a dead garden guarded by dead soldiers.

And there, in the centre of what was once the neatly trimmed lawn, stands something that presumably came from the long-lost zoo of Carsepolis: a Tyrannosaurus, quite dead, but skeletal, and moving . . .

The only other exit is a large door on the far side of the atrium. There is no way that anyone is going to be allowed simply to stroll across to it without meeting what is lumbering towards them.

Plot Summary

The Heroes fight an undead Skeletal Tyrannosaurus.

Cast List

There's only one creature here, but he's rather notice-able; and we predict that, if they ever get out of here alive, the Heroes aren't going to forget him in a hurry!

SKELETAL TYRANNOSAURUS
SKILL 12   STAMINA 25

3 Attacks, Very Large bite

Props

There are no props for this engagement. Also, we're sorry if your local games shop has just run out of models of skeletal tyrannosaurs; there's probably a lot of demand for them at the moment.

Action!

The Heroes have little choice but to fight the awesome creature. As it is so big and nasty, they can all gang up on it.

The Tyrannosaurus is a Skeleton, and all the special rules for the Skeleton warriors apply also to it, including which spells work and the damage that edged weapons can do to it.

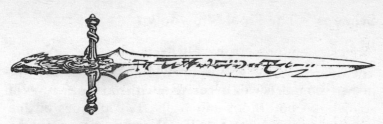

Problems?

Mumbling something about 'discretion' and 'valour', the Heroes may try to return the way they came. When they open the door, they will see the vast, perfectly aligned ranks of Xortan Throg's undead legions patiently waiting for them.

Possibly one or more of the Heroes will decide to hold off the monster while the others sneak round the distracted beast and away. That's very brave of him; he will die horribly while the rest of the group charge through the far door. Very dramatic, very tragic, very, very Heroic (it's a shame you can't give an Oscar for this, because he deserves one for such bravery).

If there are only two Heroes left at this stage, a noble sacrifice of that type may well be the best – or even only – way to get through, but don't try to arrange for that to happen. People get terribly attached to the Heroes they are playing. If they are going to go, then they should go while defending against the ravening attention of something as awesome as this little beauty.

Turn To . . .

The door on the far side of the atrium stands at the top of a pair of wide steps. It leads directly to Xortan Throg and Scene 15.

Scene 15 – The Final Showdown

Location

The door from the atrium opens into an elegantly furnished room. It is well decorated, with mosaic pictures of
soldiers on both floor and walls. Two plaques on the
walls are covered with details of the many victories of the
armies of Carsepolis. Side doors lead to other rooms
(actually the sorcerer's living and working quarters).
Xortan Throg sits in a fine chair at the far end of the
room, patiently waiting. Beside him is a table on which
lie several rolled-up maps and charts.

Plot Summary

In the thrilling final scene of the picture, our Heroes
finally dispose of Xortan Throg and the world is safe once
more.

Cast List

Xortan Throg (the real one this time, honest). His appearance is much the same as in the first adventure. This time he is wearing the full toga-like garb of an ancient Carsepolis nobleman, very similar to that worn by Sargon (though they are, quite clearly, *not* the same person).

XORTAN THROG   SKILL 10   STAMINA 28

Dagger

Magic *Skill 21, spells:* Arrow-Snake, Cockroach, Death, Force Bolt, Petrify, Raise Skeleton, Shield, Sleep, Stamina, Wall, Ward, Weakness

and many, many more

Props

None are needed to distract the players. This is the big one.

Action!

As the Heroes burst, panting, into the room, the wizard looks up and calmly welcomes his visitors with a thin smile:

'Ah, it's you. I was rather hoping it would be. So good of you to save me the trouble of coming to find you. I trust that you are impressed by my little home. Of course, it won't be long now before I move above ground, and that usurping pirate scum, Azzur, dangles from his own gibbet. When you came in I was just considering a few strategic choices in my coming campaigns. I think I shall take Chalice first – it would be so very appropriate, don't you think? And Salamonis after that, of course.

'I see that perhaps you don't altogether approve. Well, gentlemen, don't just stand there and gawp. You're not goldfish. Are you going to try to kill me or not?'

If the Heroes are following their instructions (from Sargon), they won't be advancing to attack at all; but in case they are, here is how Xortan Throg deals with them.

If a Hero tries to fire a bow, the arrow suddenly turns into a venomous snake and bites him, before crawling off into the corner. This does 1–3 points of damage (roll one die and halve the result). There is no way of avoiding this. (While the sorcerer is using his spells, don't forget the Stamina Costs they require in order to be cast. Xortan Throg is not quite all-powerful.)

Any other item which is thrown at the wizard gets reflected back, and hits the Hero who threw it, doing whatever damage is appropriate. A *Dodge* or *Test for Luck* – both at a temporary 4-point penalty – may allow a Hero to avoid the missile.

If you are not using miniatures and a floor-plan, it takes a Hero three rounds to close with the wizard, during which time the latter is able to cast more spells.

If a Hero tries to advance on Xortan Throg, the sorcerer will gesture at the character's feet and they will suddenly become stuck to the floor. As the Hero watches in horror, his boots, and the feet inside them, slowly turn to stone. The petrifaction creeps up his legs and through his body. The Hero loses 1 STAMINA point every two rounds. When he dies, the petrifaction is complete. While he has 2 STAMINA points left he can use his arms but he cannot move his feet.

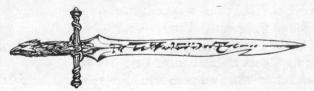

Since more than one Hero may attack simultaneously, Xortan Throg may have trouble dealing with them all. If a Hero gets close enough to strike at him, the wizard will take no chances – he uses the Death Spell. In any case, he already has a magical shield spell in place, which decreases his chance of being hit.

With any luck the Heroes will be following Sargon's suggestion and trying to goad Xortan Throg into casting a very powerful spell – and preferably the Death Spell. How they do this is up to them; but presumably they will first anger the wizard (probably by mocking his plans as being totally silly) and then question his ability as a sorcerer. Don't wait for them to perform miracles; once they seem to have said the right things, have Xortan Throg point the finger – and get the nastiest shock of his life!

What ideally should happen is as follows: in casting the Death Spell, Xortan Throg gathers together all his energies for a split second, extends a bony finger towards one of the Heroes and utters a powerful magic word: *'Die!'* A bolt of utterly black lightning leaps from his finger towards the chest of the chosen victim. One of the Heroes quickly pulls out the Crystal of Power and brandishes it at Throg. The black bolt is attracted towards the crystal and strikes it; there is a deafening noise of crackling electricity, and the bolt seems to extend back so that it links the crystal and the outstretched finger of Xortan Throg. The wizard has just enough time to utter an astonished 'Aaaaargh!' and then drops dead.

When the wizard dies, two noteworthy events immediately take place. First, any Heroes in the process of being petrified recover. Secondly, the Skeleton army standing outside the doors ceases to be animated and reverts to what it once was – a pile of mouldering old bones.

The Heroes have won.

Problems?

If the Heroes arrive at this point of the story without the Crystal of Power, their chances are very slim indeed. They *may* just manage to win through sheer force of numbers, but we doubt it. If you feel that they deserve to triumph anyway, give them a helping hand where you can and let the final decision rest on the roll of the dice.

Turn To . . .

That should be the end of the film, apart perhaps from a scene back at Salamonis where the Heroes are rewarded by King Salamon. However, if you are intending to make a sequel (and we've given you a few loose ends just in case), there are a few things you ought to sort out straight away.

The Heroes should be allowed to find their way back to Nicodemus without any further trouble (unless they are daft enough to try going up through the cellar of the Mermaid). They can then return to Halim Thrumbar, who will smuggle them out of the city.

What they do with the Crystal of Power is up to them. If they try to smash it, they will find that it doesn't break. It is probably best to leave it in the safe keeping of either Nicodemus or King Salamon; however, as it is a powerful artefact, the Heroes may wish to carry it themselves. If you fear that this could cause problems in future stories, have Nicodemus or Salamon insist that they hand it over.

Unfortunately, a very poor class of actor hangs around the studios these days. These people seem unwilling to settle for simple glory and insist on staggering away from an adventure laden with sackfuls of loot as well. Of course Xortan Throg will have had a fair amount of money; it is up to you how much you let the Heroes get their hands on – although the amount is important only if they are going to be used again. We'd recommend something in the region of 300 Gold Pieces per Hero. There is also the reward promised by King Salamon, which runs to another 500 Gold Pieces each . . . Quite a small fortune for a Hero.

The End

Coming soon?

All sorts of possibilities suggest themselves for *Dungeoneer* Adventure III. Here are a few ideas you may care to incorporate into your next blockbusting fantasy adventure movie. None of them is really strong enough for a full-length feature – but combine a few, and you could have another hit on your hands!

1. Sweeping the Sewers

The Heroes manage first to get an audience with the mysterious Lord Azzur, ruler of Blacksand, then to convince him what has been going on under his city. He may well be pleased to accept their offer to go back into the sewers and clear them of whatever nasties lurk down there. Remember that Azzur is a very wicked man and is most unlikely to deal fairly with them. Also remember that the ruins of Carsepolis extend for a great distance beneath Blacksand, both across and down. There isn't the slightest hope that the Heroes will clear out any more than a few areas, and then only temporarily, but don't tell them this. Let them discover it for themselves; finding out can be fun.

2. Holiday in Blacksand

The Heroes could certainly have further adventures in Port Blacksand before returning to Salamonis to collect their reward – perhaps they'd like to investigate the Mermaid Tavern or raid one of the pirate ships. Of course this is going to attract a certain amount of unwelcome attention towards them, and this will lead to further adventures. Just bear in mind: Port Blacksand isn't nicknamed The City of Thieves for nothing . . .

3. Zanbar Bone Lives!

If none of your players has played the *City of Thieves* solo gamebook, tell them a few rumours about the villainous Night Prince who lives in a tower not far from Blacksand, or you could even arrange for them to be hired by the poor inhabitants of Silverton. *City of Thieves* itself will give you plenty of ideas for a plot.

4. The Return of Xortan Throg!

Just what *did* the Heroes do with that Crystal of Power? Is it really quite safe? Could some wicked servant of the wizard manage to steal the Crystal of Power and restore his master to life? And if he does, how will the despicable sorcerer wreak his revenge on the Heroes and the citizens of Salamonis?

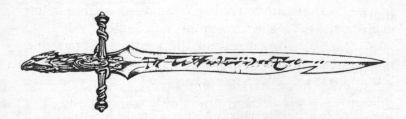

5. To Marry the Princess . . .

Somewhere along the line, one of the Heroes may have
decided that he has fallen in love with Princess Sarissa.
This is a problem, because almost certainly she wouldn't
touch a rough commoner like him with a very long
bargepole. Have King Salamon send him on a seemingly
hopeless quest in order to prove his worth, with the
promise of being knighted at the successful conclusion.
After all, if he becomes a knight he'll practically be
royalty, and Sarissa will just have to take notice of him
then . . . won't she?

6. Sargon the Dark

Well, just who is he? And what is he going to do, now
that he is alive again after close on 300 years? For that
matter, is there anyone, alive or undead, with a better
claim to the throne of Carsepolis than Sargon? What's to
stop him gathering together the undead legions and
usurping Lord Azzur's rule over Blacksand? Now that
would be a marvellous twist, wouldn't it – having Azzur
hire the Heroes to remove Sargon's threat! Can you
handle it? Certainly you can! You can do anything in a
Dungeoneer adventure!

4. FURTHER ADVENTURES

So, just what happens next? Well, the next big step – if you are a Director – is to design your own *Dungeoneer* adventures and then to set up a regular fantasy *campaign*. A campaign is simply an extended series of adventures starring the same characters in each (in film terms, think of the Conan series or, better still, all those James Bond movies). In a fantasy campaign, Heroes grow older and wiser, richer and more skilful, and generally enjoy a complete and exciting life! Some continuous campaigns deal with the Heroes' everyday life as well as all that brave stuff, while others concentrate on the Heroes when they are engaged in an actual mission.

Of course, setting all this up requires some pretty deft work on the part of the Director, since it's his job to dream up all the adventures for the Heroes to carve their courageous way through. This chapter should, we hope, provide enough information and inspiration for even the most reluctant Director to start creating his very own fantasy world! All the notes are for the Director, and we would prefer players not to consult them; the monsters, especially, will lose much of their impact if the players have already memorized their SKILL and STAMINA and know exactly what they can do.

Experience and Training

As the Heroes progress through their thrilling lives, completing more missions and adventures, they will hopefully become better at what they do. This is reflected in *Dungeoneer* by the awarding of *Experience* points. As a Hero acquires Experience, so his skills increase and he becomes ever more adept in his dealings with the barbaric fantasy world around him!

Experience Points

To simulate the increasing expertise and knowledge acquired by the Heroes as they star in bigger and better adventures, the Director awards Experience points at the end of every mission. To do this, simply consider each Hero's performance during the adventure, in terms of each of the following categories, and then rate the Hero on a scale of 1 (poor), 2 (all right) or 3 (brilliant!):

The Mission – was it completely successful? Did the Heroes achieve what they set out to do, or did they fail to spot some vital clue? Did they kill someone they were sent to capture, or let the main villain escape?

Casualties – how many of the Heroes had to die to finish the adventure? Could better tactics have saved their lives? Did any innocent people accidentally get killed by over-enthusiastic Heroes? Rate 1 for too many casualties and perhaps 3 for no needless casualties.

Heroism – just how brave is this Hero when things start hotting up? Was he there, leaping into combat or casting spell after spell, taking on any challenge thrown at him – or did he cower at the back and look frightened?

Role-playing – did the player manage to portray his Hero as a real person, or was he nothing more than a mobile sword-carrying playing piece? Award points for excellence in role-playing, even if the character played wasn't all that pleasant – at least the player was getting into character!

Once you have four ratings, add them up and divide the total by 4, to find the average score (round fractions up). This final rating – either 1, 2 or 3 – is the number of Experience points you should award to the Hero. *Note:* points are awarded only after an adventure is over, never half-way through.

Learning from Experience

These Experience points can be spent in three ways: to increase SKILL, to increase a Special Skill already possessed, or to take training in a new Special Skill or spell. The points don't have to be spent there and then (in fact, only those for increasing a Special Skill can be used in that way); the points should therefore be recorded in the appropriate place on the Heroes' *Adventure Sheet* until they are used.

Experience points can be spent by a Hero only when he is not engaged in an adventure and has time to train and practise in order to increase his powers. No character can suddenly become more proficient at something half-way through an adventure!

Increasing SKILL

Increasing a prime characteristic like SKILL will, of course, also have a considerable effect in increasing the Hero's Special Skill scores. For this reason, it costs 10 Experience points to increase SKILL by one point. Plainly, therefore, a Hero will have to save up points from several adventures.

If you are running a full campaign game in which Heroes have to account for their time, this increase in SKILL also requires a month of training and study. During this time, the Hero cannot go off on any adventures; rather, he must spend at least eight hours each day practising all his skills and abilities. At the end of this time, his *Initial* SKILL score will have increased by 1 point, and all his Special Skills will have increased likewise.

If you are running your games as a series of sporadic adventures with nothing in between, simply allow the Hero to assume that he has undergone the necessary practice in the lay-off between two adventures.

Neither STAMINA nor LUCK may be increased by experience or training, though the latter may be increased by the application of a *Potion of Luck*.

Increasing Special Skills

Alternatively, 1 Experience point may be used to increase any one Special Skill by 1 point. This Special Skill must be one that the Hero already knows, but otherwise there are no restrictions. (Learning a previously unknown Special Skill requires dedicated training and is dealt with in the next section.) The Special Skill may be increased again and again – though everyone should be aware that rolling double-6 and double-1 can mean that everyone can fail or succeed sometimes, no matter how great the skill they have.

If you are running a full campaign game in which Heroes have to account for their time, this increase in the Special Skill also requires a week of training and study. During this time, the Hero cannot go off on any adventures; rather, he must spend at least eight hours each day practising or learning about his Special Skill. At the end of this time, his Special Skill score will have increased by 1 point.

If you are running your games as a series of sporadic adventures with nothing in between, simply allow the Hero to assume that he has had the necessary practice in the lay-off between two adventures in order to increase his nominated Special Skill.

Occasionally you may have to rule that a particular Special Skill cannot be increased because the Hero hasn't used it for several adventures. After all, take the case of an Elf who spends the best part of his life at sea; plainly he isn't going to add to his *Wood Lore*! In such cases, you will have to decide what you feel can and cannot be increased. *Note also:* because of its nature as a natural skill, *Dark Seeing* cannot be increased by experience.

Training in Skills
This category applies to learning both a new Special Skill and a new Spell. Unlike simply getting better at something that one already knows something about, this category of learning requires the Hero to spend time – and money – being instructed in his new powers by another character who already knows something about the subject.

Learning 1 point of a new Special Skill costs 2 Experience points, together with the payment of 250 GPs to someone who knows the skill well enough to teach what he or she knows to the Hero.

A Hero may train in a Special Skill up to 4 points (at a cost of 8 Experience points and 1,000 GPs). Further points will have to be learnt by experience, *after* the Hero has been on his next adventure and actually gained some practice at using his new Special Skill (so that a Hero can't train up to 4 points and then immediately apply further Experience points in order to raise the skill higher by experience).

If you are running a continuous campaign-style game, you will have to decide where this teacher can be found; exotic skills, especially, may require the Hero to set out on a quest just in order to find someone! Larger city-states like Salamonis will have people who can train a Hero in the most common Special Skills. The time taken to learn the new Special Skill is one week of intensive training per point learnt.

If you are running an episodic campaign, simply assume that the Hero trains up to standard between adventures. The cost of training will still have to be paid. It is up to you whether a suitable teacher can be found close at hand; after all, having to find a teacher is a great excuse for an adventure!

Note that *Dark Seeing* cannot normally be learnt or increased by training or experience. If a Hero is really set on learning the skill, he will have to spend several years living and working underground (probably out of the game), slowly teaching his eyes to see better in the murky darkness.

Learning New Spells

This happens in much the same way as Training in Skills (see above), except that the cost is worked out in terms of the Stamina Cost of the spell a Hero wishes to learn.

Learning a new spell costs 1 Experience point per point of Stamina Cost it requires, together with the payment of 250 GPs per point to someone who knows the spell to teach what he or she knows to the Hero.

Characters who know – and who are prepared to teach – spells with a Stamina Cost of 6 or more are *very* difficult to come by. You, as Director, should be firm on this point. Tracking down someone to teach such a spell, or stealing a powerful sorcerer's spell book with a spell of so great a power in it, should require a full adventure, perhaps even several! Don't give it all to Heroes on a plate; they'll only run about blasting huge unexpected holes in your finest adventures, and the game won't be challenging any more!

Because learning sorcery is such a difficult and uncertain task, and because practising can be far too deadly, the first time any spell-caster uses a new spell, he must cast it with a −1 modifier to his *Magic* Skill. After all, who in their right mind is going to suffer all the effects of casting a *Death* spell just for practice?

Experienced Heroes

As Heroes begin to grow in stature and their fame starts to spread and their deeds are sung about in far-off lands, the game may need to adapt and expand to cater for their greater needs. Villains will have to become more deadly, or the Heroes will foil their devilish schemes with ease. Greater threats and more powerful monsters will also have to be encountered if the Heroes aren't to stroll through your adventures with one arm tied behind their collective backs.

Soon you may find the emphasis of your games turning from a series of jolly but generally inconsequential adventures into a carefully stage-managed affair which could threaten the security of all Allansia, or even the world! Everything will get bigger and more political as increasingly powerful enemies start to notice how strong those pipsqueak Heroes are getting!

On a financial level, you will probably have great fun devising different ways of ensuring that the Heroes always remain poor. This is an essential part of any extended campaign. Think about it – a poor Hero can't buy any training and will have to continue adventuring in order to gain more money. How you do it should prove no problem. If the Heroes are based in a town, let them have several run-ins with the local Guild of Thieves; if they are in open country, well, what about a famous local bandit-king? (Incidentally, if you choose to add to their worries in this way, you should find that the adventures will almost write themselves, when the recently robbed Heroes plead to be allowed to sort out their muggers once and for all!)

We would like to make the point, though, that the direction your game takes is *up to you*. If everyone is having tremendous fun playing the occasional impromptu adventure, there's no point in changing the game into a continuous campaign, full of hundreds of new and baffling complexities. All this stuff is *optional*, and is mentioned here for if you ever find your game growing more and more serious.

The Campaign

As we said above, a campaign at its most basic is a series of adventures starring the same cast of Heroes – and perhaps some of the major villains too – over and over again. This sort of campaign requires little work beyond a continuous supply of thrilling adventures for the Heroes repeatedly to risk their all against. Of course, that's plenty of work for anyone – but things do get easier, believe us!

You may decide to add a few geographical details, say letting the Heroes choose the name of a place where they'd like to be based, perhaps even deducting a few Gold Pieces every adventure for living expenses. Eventually, though, as things become more and more sophisticated, it may be time to move on.

The next major step is to upgrade the campaign so that the Heroes start to interact with their world, as well as going on adventures; in other words, live in your fantasy world day by day!

We are not suggesting that your gaming sessions suddenly have to cover every minute of every day and night. Indeed, nothing could be duller than having to do this; there are quiet moments in everyone's life, and you should concentrate on what the Heroes do best: fighting horrific monsters and going on tortuously difficult missions.

All the material here is *background*, what goes on between gaming sessions and which then leads into the next adventure. When shooting an adventure, you never waste time filming the Heroes travelling for days through endless countryside unless something very important is going to happen to them on the way. Similarly, your game should cut from one important moment to the next. All this campaign business is there to provide depth to the Heroes, to give them *reasons* for having to go out and risk their lives once more.

Heroes Day by Day

First, we recommend that the Heroes sort out a base for themselves, a home from which they can set out into the world to do what they have to do, and to which they can return once they've done it. This base could be a group of rooms in an inn somewhere, a small house in one of the city-states, or even a little tower somewhere. Initially, this home base will have to fit in with however much they can afford (towers fitted with all mod cons come expensive, especially since there's usually a long queue of evil sorcerers waiting to snap up such properties as soon as they come on the market!). You'll have to work out a range of options for them.

Secondly, there is the important matter of living expenses. After all, everyone has to eat and drink, Heroes included. You will find Heroes (and their players) really starting to fret about where the money's coming from in a continuous campaign. This is as it should be. If the Heroes want for nothing, there will be no compulsion to risk their hides doing anything as dangerous as adventuring! 'Keep them poor!' is a motto every Director should adopt!

In the short term, adventuring is generally quite profitable; but, as a freelance occupation, there may be long gaps between adventures. Some enterprises may result in the Heroes bringing back nothing but a few silver pennies; others may cost them money that they never recoup. And of course, they may keep acquiring treasure, only to have it taken off them, whether by the local bandits, or infuriating new taxes imposed upon adventurers and so on.

Living expenses soon mount up. Just think of all the items a typical Hero has to spend his hard-earned coin on every week: two or three meals a day, drink (quite a hefty sum for a Dwarf, of course!), the cost of having a roof over his head, clothes, armour, weapons, stabling and food for the horse, Adventurers' Guild fees, firewood and candles in the long winters . . . the list goes on and on.

And thirdly, there may be the small matter of regular employment. As we have said, adventuring is at best a part-time occupation; there certainly aren't enough quests to keep every Hero occupied fifty-two weeks a year. Much of any adventurer's time may well be spent travelling round Allansia searching for something to do!

Worse, adventuring takes a great deal of preparation and needs lots of time for recovery afterwards! So it may well be that the Heroes will want to sign up for some kind of gainful employment. They will probably aim for jobs which tie in with their Special Skills: a warrior could find employment as a mercenary, guarding a merchant's caravan, teaching others how to fight, and so on. A sorcerer could look after a library, become personal tutor to the king's children, set up as a healer, or whatever else suggests itself. A thief will have no problem financing his lifestyle in a busy city-state.

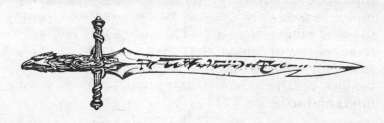

Typical Costs

The following list shows the typical cost of a range of items and expenditures. There are 3 columns for the price of articles, depending on where one is in Allansia: in a City, in a Village or in the isolated Country (and hence dependent on profiteering merchants!). All prices are for fairly basic items. Decorated or finely worked items cost around three times the quoted price. Remember that 10 SP = 1 GP.

Item	City Price	Village Price	Country Price
Ale, flagon or tankard	4 SP	3 SP	3 SP
Arrows, dozen	3 GP	3 GP	4 GP
Battle-axe	35 GP	50 GP	75 GP
Bow	15 GP	12 GP	25 GP
Candles, dozen	1 SP	1 SP	4 SP
Crossbow	90 GP	120 GP	150 GP
Crossbow bolts, dozen	6 GP	9 GP	15 GP
Dagger	1 GP	1 GP	2 GP
Dagger, throwing	3 GP	5 GP	10 GP
Horse	40 GP	40 GP	50 GP
Lantern	2 GP	3 GP	6 GP
Meal, hot, in a tavern	2 GP	2 GP	2 GP
Robe, linen	2 GP	3 GP	7 GP
Robe, silk	10 GP	16 GP	24 GP
Rope, per metre	6 SP	7 SP	15 SP
Room, per night, shared	1 GP	15 SP	2 GP
Room, per night, single	2 GP	4 GP	5 GP
Sack	2 SP	3 SP	5 SP
Saddle	6 GP	7 GP	10 GP
Shield	12 GP	15 GP	25 GP
Spear	6 GP	8 GP	12 GP
Stabling, 24 hours	1 GP	8 SP	2 GP
Sword	20 GP	40 GP	65 GP
Sword, two-handed	45 GP	90 GP	135 GP
Tunic	2 GP	3 GP	5 GP
Wine, flagon	4 SP	6 SP	7 SP

Other prices can easily be worked out from those we've given. There is a greatly expanded version of this list in *Titan*, along with plenty of other information about daily life in Allansia. While that book isn't essential for playing and enjoying *Dungeoneer*, we strongly recommend it as

the essential reference work for anyone who wants to run a full-scale campaign.

Advanced Skills

As we mentioned earlier, unless they are forever being knocked back, Heroes will eventually outgrow the adventures which were once a challenge to them. One very simple solution to the problem of having superhuman Heroes striding the land is to weaken them severely and then keep them occupied, searching for a way to restore their skills.

For a warrior, say, it is simple to set up a plot which starts with an enemy dropping into his ale something that brings on a wasting disease that slowly robs him of his powers. The only known cure is to be found on the other side of the world, but of course as he quests for it he gets weaker and weaker . . . This is even easier to inflict on a sorcerer – remember that Oops! Table on page 200, which they have to roll on every time they fumble a spell with a double-1? Be devious without your players realizing it, and your game will continue to be exciting for everyone for years!

Eventually, though, some Heroes may emerge who are just so powerful and experienced that they seriously unbalance the game. They can beat every creature you dare to throw at them, they visit the lower planes of the Infernal Pit for their holidays, they dwell in fabulous bejewelled palaces on the Elemental Planes, served over by multitudes of slaves. Heroes like this quickly becoming boring to play.

The solution? Simple: if a Hero becomes so powerful he can do anything and is afraid of nothing and no one, let him retire to somewhere warm and luxurious to live out the rest of his days in balmy splendour – and allow his player to start again with a fresh-faced new character. After all, in the movies old heroes never die; they just get replaced by younger ones!

Manufacturing
Any character with a weapon skill of 4 or more above his SKILL score may design and manufacture his own weapons (only those in which he has the Special Skill, of course). For some weapons, especially those made of metal, this will obviously require expensive specialist tools and equipment (metal-smithing will require a fully equipped forge, for example). Others, such as bow-making and fletching, require very few tools beyond a knife for carving and an abrasive file or cloth for smoothing the wood. (Of course, in any large settlement there will also be weapon-smiths who are not adventurers and who are skilled only at making weapons, not at fighting with them.)

Heroes with other skills, such as *Sea Lore* or *Trap Knowledge*, scoring 4 or more above their SKILL, can also manufacture appropriate items (boats and traps respectively, in these cases).

Making something successfully requires a roll against the appropriate Special Skill. Give each item a complexity rating from 1 to 5 (1 = plain dagger, dugout canoe; 5 = crossbow, ocean-going ship), and reduce the chance of success by that. Subtract from 10 the number of years the Hero has been manufacturing the item, and further reduce the chance of success by that. So, as an example, a Hero with *Sword* 17 who's been trying to forge swords (complexity 3) for four years, must roll 8 or less on two dice to cast one successfully.

Teaching and Training
A Hero with any Special Skill with a score of 12 or more may set himself up as a teacher or trainer of that skill. Similarly, any Hero with spells totalling 7 points or more can get away with calling himself a sorcerer: he can take on an apprentice and set up peddling the casting of spells to other people.

The cost of training *by* a Hero is the same as the cost of training *to* a Hero. Spell castings should be sold for around 50–300 GPs per point of Stamina Cost of the spell, depending upon the prosperity of the area the caster is working in and the client's ability to pay.

Designing Adventures

Sooner or later, every Director feels confident and inspired enough to rub a few brain-cells together, put pen to paper, and create his own adventure. Designing a *Dungeoneer* adventure takes a little imagination and time, but it isn't all that difficult once you get started (after all, if *we* can do it . . .)

To design an adventure, you need to do the following:

- Come up with a story, one revolving round either a commission from someone else to solve a problem, a problem that the Heroes themselves have, an interesting villain who's just started causing trouble, or whatever.
- Develop a plot round this story idea, add a reason for the Heroes being involved, and choose some suitably spectacular locations.
- Chop the plot up into a series of scenes, each one consisting of an incident that will lead to the climax in the finale.
- Fill in the details with a cast of Extras and the all-important Bad Guys! Add further details of the location and scenery, and you're away!

The Story

Think about the world the Heroes live in. It's the world of brave actions and dynamic action. It's a world of wonderful clichés, where Heroes speak grittily, evil sorcerers sneer and plot, Orcs are dumb. A world where good beats evil and right eventually wins, though not without cost. There's plenty of action, and plenty of combat. It's swashbuckling, rip-roaring and incredibly good fun to mess around in!

Typical Storylines
Can't think of a story? Turn on the TV or read a book. There are only so many ways of telling a story; inspiration could come from anywhere! If your imagination is still unfired, try fitting some names and settings to one of these simple storylines:

The Message: The Heroes must go where lesser men have failed; the Orcs are watching the passes but the message *must* get through!

Righting a Wrong: Local poachers have killed an Elf maiden who caught them inside Elven lands. The village will be put to the torch unless the culprits are caught.

The Challenge: Honour demands that one of the Heroes achieve some notable feat, or else be branded a coward (and lose the bet!).

Wanted, Dead or Alive: 'Hey, that wanted poster! Isn't that the man who passed us on the road, a few days ago? And there's a reward? Let's track him down!'

The Rescue: Find the victims, free them unharmed and, if possible, deal with their captors (see *Dungeoneer* Adventure 1).

Villainy: Someone is plotting to bring down the king. Rebellion is germinating in the dark corners of the city. Find out who, how and when – and stop them!

The Hunting Party: The Heroes try to capture or kill a rare beast for its beautiful (and very expensive) coat.

Monster on the Loose!: A peaceful village is being ravaged by a beast from the wilderlands. But there's a sting in the tail – the creature has a reason for being so angry . . .

Escort Duty: Bandits are everywhere; a merchant needs good strong men to guard his caravan. Good rates of pay. Apply Reskin, Merchant's Guild . . .

Race Against Time: Find the rare herb in the secret mountain-pass before the moon is full, or the king's daughter dies!

The Plot

Once you've got the germ of an idea, break it down into several scenes. Make each scene introduce a specific problem which must be solved before the Heroes can move on. In key scenes the Heroes can also discover a clue or something helpful which will come in handy in the final climactic encounter.

For your early scenes, sort out some *motivation* – just why should the Heroes get involved? The reason could come from an outsider: they are adventurers, after all, and adventurers are for hire. It could be the return of some-one they ran into before and would rather not meet again (like Xortan Throg perhaps?). It could be based on something in their background: what would a Hero do if the one-eyed bandit who had murdered his entire family suddenly rode into town?

Decide upon the *settings* for the adventure, and learn how to throw in those little details that make a scene come alive. *Remember:* you are serving as the five senses of your players. Convince them that they can see the scenes in their minds! The land of Allansia is a wild, overgrown country of rolling plains, fast-flowing rivers and gnarled, brooding forests. Ancient ruins dot the land, mysterious reminders of a forgotten past. Inhuman creatures lurk in the shadows of the land, preparing for the day when they shall rule. Sorcerers plot, Orc chieftains prepare for war, usurping barons form treasonous alliances with Trolls. The land is overflowing with possibilities; bring them to life!

Bad Guys

If a villain is involved in a plot, make him a good one (you know what we mean!). All villains are appalling over-actors, with more ham than a butcher's shop. Furthermore, they all seem to have something slightly wrong with them. In some this appears quite subtly, simply manifesting itself in an obsessive desire to rule the city, the land, the world. In others, there are physical problems: gammy legs, hunchbacks, missing eyes, strange speech impediments, nervous twitches, whatever seems nasty enough.

Whatever their problem, it should be plain from the outset that there is something wrong with them, that they aren't all there . . . that, well, they aren't normal! Bad Guys always have a weakness, a fatal flaw which turns them into Bad Guys, a flaw which the Heroes must discover and exploit to stop their evil plan!

Bad Guys are created like the Heroes, only in reverse; in

other words, first, work out who they are from their background and personality, and *then* assign characteristics, skills and spells. Always think up some good quotes for a Bad Guy to use – and do use them! Bad Guys are a wonderful excuse for you to act like a maniac, so make the most of their big moments!

Extras

Another way of adding greatly to the fun of any adventure is to ensure that the Heroes run into a number of interesting Extras. Even a straight swordfight will be livened up by an opponent who has a few tricks up his sleeve, a few strange skills (your players will be impressed – or should that be dumbfounded? – by an opponent who somehow manages to back-flip out of their Hero's way just as he is about to be run through).

If you want to add some memorable Extras to an adventure, think about what makes them interesting.

Appearance

What does the Extra look like? If you like, think of a real person (film star, TV actor, friend, it doesn't matter who) he most resembles. Alternatively, jot down just one or two adjectives to describe his appearance; when the Heroes meet him, their players will be able to picture him in their minds. Non-human beings and monsters are even easier to describe and characterize because they are so different from humans (we'll get on to monsters in the next section).

Speaking

Just like any other land, Allansia is riddled with different accents and ways of speaking. In the large city-states, educated characters may talk extremely formally or snootily, while gutter-thieves converse in lazy slang. Out in the isolated regions, people talk like country folk anywhere, long and slowly with drawn-out 'oo-arrs'.

As well as his accent, vary a character's vocabulary. Farmers talk in terms of the weather and their crops, measure time by the moon and are much given to superstitious sayings and proverbs. Courtiers refer to themselves as 'we'. Orcs tend to dribble and miss out every other word, and they adapt words to the way their mouths work ('humans' becomes 'yoomans!', for example). If necessary, scribble down a few quotes for the Extras to use.

What They Want
In any encounter between Extras and Heroes, each side will probably want something from the other. Heroes may want information, help, a special item, that sort of thing. Extras (being little more than plot devices in many cases) have lower objectives: giving out information, helping someone, having a conversation, money, fame, power, an exciting time, and so on. Knowing that an Extra wants some specific thing will make him easier to play.

How They Intend to Get It
If you intend Extras to use some skills, or to get into a fight with the Heroes, they'll need some specific characteristics, maybe some Special Skills or spells. Decide on these before the adventure starts; but only note the ones you think your Extras will need. Like Bad Guys, Extras are created backwards, starting with who they are and

then filling in any appropriate numbers. If, during an encounter, you suddenly find that an Extra needs to use another skill, make it up or roll against his SKILL score.

Repeats
It's always entertaining to have certain successful Extras come back to help, hinder or haunt the Heroes time and time again. They can provide light relief in the manner of a running gag, and they can even cause your players to bang their heads on the table in disbelief at their bad luck in running into him *again*. Extras who are always turning up at exactly the right moment to help the Heroes out of a fix may quickly develop into more important members of the cast – how does he always do it, and why? You'll quickly learn who to repeat, from watching your players' reactions. If a character raises a laugh, or an exasperated groan, bring him back!

Monsters

As well as the more intelligent Extras for the Heroes to parley with, there are also the Monsters, the ravening creatures and the nasty, scheming humanoids. Some skill is required in playing a Monster, for not all of them are simple sword-fodder, designed solely for the Heroes to chop into little pieces in a moment of blood-crazed battle-frenzy.

Many Monsters possess something approaching intelligence; truly Heroic characters will allow many to live, preferring to bribe or con them into allowing them to pass rather than hacking them down. Some Monsters may even have specific Special Skills, which they will certainly use to defend themselves.

Having said this, of course, there are also dozens of truly horrific beasts which must be dispatched immediately. Some will even be so powerful that the Heroes will have to run away if they wish to stay alive. If you manage to vary the way Monsters react and behave, however, your adventures won't end up as a sort of shooting gallery for Heroes to practise their *Sword* skills in.

The range of Monsters we list below extends from the hostile humanoid races (Orcs, Goblins and their ilk) to giant mutant creatures, from spooky undead to real ravening monsters! We haven't gone into long descriptions of their history, politics, demographical spread or any of that; you'll find all such information in *Out of the Pit*, to which you are referred for more details of these creatures, and over 200 others.

In the list that follows, every creature has been given 'typical' SKILL and STAMINA scores. Plainly, some creatures will be weaker and some stronger than this, so you are welcome to personalize them a little by varying their scores by one or two points.

Monster List
The following are some of the more commonly encountered creatures in Allansia. Each creature is described in the following order: Type of Monster; Habitat; Number Encountered (increase or reduce according to the number of Heroes); Reaction; Intelligence (believe it or not, humans count as High); SKILL; STAMINA; Weapon used; together with any special notes on the creature's appearance, special attacks and so on.

Bird Man: Humanoid – Hills – 1–6 met – Neutral – Average–Low – SKILL 10 STAMINA 8 – Large claw

Winged, bird-headed humanoids, typically found in the Moonstone Hills. If they hit and make a SKILL roll, they can hoist their victim high into the air before dropping him again.

Boulder Beast: Magical creature – Anywhere wild – 1 met – Hostile – Low – SKILL 8 STAMINA 11 – Large fist

Elemental spirits trapped inside rocks, who form themselves into humanoid shape to attack. Edged weapons do only 1 point of damage to them.

Centaur: Humanoid – Anywhere wild – 1–6 met – Neutral/Unfriendly – High – SKILL 10 STAMINA 10 – Bows and spears

These half-human/half-horse beings roam open plains, away from human civilization.

Giant Centipede: Insect – Underground – 1–2 met – Unfriendly – Low/None – SKILL 9 STAMINA 7 – Large bite

Some of these giant creatures have poison bites, causing an extra 2 points of damage.

Cyclops: Humanoid – Hills/Caves – 1 met – Hostile – Average – SKILL 10 STAMINA 10 – Battle-axe (+1 damage for *Strength*)

One-eyed and brutish, like a deranged, mutant Ogre.

Dragon: Monster – Anywhere wild – 1 met – Neutral – High – SKILL 16 STAMINA 25 – 4 Attacks – Very large claws

This is an example of a young Gold Dragon; there are many types and ages. This Dragon can also breathe flame every second Combat Round, causing 4 points of damage (a *Test for Luck* or *Dodge* to reduce to 2 points).

Giant Eagle: Bird – Anywhere wild – 1–2 met – Neutral – Low – SKILL 7 STAMINA 11 – Very large claws

First attack will be a powerful dive at +3 SKILL. If it scores 2 hits in a row, it will hoist its victim aloft and fly back with him to its mountain-top nest.

Fish Man: Humanoid – Rivers/Caves – 1–4 met – Unfriendly/Hostile – Low – SKILL 7 STAMINA 6 – Trident (as Spear)

These bulbous-eyed beings are half-fish/half-human (see *Dungeoneer* Adventure II).

Fog Devil: Monster – Forests – 1–3 met – Hostile – Low – SKILL 8 STAMINA 6 – Large claw

These insubstantial mist-creatures are vaguely human-oid in shape. Fighting such a wispy, transparent creature is done with a 2-point penalty to the Hero's SKILL.

Ghoul: Undead – Ruins/Underground – 1–3 met – Hostile – Low – SKILL 8 STAMINA 7 – 2 Attacks – Human fist

If a Ghoul – a rotting, reanimated corpse of quite horrific appearance – manages to score 4 hits on one target, the victim will be paralysed for fifteen minutes, and may be devoured by the creature.

Giant: Humanoid – Caves/Underground – 1–3 met – Hostile – Low – SKILL 9 STAMINA 10 – 2 Attacks – Large fists

There are many races of these enormous humanoids; the one detailed above is a Cave Giant. Their grey skin allows them to surprise opponents, for a first Unopposed Strike, 5 times in 6.

Goblin: Humanoid – Hills/Plains/Underground – 1–6 met – Hostile – Average – SKILL 5 STAMINA 5 – Sword, axe, throwing dagger

Like smaller and stringier Orcs (but just as disgusting in their habits), Goblins prefer to live close to nature, though they are also found serving alongside Orcs in the armies of evil.

Imitator: Monster – Underground – 1 met – Hostile – Low – SKILL 9 STAMINA 8 – Large fist

This shapeless blob of grey matter can transform itself into a common dungeon object, say a chest or a door. When potential prey investigate, they become stuck, and the Imitator forms part of itself into a fist. Stuck victims fight with a 2-point SKILL penalty.

Lizard Man: Humanoid – Jungles/Marshland/Ruins/Underground – 1–6 met – Hostile – Average–High – SKILL 8 STAMINA 8 – Spear, sword, crossbow

These tall, strong, reptilian humanoids are evil and warlike, and are feared for their habit of taking humans as slaves for their gold mines.

Manticore: Monster – Anywhere wild/Underground – 1 met – Hostile – Average – SKILL 12 STAMINA 18 – 2 Attacks – 2 Large claws and sting

This bizarre and highly dangerous creature has a human

face, the mane and body of a lion, leathery bat-like wings, and a scorpion's tail. After a successful claw hit, a victim must successfully *Test for Luck* or *Dodge* or be hit by the poisoned sting for 6 further points of damage!

Minotaur: Humanoid – Underground/Ruins – 1 met – Hostile – Average – SKILL 9 STAMINA 9 – 2 Attacks – Large fists

This bull-headed humanoid typically dwells at the heart of an underground labyrinth.

Ogre: Humanoid – Anywhere – 1–6 met – Hostile – Average–High – SKILL 8 STAMINA 10 – 2 Attacks – weapon or Large fists

These huge, animalistic humanoids are related to Orcs and their like, and may be found leading a band of them.

Orc: Humanoid – Anywhere – 1–6 met – Unfriendly/Hostile – Average – SKILL 6 STAMINA 5 – Sword, spear, pole arm

Orcs are the most common of all evil humanoids, and they infest all of Allansia. They are vicious, cowardly, cruel and totally disgusting!

Giant Rat: Animal – Underground – 2–7 met – Unfriendly – Low – SKILL 5 STAMINA 4 – Small bite

Giant Rats are a menace to anyone exploring old ruins, dungeons or ancient town sewer systems.

Rat Man: Humanoid – Underground/Ruins – 1–6 met – Unfriendly – Low – SKILL 5 STAMINA 6 – Small claw or weapon

These rat-headed mutant humanoids are adept at surrounding their isolated domains with traps and snares.

Rock Grub: Insect – Underground – 1 met – Unfriendly – Low/None – SKILL 7 STAMINA 11 – Large bite

These huge, rock-boring beetles chew their way through the underground world.

Skeleton: Undead – Underground/Ruins – 1–6 met – Hostile – Low – SKILL 6 STAMINA 5 – Sword, bow, axe

The commonest undead beings, Skeletons can be damaged properly only by crushing weapons; edged weapons do only 1 point of damage to them.

Giant Spider: Insect – Anywhere wild – 1 met – Hostile – Low – SKILL 8 STAMINA 8 – Large bite

Anyone caught in a Giant Spider's web must make a SKILL or *Strength* Skill roll successfully twice in order to escape, or suffer Unopposed Strikes from the Spider.

Troglodyte: Humanoid – Underground – 2–12 met – Unfriendly – Average – SKILL 5 STAMINA 4 – Dagger, bow

These small, misshapen humanoids dwell in caverns far beneath the surface of the world.

Troll: Humanoid – Anywhere – 1–3 met – Neutral/Hostile – Average–High – SKILL 9 STAMINA 9 – 2 Attacks – Battle-axe, pole arm, sword

These large, ugly humanoids are related to Orcs and their kind. They are gruff and surly, but they do enjoy jokes in which other creatures get severely injured. This is a Common Troll; there are many other races.

Werewolf: Humanoid – Anywhere – 1 met – Hostile – Average – SKILL 8 STAMINA 10 – 2 Attacks – Large claws

When the moon is full, some humans turn into were-creatures and roam the night killing all they meet. Anyone bitten by a Werewolf will himself turn into one at the next full moon. The statistics are for a human in Werewolf form only.

Wolf: Animal – Anywhere wild – 1–6 met – Hostile – Average–Low – SKILL 7 STAMINA 6 – Large bite

Wolves may be found roaming in hunting packs throughout Northern Allansia.

Zombie: Undead – Underground/Ruins – 1–6 met – Hostile – Low – SKILL 6 STAMINA 6 – Small claw

Looking like a recently deceased corpse, these undead beings are usually commanded by a nearby sorcerer, for they are slow and stupid.

Treasure

Many intelligent creatures will have their own treasure, be it in the form of Gold Pieces, a few sparkling gems, a finely wrought weapon, or even something magical. For some creatures, you will have a specific article in mind: a key to open a door further into the adventure, a helpful potion or weapon, that sort of thing.

For those occasions when there is no special treasure and you want to pick some at random, simply roll one die on the table appropriate to the type of creature involved; roll once for each creature present. *Note:* most creatures keep treasure in their lairs; if encountered away from it, they will not be carrying anything. Treasure is usually hidden; however, if a humanoid creature has a magic weapon, it may well be using it.

Roll	Humanoid	Monster	Undead	All others
1	nothing	nothing	nothing	nothing
2	1–3 GP*	nothing	nothing	nothing
3	1–6 GP*	1–3 GP*	nothing	nothing
4	2–12 GP*	1–6 GP*	1–6 GP*	nothing
5	Special item†	2–12 GP*	2–12 GP*	1–3 GP*
6	Special item plus 1–6 GP†	Special item†	Special item†	1–6 GP*

* – *Gold Pieces*
† – *Roll two dice on the Special Items table, below*

Special Items

Roll   Item and explanation

2   Enchanted battle-axe; adds 1 to user's SKILL

3   Potion of Invisibility (as the spell)

4   Magical sack; can hold five items as if they weighed one

5   Silver arrow, not magical but useful against certain beings

6   1–6 jewels, worth 10 GP each

7   1–3 gemstones, worth 25 GP each

8   Scroll containing *ESP* spell – may be used once by anyone

9   Healing potion – as *Stamina* spell

10   Magical dagger, so badly made it reduces SKILL by 2 (unknown to the wielder)

11   Poisoned potion; causes 1–6 points of damage

12   Enchanted sword; adds 2 to user's SKILL

Feel free to substitute your own favourite items for the ones on this table. Give a powerful item a high or low number on the table so it isn't found quite as often as a weaker one, and always include a few nasty items to balance all the nice ones and keep the Heroes on their toes!

ADVENTURE SHEET

N A M E : Aspen Darkfire

PLAYER:

A G E : 25

M / F : F

RACE/
PROFESSION:
Elf adventurer

SKILL	STAMINA	LUCK
Initial: 8	Initial: 17	Initial: 11
Current:	Current:	Current:

SKILLS	Value	SPELLS	Stamina Cost
Bow	11	Darkness	1
Hide	9	Fire Bolt	1
Wood Lore	10	Illusion	1
Awareness	10	Mirror Selves	2
Magic	10	Stamina	1

MONEY : 8 GPs   4 SPs

TREASURE

EQUIPMENT

Sword
Bow

PROVISIONS : 2

EXPERIENCE
POINTS :

BACKGROUND

Aspen Darkfire is the disowned daughter of a minor Elven prince from the Forest of Yore. Driven by an insatiable curiosity to find out about life 'outside', she forsook a life of endless balmy days in the golden forest four years ago. She knows she can never return to her family, though she sometimes receives news of them from other Elves. Since then she has wandered the lands north of the Whitewater River, seeking out and finding adventure in many lands.

PERSONALITY

Those Elves who have left their sacred forests to venture out into the world are cheerful, happy-go-lucky folk who never seem to get upset about anything. Aspen is always making jokes, even in the most dangerous situations. She is very elegant and graceful, and just about the only way to get her really annoyed is to ask her to do something that would lead to her getting smelly or dirty. She is wise beyond her years, but most of the time she seems to regard everything just as tremendous fun!

Aspen Darkfire dresses in dull green clothes that have plainly seen a lot of action, if one is to go by the number of repairs and patches!

QUOTES

'I say, chaps, outnumbered again, eh? Jolly good show!'
'You would have thought the old wizard could have managed to hire some Orcs that didn't have bad breath for a change!'
'I wouldn't do that if I were you…'

NOTES

ADVENTURE SHEET

NAME: Jerek Stormgard   PLAYER:

AGE: 25   RACE/
PROFESSION:
M/F: M   Human mercenary

SKILL	STAMINA	LUCK
Initial: 10	Initial: 20	Initial: 8
Current:	Current:	Current:

SKILLS	Value	SPELLS	Stamina Cost
Sword	13		
Crossbow	11		
Dodge	12		
Ride	12		
World Lore	12		

MONEY: 12 GPs   0 SPs

TREASURE

EQUIPMENT

Sword
Crossbow
Dagger

PROVISIONS: 2

EXPERIENCE
POINTS:

BACKGROUND

Jerek Stormgard hails from the minor city-state of Kaan, just to the north of Port Blacksand. He has served as a hired warrior all over Allansia since running away from home at the age of fifteen, after he accidentally killed his best friend while practising sword-fighting.

PERSONALITY

Despite his comparatively tender years, Stormgard is a tough, experienced mercenary. He has travelled all over Allansia and has killed just about every sort of monster there is to be killed (and more than a few that weren't supposed to be killed as well). Twin scars to one side of his left eye attest to his battle experience.

Physically, he is in excellent condition; but there seems to be something calculating and emotionless about him. He is a quiet person most of the time, and usually allows others to make the decisions; but he's very confident of his own ability – and quite ruthless, once he gets into a fight.

QUOTES

'Hurumph!'
'Let's GOOOOO!!'
'Come on, Orc, make my day!'

NOTES

ADVENTURE SHEET

NAME: Gordo Brondwyn

PLAYER:

AGE: 18

RACE /
PROFESSION:

M/F: M

Human thief

SKILL	STAMINA	LUCK
Initial: 9	*Initial:* 17	*Initial:* 12
Current:	*Current:*	*Current:*

SKILLS	*Value*
Dagger	10
Climb	10
Con	12
Sleight of Hand	11
Sneak	11

SPELLS	*Stamina Cost*

MONEY: 13 GPs   2 SPs

TREASURE

EQUIPMENT

3 Daggers
Rope and spikes
Lockpick tools
Loaded dice

PROVISIONS: 2

EXPERIENCE
POINTS:

BACKGROUND

This shadowy Hero was raised in the crowded backstreets of the city–state of Fang in northern Chiang Mai. After losing both his parents in the plague at the age of eleven, he and his four brothers grew up in the gutters, snatching food from shops, sleeping in corners, struggling just to stay alive.

At twelve, Gordo (a nickname, short for another name he hasn't used since his parents died) committed his first burglary; at fourteen he was drafted into Fang's Thieves' Guild and learned much of the art of crime. Two years ago, though, the wanderlust took him and ever since he has been travelling round Allansia as an adventurer.

PERSONALITY

Gordo is as silent as a cat, as slippery as an eel and can climb faster than a monkey. He is also very smart and resourceful, but he doesn't make a great show of this because he doesn't like drawing attention to himself. If ever the Heroes are in real trouble, he is the one who will come up with a smart plan to get them out of it.

Despite his criminal connections, Gordo has strong principles, chief of which is his loyalty to his Hero friends. He will not steal from them – or do anything to harm them deliberately in any way.

QUOTES

'I thought that would happen!'
'That should give them something to think about!'
'Luckily, I happen to have with me...'

NOTES

ADVENTURE SHEET

N A M E : Grimbold Tornhelm

AGE : 27

M / F : M

PLAYER :

RACE /
PROFESSION :
Dwarf warrior

SKILL	STAMINA	LUCK
Initial: 9	Initial: 22	Initial: 7
Current:	Current:	Current:

SKILLS	Value
Axe	12
Dark seeing	11
Unarmed Combat	10
Trap Sensing	10
Underground Lore	11

SPELLS *Stamina Cost*

MONEY : 14 GPs   0 SPs

TREASURE

EQUIPMENT

A very big battle-axe

PROVISIONS : 2

EXPERIENCE POINTS :

BACKGROUND

Grimbold, son of Hakkim, chief of the Tornhelim clan, was reared in a small Dwarven mining community in the Moonstone Hills. For a time he too worked in the gold mines, but his penchant for strong liquor – and brawling when drunk – made him unpopular. Since leaving the family mines, he has wandered the Windward Plain rather aimlessly, squabbling and boozing, looking for something to give shape to his life.

PERSONALITY

The typical Dwarf is sour, grumpy and short-tempered, and Grimbold is a typical Dwarf. Annoying him is very easy and not at all wise, because he has a very big battle-axe and loves hitting things with it – especially Orcs.

He is also very greedy, especially for treasure. He is fascinated by glittering and shining objects, especially if he knows they are precious. For Grimbold, money is the route to all pleasure. Besides money, he takes greatest enjoyment in food and drink. Unless carefully watched he will indulge himself to the full at every opportunity.

QUOTES

'You say that again, and I'll split your stupid face from ear to ear!'
'Isn't it time we stopped to eat yet?'
'GOLD!!!'

NOTES

ADVENTURE SHEET

NAME : Axel Wolfric

PLAYER :

AGE : 20

RACE/
PROFESSION :
Human (barbarian) warrior

M / F : M

SKILL	STAMINA	LUCK
Initial: 8	*Initial:* 21	*Initial:* 8
Current:	*Current:*	*Current:*

SKILLS	*Value*
Two-handed Sword	10
Sneak	10
Strength	10
Wood Lore	10
Magic	9

SPELLS	*Stamina Cost*
Fear	1
Luck	1
Stamina	1

MONEY : 6 GPs   3 SPs

TREASURE

EQUIPMENT

Massive two-handed
sword
Spear
Lucky rabbit's foot

PROVISIONS : 3

EXPERIENCE
POINTS :

BACKGROUND

Reared among the snowy steppes of northern Kaypong in far north-east Allansia, Wolfric is the son of a barbarian Snowdeer hunter and leather-worker of the Stormchild tribe of hunting barbarians. He has been wandering the northern lands for several years without enjoying much fortune, and has recently headed further south in search of real adventure.

PERSONALITY

Two metres tall and of solid muscle, in all directions, Axel could carry an adult Yeti on his shoulders. For all his strength, however, he is a simple fellow, unused to civilized lands. Although he is overawed by cities, he tries not to let this show and boasts about how strong his own people are, compared to civilized folk. When put in an unfamiliar situation, though, he will be confused and will probably offend someone by accident.

Although the barbarian knows a few spells, none of them go flash-bang or do obviously unnatural things; he regards them as just natural talents and nothing special. He will righteously hit anyone who accuses him of using 'sorcery', which he regards as a great evil.

QUOTES

'I don't like the smell of these stone floors.'
'In my tribe we train our daughters to kill Orcs by the age of six!'
'Never trust a wizard!!'

NOTES

ADVENTURE SHEET

NAME : Baradas Rangor
PLAYER :

AGE : 19

M / F : M

RACE/
PROFESSION :
Human wizard

SKILL	STAMINA	LUCK
Initial: 6	Initial: 18	Initial: 11
Current:	Current:	Current:

SKILLS	Value
Dodge	7
Languages	8
Sleight of Hand	7
World Lore	8
Magic	9

SPELLS	Stamina Cost
ESP	2
Fire Bolt	1
Levitate	2
Sleep	2
Stamina	1
Weakness	1

MONEY : 15 GPs   0 SPs
TREASURE

EQUIPMENT

Sword
Staff
Spell book
Dead toad (fresh)

PROVISIONS : 2

EXPERIENCE
POINTS :

BACKGROUND

Son of a much-travelled merchant from Silverton in central Allansia, Rangor was apprenticed at a very young age to an elderly sorcerer and sage. When his master was killed as the result of a badly translated enchantment from ancient Allansia, Rangor gave in to his thirst for knowledge and experience, and set out into the world.

PERSONALITY

Most wizards are very studious types who spend their early years poring over old books. For this reason they very rarely become Heroes. When they do, it is probably because they are so intensely curious about the world that they cannot bear to stay in one place for more than a day.

Rangor is young, keen, eager and painfully inquisitive. If there is trouble to be found, he will be in the thick of it; it's almost as if he is under some curse to see everything there is to be seen in this world before he reaches thirty!

QUOTES

'Great, let's go!'
'I wonder what's behind this door...'
'I wonder how you summon up one of those...'

NOTES

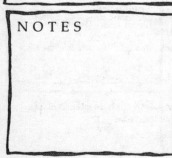

FOR THE BEST IN PAPERBACKS, LOOK FOR THE 🐧

In every corner of the world, on every subject under the sun, Penguin represents quality and variety – the very best in publishing today.

For complete information about books available from Penguin – including Pelicans, Puffins, Peregrines and Penguin Classics – and how to order them, write to us at the appropriate address below. Please note that for copyright reasons the selection of books varies from country to country.

In the United Kingdom: Please write to *Dept E.P., Penguin Books Ltd, Harmondsworth, Middlesex, UB7 0DA*

If you have any difficulty in obtaining a title, please send your order with the correct money, plus ten per cent for postage and packaging, to *PO Box No 11, West Drayton, Middlesex*

In the United States: Please write to *Dept BA, Penguin, 299 Murray Hill Parkway, East Rutherford, New Jersey 07073*

In Canada: Please write to *Penguin Books Canada Ltd, 2801 John Street, Markham, Ontario L3R 1B4*

In Australia: Please write to the *Marketing Department, Penguin Books Australia Ltd, P.O. Box 257, Ringwood, Victoria 3134*

In New Zealand: Please write to the *Marketing Department, Penguin Books (NZ) Ltd, Private Bag, Takapuna, Auckland 9*

In India: Please write to *Penguin Overseas Ltd, 706 Eros Apartments, 56 Nehru Place, New Delhi, 110019*

In Holland: Please write to *Penguin Books Nederland B.V., Postbus 195, NL–1380AD Weesp, Netherlands*

In Germany: Please write to *Penguin Books Ltd, Friedrichstrasse 10–12, D–6000 Frankfurt Main 1, Federal Republic of Germany*

In Spain: Please write to *Longman Penguin España, Calle San Nicolas 15, E–28013 Madrid, Spain*

In France: Please write to *Penguin Books Ltd, 39 Rue de Montmorency, F-75003, Paris, France*

In Japan: Please write to *Longman Penguin Japan Co Ltd, Yamaguchi Building, 2–12–9 Kanda Jimbocho, Chiyoda-Ku, Tokyo 101, Japan*